SEDUCTION WAS BACK
IN HIS EYES

His lips touched hers—gently, teasingly, warming her with the sensation. Elizabeth sighed. Ian felt her give in, felt his own immediate arousal at the touch and taste of her. Her body was lithe, her curves firm but womanly soft.

Elizabeth knew she was tempting fate, but she couldn't seem to stop her reaction to him. Everything about him excited her. Never had a man been able to ignite her passion like this....

But while Ian kissed her deeply, tantalizing her with his lips and tongue, his mouth never went farther than her throat. And though his hands caressed her body, they didn't touch the overheated skin beneath her dress. It was as if he were exploring, learning her for future, more intense loving....

ABOUT THE AUTHOR

Life in Sharon Brondos's household—which includes a husband, four teenagers, a dog, two cats, two rabbits and a gerbil—is understandably hectic. But somehow this Wyoming author found the time to write her third Superromance, and not surprisingly, it's filled with humor. Sharon's many fans will be happy to know that her fourth Super is in the works.

Books by Sharon Brondos

HARLEQUIN SUPERROMANCE
153–A MAGIC SERENADE
183–PARTNERS FOR LIFE

HARLEQUIN TEMPTATION
70–IN PERFECT HARMONY

These books may be available at your local bookseller.

Don't miss any of our special offers. Write to us at the following address for information on our newest releases.

Harlequin Reader Service
901 Fuhrmann Blvd., P.O. Box 1397, Buffalo, NY 14240
Canadian address: P.O. Box 2800, Postal Station A,
5170 Yonge St., Willowdale, Ont. M2N 6J3

Sharon Brondos

A PRIMITIVE AFFAIR

Harlequin Books

TORONTO • NEW YORK • LONDON
AMSTERDAM • PARIS • SYDNEY • HAMBURG
STOCKHOLM • ATHENS • TOKYO • MILAN

Published June 1986

First printing April 1986

ISBN 0-373-70215-9

Printed in Canada

To Margaret Learn,
my first editor and long-distance friend.

CHAPTER ONE

IT WAS SEPTEMBER SMOKE, Elizabeth Marlowe decided as she lifted her soft-sided weekend case from the back seat of her Mercedes. The Long Island air was hazy with it. She took a deep breath, appreciating the scents of the autumn evening—the musty sweetness of the fallen leaves, the tang of wood smoke. This was the perfect weekend to have gotten out of Manhattan, away from the smells and sights of commerce and chemicals and concrete.

She adjusted the strap of the handbag that hung from her shoulder and turned to look for a moment at the mansion that had been her home until recently. Her home since the plane crash that had claimed her parents' lives when she was a child, leaving her to the care of her beloved Uncle Robert and Grandmother Adelaide, and gaining her a brother-sister relationship with her zany cousin, Michael.

The home was huge, constructed generations ago out of enduring New England stone by nineteenth-century Marlowes. She smiled to herself. If fate was up to her uncle, a Marlowe family would live in the place until the end of everything.

She started up the driveway, her high heels making clicking sounds on the old cobblestone, the noise

an affront to the peacefulness of the early evening.
The thick woods dominating the estate right up to the
lawn around the house isolated the place from noise
and made it seem distant from the millions of people living next door in the city. Elizabeth felt a wave
of nostalgia as she remembered how she had explored the woods as a child, her small feet clad in
moccasins ordered from the L. L. Bean catalog. Occasionally she had even been able to cajole her
grandmother into arranging her long blond hair into
braids, and she pretended to be an Indian maiden,
adventuring in an uncharted wilderness.

But those times were past. Now her environment
was the concrete, steel and glass of Wall Street, and
her life was that of a free-lance financial adviser. She
would probably be hopelessly lost in the trees in a
matter of minutes. She gave a small sigh and looked
back to the house, wondering why the huge front
door hadn't already opened in greeting for her.

It was odd, considering how bitterly her family
had opposed her moving out. Her settling into an
apartment in Manhattan had been an emotionally
wrenching experience for all of them, even though it
did make much more sense for her to live closer to
her place of business. And she found that she loved
the bustle and excitement of the inner city as much
as she had the peace and solitude of the estate. In
fact, at twenty-seven, on her own with a healthy inheritance from her parents and a highly profitable
profession, she would be hard-pressed to give up her
privacy and freedom to share space with *anyone*,
however beloved.

But Robert and Adelaide were expecting her, and someone in the house should have heard her drive up, should have heard the electronic beep when she opened the gates at the end of the driveway with the small device she had dubbed the "gate zapper." And Michael! She should already be suffering from some practical joke at her irrepressible cousin's hands. She paused, listening for signs of life on the evening air.

Nothing. A frisson of anxiety moved up her back, tightening the muscles between her shoulder blades. Could something have happened? An emergency that had caused them all to leave before she could be contacted? She had driven across the Queensboro Bridge in bumper-to-bumper traffic and had been away from a telephone for several hours. Concern for the family she loved filled her. Then she heard a sound.

An animal growled in the trees directly behind her, an area fronted by large lilac bushes. Elizabeth froze, not believing that she had actually heard such a primitive, chilling noise in this familiar, civilized place. Tilting her head, she wondered if in her anxiety, she had misinterpreted the sighing of the wind in the tall pines.

But it wasn't the wind that snaked through the darkening twilight and made her flesh creep and her blood ice. It was a low, thrumming sound, like the growl of a jungle cat. She turned and faced the woods, unwilling to keep her back to the menace.

She could see nothing because of the barrier of the lilacs, but realized that a wild animal *could* be out there, because the New York area contained numerous zoos. It was possible, but most unlikely. Yet as the growling continued, the hairs on her forearms rose underneath her suit jacket and the coldness inside grew as her body reacted instinctively to the threatening sound.

Her mind was another matter, however. Logic ruled, and she decided that it *had* to be Michael Marlowe out there with some kind of recording device. *Up to his old tricks,* she thought, anger mixing with affection. Michael, two years her junior, had given her about a month to grieve for the loss of her parents before he started putting rubber spiders in her shoes, short-sheeting her bed and hiding coiled spring snakes in her lunch box. A natural tease, he had actually helped her come out of the state of horrified shock that the loss had plunged her into, but now he was a responsible businessman, married to beautiful, gentle Jennifer, and he *ought* to behave like an adult.

Instead she figured that he was out there, laughing himself silly because she was standing stock-still, hesitating like an idiot instead of calling his bluff. She waited another moment, trying to calm the anger and granting him that he had somehow acquired a very realistic recording. Then she put the hand that wasn't carrying the suitcase on her hip.

"Michael!" She tried to inject just the proper displeasure into her voice. "I know it's you out there. Will you just stop that stupid tape and come say hello to me like a normal human being?"

For a moment the growling stopped, and Elizabeth began to congratulate herself on having won this particular encounter. Then the air erupted with an earsplitting roar. She managed to hold her ground until she saw the bushes start to shake, then instinct conquered intellect. She fled for the house, hearing the muffled laughter that punctuated the roar only after she had made it all the way up the stone steps to the massive door.

It opened just as she reached it, and she found herself facing the tall form of Alan Charters, her uncle's butler and her old friend. She pushed past the white-haired man, giving him only a civil greeting. When she had heard the laughter, her fear had changed instantly to fury, and she decided that family ties or no family ties, she was going to flay Michael verbally right down to his many immature funny bones.

"I take it that you've had a brush with Mr. Michael and his friend, Miss Elizabeth." Alan Charters's dry words drew her attention to him. She turned and gave the dignified man a quick hug, apologizing for her rude and abrupt entrance.

"What about this friend?" she asked, handing her luggage to the butler. "Do you mean to tell me that Michael has an accomplice helping him make those absurd jungle noises?"

Charters nodded, his snowy eyebrows rising and his lips turning in a shadow of a smile. "He's an old chum from college. One Michael never brought home. Quite an odd chap. Some kind of animal scientist, I believe, hence the familiarity with nature's music. Young Michael has been using the chap's talents as a mimic to keep the household in an uproar all day." His light-blue eyes held an amused twinkle. "Quite literally, I'm afraid. As you've just experienced."

Elizabeth glared at him. "You'd better not have been in on this, too," she warned. Alan Charters was the ideal English-style butler, but in the past he had lapsed occasionally and assisted Michael in one of his many pranks. Or at least, she reflected, covered for the scamp.

But the older man gave her an innocent look. "I did hear your car drive up, but neglected to inform the family immediately. They're in the den, having cocktails before dinner. Would you care to join them?"

"Is Michael there?"

Charters glanced at his watch. "By now he and his friend should have made their escape to the back of the house and are undoubtedly awaiting your appearance with great glee."

Elizabeth eyed the butler. "Would you be willing to help me turn a few tables?"

Charters's smile widened a bare millimeter. "I do believe that I have been known to in situations such as this one."

She rubbed her hands together. "Good. Go tell them that I've gone berserk, that I've gone hunting for what scared me! Tell them that they must bring me in or I might hurt myself. But don't tell anyone but Michael and his friend. I don't want Robert or Adelaide upset, or Jennifer." Charters agreed.

Leaving him to carry out his part of her plan, Elizabeth hurried to the room where generations of sporting Marlowes had left their legacy of weapons. Familiar with guns and rifles, as she had been taught to shoot by Robert, she was able to quickly select the kind of rifle that could bring down large game. She checked it carefully to make sure that it was empty. This was a joke, not serious revenge. Then she went back outside to inspect the scene of the crime, thinking how strange she must look in her fashionable suit, lugging the heavy rifle.

Parting the lilacs, she located marks in the dirt beneath the bushes. Undoubtedly made, she deduced angrily, by the two rascals as they rolled on the ground, hysterical at the sight of her undignified flight. While she had learned the hard way over the years to be at the receiving end of her cousin's pranks with fairly good grace, she still hated to have her dignity ruffled. It was a character flaw, she had long ago decided, that came with Marlowe blood. Michael clearly had no problem with it, though she knew that in the business world of Marlowe Industries, he had a fine reputation. Only at home...

She headed toward the ornamental garden behind the mansion, thinking that the two were most likely to come out the back.

It took her a few minutes to make the trip since she was still wearing high heels and didn't want to turn an ankle. That would really be terrific, she thought. Michael would find it unbelievably funny if he found her sprawled on the grass.

She saw that the garden was deserted and assumed that Charters hadn't made contact yet or hadn't been able to get Michael and his friend aside. She located a stone bench and sat down to wait. When they appeared, she would wave the rifle around and scare at least the pants off them!

Smiling in anticipation, Elizabeth wondered if her cousin's friend could take a get-back joke as well as

Michael could. After all, he had actively participated in gulling her.

The breeze freshened, making her shiver a bit and sending a few tickling strands of hair across her face. She started to brush them back, and then became motionless as she heard a rustle in the boxwood hedge behind her. The same thrumming growl that had caused her alarm earlier sounded from directly behind her. Controlling her fear with difficulty, Elizabeth turned her head, but she could see nothing in the darkness beyond the hedge.

This time she knew it couldn't be Michael. There was no way he could have slipped past her either from the front or from the back. She would have seen him. So what was in the darkness?

The menacing tone of the growl increased, and she wished fervently that she had loaded the rifle. Impossible though it seemed, there just might be a dangerous animal out there. And except for the empty weapon, she was exposed and helpless.

She could scream, but that would bring her family out into the danger with her. No, she thought, she would handle this alone, regardless of the consequences. Clutching the empty rifle, she stood and faced the darkness.

A chittering noise greeted her movement. That, she thought, sounded exactly like a monkey. Fear left, and anger fired her again. She pointed the rifle at the hedge.

"Listen, whoever you are," she said, putting as much fury into her voice as she could. "You had better show yourself right this minute, or I swear I'll start blasting away! I'm mad enough to not care who or what I hit!'' she added, aiming the rifle and hoping that her bluff wouldn't be called.

But it was. She heard the brush and rustle of someone or something moving deeper into the woods. Elizabeth took a long, shaky breath and followed, determined to discover and humble whoever or whatever was responsible for treating her in this manner. It was a matter of pride now.

Her prey led her on a merry chase, especially since she was navigating on heels over pine needle-strewn loamy soil. But she had the bit in her teeth now and was set on finding her tormentor. Several times she was certain that she had been led astray and abandoned, but then a snapped twig or soft sound would cause her to move on deeper and deeper into the woods.

Gradually Elizabeth began to enjoy the game. In spite of its emotional cause, this hunt was like one of her childhood fantasies come true, and the experience now wasn't just one of anger, but curiosity and excitement. She heard the rustle of leaves off to her right and knew that the object of her search was in the clearing by the spring. She congratulated herself on her memory of the woods, amazed that she hadn't been hopelessly lost as she had thought she would be. More rustling from the clearing, and the gurgling noise of disturbed water from the spring.

She had him/it now! Moving as stealthily as possible, she circled the clearing, getting between her quarry and its escape route to the house. Then she ducked low and began to enter the open space, rifle held ready as if she meant to use it. The twilight had faded to dark night, but the sliver of moon gave her enough light. Slowly she parted the last of the foliage screening her from the clearing.

"Give me that damn thing!" A deep male voice whispered the words with intensity as a huge hand closed down over the stock of the rifle and jerked it out of her grasp. Since she had been moving on tiptoe, this propelled her into the clearing and sent her sprawling onto the soft ground. She felt her panty hose pop at the knees.

"You must be out your mind!" the male voice went on. "Coming after us with a *rifle*." Elizabeth shook her head to regain her senses and then rose to her feet with as much dignity as she could muster. She heard the sound of the rifle being opened, and then words muttered about the thing not even being loaded.

"Well, the idea wasn't to *shoot* you," she snapped, turning and trying to locate the man. "I was only planning on scaring you just as you did..." Her words trailed off as she focused on him.

The man was undoubtedly the largest human she had ever seen. She had difficulty making out his features in the moonlight, but she could tell that he had dark hair, a hawk's hook of a nose and a wide mouth that was pulled down in a disapproving scowl. She didn't have difficulty seeing that his body was muscular and well formed.

"I only wanted to even things up," she managed to say.

To her surprise, the man chuckled. "That's what Alan Charters told us. You need to be a bit more careful whom you choose as an ally, Liz. Your butler finked on you, and Michael suggested that I come out and make our mutual apologies. But when I saw that you really did have a weapon, I decided to give you a little more medicine.''

Elizabeth experienced a flood of outrage. How could Charters have let her down? And how dared this man treat her as if she were a child who needed a lesson. "My name is *Elizabeth*," she said, almost sputtering.

"That takes too long to say." His tone was clearly amused.

"You are no gentleman!" She balled her hands into fists.

"Never claimed to be, Lizzie."

Elizabeth was furious. The man, the situation, her inability to put him in his place without getting a retort... It was like playing tennis with a whiz like Jennifer Marlowe. You played, but you knew from the beginning that the lean little tennis nut was going to return every ball and finally whop the socks off you. But her cousin-in-law she liked. This man, she did not!

"I don't think we have anything more to say to each other," she declared, her voice icy. "If you'll give me the rifle, I'd like to go see my family now." She held out her hand.

"Not so fast." He held the rifle away from her. "I think we need to clear the air here first."

"I have no intention of wasting my time with you!" A small flicker of concern sparked. She really had no concrete reason to believe that this unmannerly giant was in fact Michael's friend. And if he proved to be even more ungentlemanly than he had already been, she was now much too far from the house for a scream to be heard. She was literally at the man's mercy. But she was damned if she would give him the slightest hint that she was frightened. "Give me the rifle," she repeated. "Or I'll just leave without it." She folded her arms across her chest and glared up at his face defiantly.

Ian Bradshaw studied the woman who stood before him with great interest. The cloud of blond hair that framed her face and the soft curves that made up a perfectly luscious body seemed at odds with the hard glint in her big eyes and the set of her squared shoulders. He knew the eyes were blue because earlier he had seen a painting of her in the mansion. Mike had told him that the portrait was more than a decade old, and he'd imagined that the teenage beauty had grown even more lovely as time had passed. She had also obviously acquired a stubborn and gutsy spirit.

"Calm down, Elizabeth," he said gently, conceding her right to be called what she wanted to be called. "There's no need to stay upset. I'm afraid I've already done enough damage to my relationship with your family. I'd like to be friends with you."

He saw her expression and stance soften slightly and knew that if he were confronting one of the many exotic women he had romanced over the years, he would try now to make physical contact. But Elizabeth Marlowe didn't strike him as the type who would appreciate that—it was far too soon. Maybe later....

"Charters did mention that you'd caused trouble," she said in a thoughtful tone. "Maybe that's why he decided to tell you what I was up to. When we were children, he often settled disputes between Michael and myself.'' She smiled. ''He's sort of an uncle, you see.''

What Ian saw was one of the most beautiful women he'd ever been privileged to meet. The smile brought a sweetness to her classic, aristocratic beauty that made her seem accessible, even to a ''commoner'' like himself. He grinned in reply.

''I did worse than cause trouble,'' he admitted. ''I was stupid enough not to remember your cousin's delight in practical joking. He told me that everyone would be absolutely wild about my mimicking abilities and encouraged me to try to convince those good people that I'd brought the whole damn jungle back with me. They bought it hook, line and sinker. Your poor uncle actually called the animal control officers.

''Oh, no!'' she laughed, putting her hands to her face in a gesture of amused horror. Hands, Ian noted, that were long and slender with nails that were neatly manicured, but short. It was too dark to see if they sported polish, but he figured that if they did, it would be pale and practical. The lady was fashionable, but conservative.

''That's when I decided that my good old buddy had slipped me one and 'fessed up,'' he explained.

''I'm surprised you weren't tossed out on your talented ear,'' she said, laughter still in her voice.

He shrugged. ''The possibility was discussed with some heat. But your uncle's basically a kind man, and he calmed down after being out voted. Jennifer and your grandmother took my side, as did Mike, of course. The whole thing was, after all, his fault." He put his hand to his forehead. "But then I had to go and believe him when he said you'd love being tricked. I swear that's the last time I'll believe a word he says."

"If I had a dime for every time I swore the exact same thing, I'd be wealthier than Uncle Robert." Another smile, and Ian noticed that she had a small dimple in her left cheek. "Michael is a magician of manipulation. It's one reason why he's been so successful so young. I always thought he'd wind up as a con man, but I suppose the education we both received as children saved him from a life of crime." She raised one blond eyebrow. "You know, we've been talking for quite some time, and you haven't even introduced yourself."

Remembering her stinging remark about his manners, Ian gave her a slight bow. "Ian Bradshaw, Miss Marlowe. At your service and full of apology for any embarrassment I may have caused you."

Elizabeth held out her hand. "Accepted. I apologize for being so bad tempered, Ian. I've had a long and tiring week, and I guess I just ran low on 'cope.' "

"New York will do that to a person." He took her hand and held it gently. The skin was soft and the bones fine, but she gave him a healthy squeeze instead of just limply shaking his hand.

"That's true," she admitted, "but I love the city."

Ian frowned. "I'm afraid it's just not my style. I prefer more open spaces. Shall we head back, now that we've settled our differences?"

Elizabeth started to walk beside him. "We can go back, but I hardly think we've settled all our differences, Ian. I'm a New Yorker to the heart."

"Suit yourself."

He moved easily through the trees, and Elizabeth found that she was making more noise than he was. The discovery prompted her to ask how he had managed to get behind her in the garden.

"Piece of cake." His teeth gleamed in a smile. "When you've spent years in the wild, sneaking up on wary animals, a city dweller like yourself was child's play to stalk."

His words made her shiver. "You're a hunter?" The profession disgusted her, but it seemed to fit the large man. He certainly had a ruthless look about him.

But Ian laughed. "I *skin* game hunters. They kill the very beings I love. No, Elizabeth, I'm an ethologist. I took my doctorate at Harvard. That's where I met and became friends with good old Mike."

"I see," she replied, unwilling to admit ignorance as to what an ethologist was. It clearly had something to do with animals, and she determined to look the word up the first chance she got. Her heel caught on a fallen branch, and she started to trip, but a large hand at her elbow steadied her.

"Thanks," she said. "Ordinarily I don't traipse about out here in heels."

"Do you 'traipse' much?" he asked, surprising her with his interested tone. "Do much traveling outside your native territory?'

"No." She didn't want to elaborate, to admit to this stranger that she suffered from a crippling fear of flying, and that even minor heights gave her the willies. Quickly she thought of a way to change the subject. "Before we get back to the house, Ian, would you please do something for me?"

Ian felt his blood start to race. Could he have read her wrong? Was she going to come on to *him*? Could he be that lucky so soon?

No such luck. He was disappointed when she asked him to give her a demonstration of his mimicking talents while they were still far enough away from the house not to scare the family.

"I can't believe human vocal cords can actually make the sounds I heard," she said, looking up at him and making it difficult for him to resist taking a kiss from those sensual, full lips. Then a wicked thought occurred to him.

Wordlessly Ian lowered the rifle to the ground. He assumed a half crouch and fixed her with a leopard's hunting stare. He began to move, making the low rumbling of a cat that knows its prey is doomed.

Elizabeth felt her body turn to cold stone. She couldn't have moved if she had wanted to. It was horrifying and exciting at the same time. Ian seemed to have really transformed into a jungle cat. He circled her, making that menacing sound deep in his chest and throat.

He moved closer and closer, using a slow, measured, confident pace. Closer, until she could feel the heat of his body. He stopped, staring at her intently. She waited, feeling a trembling start in her leg muscles. Then Ian roared.

The cry was like the one that had sent her scurrying for dear life up the steps, and she instinctively screamed in response. Ian stepped back, laughing.

"Sorry," he said. "I just couldn't resist doing that. Now we really had better get back before your uncle sends out the Marines."

CHAPTER TWO

WORDLESSLY ELIZABETH ALLOWED Ian to guide her back through the trees to the house. He carried the rifle in one hand and the other rested lightly on her elbow, as if he knew how weak her muscles were after she'd been subjected to such an experience. She considered protesting the gallantry, but she really was still shaken by his stalk and scream, and she doubted Ian Bradshaw was the kind of man to take exaggerated women's liberation seriously. In fact, he seemed to be as primitive as the creatures he imitated. For Ian Bradshaw, doctoral degree or not, civilized behavior was probably just a thin veneer. The thought made her shiver, but the feeling wasn't entirely a negative one.

He led her into the mansion, turning to shut the front door behind him. "You go on and join your family," he said. "I'll put the cannon away and change for dinner. Be with you in a little while."

Elizabeth nodded, still unable to speak, but now for a different reason than shock. Outside, seen by the light of the moon, he had seemed passably handsome, as well as intimidatingly huge. In the full light from the vestibule chandelier, he was far, far more than passable, and the very size of his muscular frame made him even more attractive.

His skin was darkly tanned, his hair so black and shining that it actually had bluish highlights, and his eyes were the most extraordinary color of gray she had ever seen. So clear and bright that they seemed made of silvery crystal. His features were firmly sculpted, and his chin had a very masculine cleft in it.

But she knew that it was more than just his appearance that made her mouth go dry and her pulse increase. Elizabeth was no stranger to handsome men, though his attractiveness certainly had a wild quality that she wasn't accustomed to. He had, she realized, a rare and powerful kind of magnetism—a sensuality that seemed to surround him like an aura and made her want to move into his arms. *This is completely unlike you,* she scolded herself, but she had to admit that Ian Bradshaw, eth...whatever the heck he was, had sex appeal!

"Was it something I said?" he asked, an amused smile on his face. She felt herself redden and realized that she had been staring at him.

"I—I'm sorry," she stammered. "Forgive me, Ian, but you must know that you're an exceedingly...unusual-looking man."

He bowed his head slightly as if acknowledging the compliment. Then he started to laugh. "Look at your knees," he said.

She glanced down and saw the two large holes that had popped in the nylon when she had fallen in the clearing. Her skirt was also littered with leaves and pine needles.

"You'd probably better change, too," he suggested, his tone gentle. "Or your protective uncle will think I took advantage of you and be after me with this *loaded*.'' He gestured at the rifle. "I'm sorry I got too rough taking it away."

"I doubt very seriously that anyone in their right mind would try tangling with you, loaded rifle or not." She studied him again, and decided that in addition to being devastatingly alluring, he also looked dangerous. He carried the weapon with easy familiarity in the crook of his elbow. His other hand was hooked casually by his thumb through the belt loop of his jeans. The khaki shirt he wore was open at the throat and the sleeves were rolled up to his elbows, revealing dark chest hair and black-sprinkled forearms. If someone did walk in and see them right now with her clothing in this condition, they would undoubtedly come to the conclusion that Ian was a bandit about to ransack the mansion and carry her away to satisfy his lusts. Images of dashing pirates and bold highwaymen flashed through her mind. *Elizabeth Marlowe,* she told herself, *you are thinking like a romantic. Cut it out!*

"You're forgiven," she told him. "If I'd had any idea the kind of quarry I was up against, believe me, I wouldn't have left the house."

His eyes narrowed. "I think, Elizabeth Marlowe, that you would have come out even if you'd known King Kong was waiting. I think you're a very gutsy lady."

His compliment warmed her, and she was about to reply when she heard her name uttered from behind in a horrified tone.

"Elizabeth! Good Lord, Bradshaw. What the devil are you up to now? If you've laid a hand on her . . . !"

She turned to see her Uncle Robert standing in the archway that led from the vestibule to the front parlor. On his lean, aristocratic face was both outrage and apprehension. She had never seen him so upset, not even over her own rebellions against his ideas of how she should live her life.

Robert Marlowe barely controlled himself as he viewed the two people before him. His beloved adopted daughter, so dear to him in spite of her infuriating independence, her usually neat appearance marred by torn stockings and foliage. And that ungodly friend of Michael's, looking so uncivilized and seeming quite pleased with himself. What had the man been up to with her?

"Nothing's wrong," Elizabeth said, her tone of voice assuring. "I just tripped and got a bit mussed. Ian helped me."

But Robert saw a blush on her cheeks and knew he wasn't getting the whole story. Bradshaw's stance was too arrogant, and Elizabeth actually looked flustered. A state of mind he had never known his niece-daughter to be in. Not even when Michael had been at his worst, teasing her.

"Why the rifle?" he asked, glaring at the bigger man.

"It's a long and funny story." Elizabeth went over to her uncle and gave him a kiss on the cheek. "Why don't you welcome me home, then I'll change and tell you all about it."

Robert's love for her washed away his anger. Embracing her warmly, he did welcome her back to the mansion. "This is always your home," he said. "You must never forget that, Elizabeth."

"I won't, and you know it." She kissed him again. "Go tell everybody I'll be right down."

Robert gave her a careful look, one that she had seen only a few times in her life and one she knew meant he was worried about her. "You're sure you're all right?" he asked, confirming her analysis. Robert's love for her was great, but sometimes she thought he still considered her to be the terrified and grief-stricken child he had welcomed into his home so long ago. "I'm *fine*," she insisted, turning to ask Ian to confirm her words, but to her amazement, the man had disappeared.

"He's been doing things like that all day," Robert said in a disapproving tone. "One minute he's right beside you, and the next, he's vanished." He gave a visible shudder. "I don't mind admitting it, Elizabeth, the man makes me highly nervous. He's unpredictable."

"*That* from the man who loosed Michael on the unsuspecting world?" She laughed and hugged her uncle again. "I'll tell you what we were doing. Michael conned poor Ian into thinking I'd love his mimicking, too, and the man fell for it. He was apologizing to me, for goodness' sake."

Robert's features took on a worried expression. "My son has been acting up more lately. It's almost the way he behaved after his mother died, before you came to live here. Antic. Even a bit manic."

"Trouble with the Industries?" she asked, knowing that Robert had been giving Michael more and more responsibility as the older man prepared for retirement. Maybe Michael just wasn't ready to handle the Marlowe industrial empire, which included such diverse enterprises as overseas trade, local manufacturing of factory equipment, investments in the garment industry and several other businesses that the family had accumulated over the generations.

"No." Robert shook his head. "If anything, he's doing a better job than ever. And at the office, he's an entirely different person. Serious, clearheaded, resourceful. I'm very proud of my son, just as I'm proud of you." He gave her a glance that held a shadow of teasing in it. "Only I still wish that you'd come into the fold and offer us your financial wizardry instead of forging out on your own."

"Let's not get into it," she warned. "I came to visit, not to refight old battles."

"Okay, darling. I promise to try to keep my controversial opinions to myself. Get dressed for dinner, and I'll see you in the dining room." They parted, and she ran up to her old room to change.

IAN PUT THE RIFLE AWAY, then started to go to his guest room, but something impelled him to go into the main living room once more and look at Elizabeth's portrait.

Hanging on one long wall dedicated to paintings of her relatives and ancestors, she stood out to him like an angel portrayed alongside ordinary humans. The artist had captured something of the present woman, Ian decided. He had given her small chin just the right stroke of defiant stubbornness, and her blue eyes smiled but dared anyone to cross her. He knew from Michael that she had been orphaned as a child, and decided that had probably given her the strength to make her own decisions and enforce her own will in matters. A formidable woman as well as a beautiful one. A dangerous but fascinating combination, and one he intended to investigate this weekend as thoroughly as possible—in his own way. He smiled to himself. *Lizzie* Marlowe might be used to getting her own way with most people, but he was certain her strong character had some flaws in it, some weakness he could use to get a taste of the real woman under the aristocratic facade. Literally a taste. Ian felt anticipation as he thought of kissing those lips.

"She's a lovely young woman, isn't she, sir?" The butler's British-accented words cut into Ian's romantic thoughts. He turned and saw the man standing in the wide doorway.

"She is," he agreed. "And you're very good, Mr. Charters. Not many people are able to get near me without my knowing it."

The butler approached. "Perhaps you were too...distracted," he suggested, glancing meaningfully at the portrait of Elizabeth.

"Perhaps I was," Ian admitted.

"This is a very close family," the butler went on. "I feel very much a part of it, though my role is that of a servant." His blue eyes were fixed on Ian's.

Subtle warning, Ian thought. *Hands off the lady, stranger.* "The role of servant is a noble one," he countered. "I recall a number of admirable people who deliberately made themselves serve others out of love and concern."

The butler blinked, and Ian knew he had scored. Perhaps the man would trust him more after this exchange. He had no intention of harming Elizabeth. Far from it!

The other man did seem somewhat mollified. He looked at the portrait. "I remember when she first arrived here after her parents' deaths in that plane crash," he said. "She witnessed it. She'd been watching her father fly his plane in, when a gust forced it down. The poor child's heart and mind seemed to turn to stone. Then one day—"

"One day she came out of it and has been running life pretty much her own way ever since," Ian hazarded.

"Very astute of you, sir," the butler conceded. "Yes, Miss Elizabeth is a strong-willed young woman." He smiled slightly. "As many young men have discovered, to their dismay."

"I'll hold the thought," Ian replied.

WHEN ELIZABETH ENTERED the large formal dining room, she was immediately surrounded by her family. Michael, tall, dark blond and clearly unrepentant about his trick, grabbed her in a bear hug.

"You were *so* funny," he told her. "If only you could have seen the look on your face when Ian screamed. I thought I'd die laughing."

"Too bad you didn't." She softened the words with a grin.

"Aw, you're not still mad, are you?" Michael looked hurt. "I mean, it was just a joke."

"If you had him do that panther roar," Jennifer interjected, winking at Elizabeth, "she ought to still be angry." She widened her brown eyes. "Wasn't that the scariest thing you've ever heard?"

Elizabeth agreed, thinking that what he had done in the woods, openly stalking and then screaming, had been almost enough to do her in.

"Well, *I* think he's charming." Adelaide, Elizabeth's silver-haired grandmother, gave her a warm hug and a kiss on the cheek. "And I think it's perfectly delightful that Michael chose to invite him to visit the same weekend you planned to come."

Oh, did he? Elizabeth thought. *How interesting . . .*

Alan Charters entered the room and told them that their houseguest was on his way and that dinner would be served in a few minutes. Elizabeth took advantage of the interruption to study her family, because it had been weeks since she had seen them, and from what Robert had said to her in the vestibule, things seemed a bit out of whack, especially where Michael was concerned.

Jennifer, tanned from her fanatical tennis playing, was as pretty as ever with her curly short brown hair, highlighted with red streaks from the summer sun. But Elizabeth thought she detected a shadow of sadness in her brown eyes. And the edges of Jennifer's smile seemed to slip when she thought no one was looking at her.

Adelaide looked wonderful. The seventy-year-old woman was petite, her figure was straight, and the pale lilac dress she wore was quite becoming. Her white lined skin showed more color than usual, which Elizabeth put down to excitement over having company. Especially company like Ian, she thought wryly. He'd put color in any woman's cheeks.

Robert was, as usual, impeccable, every graying blond hair in place, and his dark business suit fitted his trim form perfectly. A regular squash player at fifty, Robert was a handsome man. She was proud to be his adopted daughter.

Then there was Michael.

Her brother-cousin seemed unusually nervous, his laughter a bit too loud and forced. A practiced comic, Michael seemed to have lost his sense of timing, and the jokes he told fell on their verbal faces. Robert was right: something was wrong.

Adelaide queried Elizabeth about her social life, asking if she had found any young men especially to her liking in the city. When Elizabeth confessed that most of her socializing was just with friends and that she had no romantic involvements worth reporting, her grandmother looked disappointed.

"You'll never find a husband at this rate," she said. "Heavens, I was married at eighteen and had your uncle when I was twenty."

Elizabeth sighed. It was another old bone of contention with her family that she had chosen a career over marriage, at least for the present. "I'm not living like a hermit," she said defensively. "I'm just not ready to settle down yet."

"That's because you haven't met the right man, dear," Adelaide declared.

At that moment, punctuating the sentence with his presence, Ian Bradshaw made his entrance. He strode through the doorway and into the dining room, looking for all the world as if this was his home and the Marlowes were the guests. If she hadn't met him before, Elizabeth would have assumed that he was a businessman, or at least a New Yorker with a prestigious profession. Certainly she would never be able to picture him crouching on all fours in the bushes and making lion noises.

He wore dark-brown slacks and a jacket of slubbed beige silk cut perfectly for his broad-shouldered form. His black hair was neatly combed, and in contrast to the khaki shirt he had worn earlier, his dress shirt didn't seem to have a wrinkle in it.

He greeted everyone politely, giving Elizabeth no more and no less attention than anyone else. His manners were smooth and beyond reproach, and she found herself reevaluating him as dinner progressed.

He was a chameleon, she decided. Just as he was able to mimic wildlife, he had the ability to blend with and behave according to his surroundings. She wondered about his background, his childhood, and hoped that she would have a chance to ask him about them later. Probably, she speculated, he could be dropped into any culture in the world and in a short while be indistinguishable from a native. Now that he knew Michael had misguided him about the family, he had changed his behavior and was settling in to charm away the first poor impression he had made.

Robert even thawed a bit when Ian displayed an interest in the family history. Her uncle spoke with pride of the lineage and of the tradition of industry and time-honored values that had kept the Marlowes strong for generations. But she winced inwardly as the subject moved to the importance of heirs.

"Without children to inherit and carry on," Robert stated, "all the money and power in the world will do a family no good whatsoever. Fortunes and estates just disintegrate, scattered to uncaring, distant kin."

"Dad, there's no point in bringing that up now," Michael interjected, a note of anger evident in his voice. Elizabeth glanced at him, surprised. The no-heir bit was usually reserved for her unmarried self. Michael's face looked strained, and she noticed that Jennifer was staring down at her plate, picking at her food.

"Lines do die out," Ian commented. "Some believe it's nature's way of making room for new, stronger breeds."

"We're not animals," Robert retorted. "We're the *Marlowes*." Ian just smiled and directed his attention back to his dinner.

Adelaide spoke up, changing the subject, much to Elizabeth's relief. "Dr. Bradshaw," she asked, "I've been wondering all afternoon just exactly how you learned to do those fantastic imitations. Would you mind satisfying an old woman's curiosity?"

"And mine, too," Elizabeth added. "When I'm the target of a practical joke, I'd like to know how the perpetrator was able to carry it out."

Ian was sitting directly across from her, but he had avoided looking her straight in the eye, concerned that his growing attraction to her would become obvious to the other family members and make it more difficult for them to accept him, thinking that he might be planning a little weekend seduction. To a limited extent, he realized, he was.

But he wanted acceptance. Not only because he enjoyed Michael as a friend—they still shared the same wacky sense of humor that had bonded them at Harvard years before in spite of the differences in their ages and backgrounds—but also because of Elizabeth. She intrigued him, and he sensed that he would have a better chance at getting close to her if her relatives weren't antagonistic toward him. However, now that she had addressed him directly, he couldn't resist gazing into her eyes.

Elizabeth had difficulty not exclaiming aloud at the strong current of sensuality she felt as his gaze locked on hers. It was as if they were suddenly the only two people in the room and something wonderful was about to happen.

But when Ian spoke, it was in a perfectly normal, no-nonsense tone. "I'm an ethologist. I watch animals. After years of doing it, I've managed to pick up on some of their various verbalizations."

And mannerisms, Elizabeth thought.

"You're *paid* to just observe wildlife?" Robert sounded incredulous.

"Scientific grants, Dad." Michael jumped to his friend's defense. "Ian's also written a number of books and does free-lance consulting work for motion pictures."

As the conversation continued, Elizabeth learned that Ian had spent years in Africa, Malaysia and Indonesia, studying primate behavior. His doctoral work had been on lions and other large felines, but he had changed his focus of interest after that.

"Primate life had almost been overstudied," he said, citing several scientists whose names she recognized. "But though the groundwork's already been done, as Africa and Asia continue to develop, wild land will continue to be lost in the same way it was in North America. Eventually, the only home for many species will be zoos and fauna parks. My hope is that the observations I've recorded will help make those places better environments for the survivors."

Ian's passion for his work was obvious. He had a cause, and he was crusading for it. It made the financial wheeling and dealing she did seem petty by comparison. Elizabeth's admiration for him grew, and she hoped the weekend would turn out to be a time to get to know him better. Since he had indicated a distaste for city living, and since his profession obviously kept him in the wilds most of the time, she doubted she'd have another chance.

But the rest of the evening passed without any opportunity for her to speak to him at all. Her family seemed to hedge around her as if trying to keep her away from Ian, the outsider.

"Come over and sit with with me, dear," Adelaide said as they entered the den to take coffee and after-dinner drinks. She put her hand on Elizabeth's arm. "I must fill you in on the neighborhood gossip."

Elizabeth went, as Ian, Michael and Jennifer clearly were planning an evening of reminiscing about shared college days, a bottle of cognac at hand to sharpen memories. They settled in one part of the room, while Robert, Adelaide and she sat in another. Adelaide started in, and Elizabeth forced herself to sit patiently and listen.

"Of course," her grandmother said, "you must have heard that your old boyfriend, young Billy Stockdale, broke off his engagement to Muffy Turner." Elizabeth said that she hadn't, not adding that she couldn't have cared less. She had dated the man occasionally last summer before she had moved into the city, but had found him to be outwardly handsome and inwardly dull, a condition she was already certain Ian Bradshaw didn't share.

"Well," Adelaide went on, "I understand that Muffy was crushed, and that she blames the torch he's still carrying for you as the cause."

"That's nonsense," Elizabeth commented. Robert agreed, saying that he was certain the Turners' financial reverses were the real cause, since he felt Stockdale was a fortune hunter. Elizabeth silently concurred.

She participated in conversation for a while longer, then excused herself saying that she was exhausted from the week of work she had put in. When she waved good-night to Michael and Jennifer, Ian didn't even seem to notice her. *To heck with him,* she thought.

Her mood didn't improve as she readied herself for bed. She felt nostalgia, being in the room she had called her own for so long, but she also experienced a sense of not belonging that bothered her. And she had to admit that tonight she'd felt a certain dissatisfaction with her life. Something was missing.... She turned off the light, hoping that sleep would come quickly and relieve her of her moodiness.

But it didn't. The moment she closed her eyes, the image of Ian Bradshaw filled the motion picture screen of her imagination. She saw him stalking her in the woods; standing in the vestibule looking like a guerrilla warrior; entering the dining room as if he owned the place; ignoring her after she had been certain she had seen interest in his gray eyes.

She rolled over and punched the pillow. Ian was a fluke, a man with an unusually sexy aura, and she had no reason to let herself dwell on him. Darn Michael anyway for inviting the man here when he knew—

Could Michael have planned for the two of them to meet and perhaps hit it off well? Oh, no, she thought. That was just too Machiavellian for him. Too devious. But then, parading such an unusual man in front of her might just appeal to his Falstaffian turn of mind. Drat!

All this thinking, she told herself, was wasted mental energy and no way to get to sleep. She might as well read. Turning on the light, she padded to the bookshelf and selected an old childhood friend, *Winnie the Pooh*. With Winnie she could hardly dwell on Ian, sex or Michael's scheming. Fluffing her pillow, she sighed, settled in and began reading.

After a few chapters, she slipped into a warm sense of security and drowsiness. Good old Winnie, she thought, putting the book aside. He did have a way of setting life into gentle perspective. She could sleep now, with no "ape men" haunting her dreams.

Elizabeth reached to turn off the lights, but a movement at her window caught her attention. She blinked, rubbing her eyes and wondering if she was so tired that she was beginning to see things. Her room was on the second floor, too far up for anything but a bird to be outside.

There it was again. Something pale, flapping at the lower pane. Maybe it was a bird, she thought. An owl, perhaps, caught in the ivy while hunting mice. She got out of bed and went over to see.

The window looked out on the ornamental garden and the woods beyond. Elizabeth had spent many an hour as a child daydreaming as she sat on the window seat. Some of the dreams had been good ones, in which she was a fairy princess and a handsome prince had carried her out of danger to his castle. Some had been waking nightmares about her parents' fiery deaths. As she grew older, the prince had been replaced by plans for her future and career. She unlocked the sash and eased the window open, then peered out, gripping the frame in case the dizziness of her phobia overcame her. What she saw made her cry out in terror.

Ian Bradshaw was skillfully making his way up the wall. She watched, horrified, until he crouched on the outer sill.

"Unhook the screen and let me in, Liz," he said. "I swear I'm not Dracula."

CHAPTER THREE

HURRIEDLY, WITH FINGERS THAT SHOOK not only from her own fears, but also terror that Ian might plunge to the stone terrace two floors below, Elizabeth worked the screen loose. When she stepped back, she saw that he looked pleased and that he seemed no more anxious about his precarious position than if he was standing outside her bedroom door. With a lithe movement, he entered the room.

"Just what do you think you're doing?" she whispered impatiently, not wanting to bring anyone else's attention to the fact that he was in her room. "You could have been killed."

"Not likely." He brushed twigs and ivy leaves from his hair and clothes. He had changed into khaki shorts and a white T-shirt. No shoes. "I've made far more difficult climbs under much worse conditions for objectives that were far less compelling."

"Wha—what do you want?" She no longer felt the grip of terror, but her body was reacting by sending her into a shivering fit.

Her reaction puzzled Ian. He had expected outrage, perhaps, that he would have the nerve to climb to her bedroom. But she looked genuinely terrified. Surely she didn't care that much for him already.

"I just wandered up here to talk," he said, wondering if he should comment on the shudders that were racking her body. "We had no chance after dinner, so when I saw that your light was still on, I figured I'd take a chance on a midnight call."

She turned away, hugging herself, the shakes obviously getting worse. "We...we can talk tomorrow, Ian. Please leave by way of the door. You shouldn't be in my bedroom, anyway. We just met, after all."

He went up behind her and put his arms around her trembling body. "You ought to know by now that I don't obey conventions, Elizabeth. And you don't strike me as the kind of woman who gets all fainty and trembly when a relatively strange man is in her room. What's really the matter?" He pulled her close, marveling at how wonderful she felt, wearing just the thin, silky nightgown. Not see-through, but darned close. Close enough to satisfy him for the moment. She seemed to accept his nearness, huddling against him like a child or a frightened animal seeking comfort.

"I—I don't like heights," she whispered. "Seeing you out there, so high up with no protection..."

Mentally, Ian slapped himself. Of course. She had seen her parents die in a plane crash. It made sense that she might have developed a phobia about high places. Still holding her, he led her to the bed and sat her down, wrapping her with a mohair throw blanket lying across the foot.

"I'm sorry I scared you," he said as gently as possible, sitting beside her. "I didn't know. Want to talk about it?"

Elizabeth felt her body start to relax. His kindness warmed her as much as the blanket, and she knew she would be back to normal soon. But she shook her head. Talking about her problem never had seemed to help, and she had been shaken up enough as it was.

"Sometimes it helps—" Ian's hand touched her shoulder.

"I've tried!" she snapped, ignoring his small caress. "I've been to every specialist in the city, and not one of them has been able to help me deal with it. Remember when you asked if I'd 'traipsed' outside my territory? Well, I haven't, Dr. Bradshaw, because I *can't fly*."

"Neither can I." He began to stroke her back soothingly. "You have to have wings for that."

"Listen, it's not funny to me," she said, glaring at him.

"I can tell that." His expression was one of kind concern. "But I've found that humor can help when something's bothering me deeply. I'm sorry if I offended you."

Elizabeth smiled slightly. "You seem to be apologizing a lot tonight." His hand felt good on her back, making the tense muscles relax.

"I have, indeed. We all have our weaknesses, and annoying members of the Marlowe clan seems to be one of mine."

"Any others?" She lifted an eyebrow.

"Just beautiful blondes who are afraid of flying."

Elizabeth surprised herself by starting to laugh. It felt wonderful, and she confessed to him that perhaps he was right about humor. "I've often been told," she added, "that I tend to be too serious about things."

"Well," he said softly, "people can change, you know. We are the most adaptable of all species."

Elizabeth looked at him, feeling a new kind of warmth, the kind that had washed through her when she had first got a clear look at him. Now that her fear was past, his sensuality began to tantalize her. "I suppose you're right," she said, her voice low.

Ian kissed her. Gently, just a brush of touching, but the warmth inside her grew.

He held himself in check with difficulty. Her lips were so full and soft that he longed to taste them more intensely. But, he warned himself, he had to go slowly. The Elizabeth he was getting to know would hardly appreciate an intrusive smooch at this point. Regretfully, he pulled back.

"That was nice, Ian." Her voice was soft, and he knew he had done the right thing by not getting pushy. He saw a new light in her blue eyes.

"Tell me more about yourself," she said.

He shrugged. "I told you at dinner. I—"

"No, no." She shook off the blanket and stood, walking across the room to a large closet from which she took a disappointingly opaque bathrobe. "I mean, tell me what you like. Where you came from. How you met Michael. Things like that."

Ian smiled. The fact that she was showing some interest in his background was a good sign. Then it occurred to him that once she knew about it, she might not be very impressed. She was, after all, a true blue-blooded society lady. But if he did decide to pursue her romantically—a possibility that grew stronger with each passing moment—she would learn the truth, anyway. Might as well get it all out in the open now. At least then he would have an idea where he stood with her.

Elizabeth could see that he was hesitating. Was his past so embarrassing to him that he didn't care to share it with her? Puzzled, she took a seat on the chaise longue that graced one corner of the room. Ian cleared his throat.

"My background is very different from yours," he said slowly, rising and beginning to pace the room. He didn't look directly at her. "I'm originally a Nebraska farm boy. I grew up attending a one-room schoolhouse in the middle of the Sandhills. My parents are proud, good people, but neither one got past the eighth grade, and my father used to whip me when he found me reading instead of doing the chores." He smiled. "Until I got too big to whip, that is."

She laughed again. "Tell me about that."

Relieved that she was still displaying interest, Ian regaled her with the tale of the day he respectfully but firmly told his dad that he was going to college instead of staying on the farm. By then he was seventeen, and the chores had shaped him into the man he was now. Sam Bradshaw had glared at his son for a long moment, and then declared that if the boy wanted to waste his time and life in "book-larnin'" he reckoned that was Ian's business.

But he had had to make his own way.

"I was fortunate enough to have a teacher at that little schoolhouse," he told Elizabeth, "who approved of my intellectual ambitions. He worked my brain harder than my father worked my butt, and I got a full scholarship to the University of Nebraska. I worked part-time as a mechanic—I'd learned to fix machinery at home—and I managed to keep body and soul together while finishing my undergraduate work.''

Elizabeth listened, amazed. Her own life, in spite of the loss of her parents, had been luxurious by comparison. She couldn't imagine the strength of will it must have taken to pull himself out of his original environment and eventually graduate from Harvard with a doctorate. It certainly explained his ability to adapt. The man must be highly intelligent and capable.

"My parents are proud of me," he went on. "But I don't think they've ever really understood why I went the route I did."

"Do they still farm?"

Ian grinned. "My old man only had an eighth-grade education, but he wasn't dumb. He sold the farm a few years back for a whopping profit, and now they live in a quiet little town in Nebraska, enjoying retirement."

"Now what about meeting Michael?" Elizabeth asked. She didn't feel the least bit sleepy, and since Ian seemed to be in a talkative mood, she was going to get all she could out of him.

"Michael." Ian laughed. "I took my master's at Nebraska, then applied to Harvard just for the hell of it, to see what would happen. No one was more surprised than me when I was accepted *and* received another scholarship. But boy, oh, boy, was I unprepared for Boston and the Harvard social life. I was a hick in spite of all of my education. Your cousin has a very kind side to his crazy personality, and he took me under his wing, teaching me how to adapt."

"I imagine you caught on fast."

He stopped pacing and faced her, hands on his hips. "Now why would you think that, Elizabeth?" His silvery eyes gleamed amusement.

"I've seen you in action, remember?" She lay back on the lounge. "Robert loathed you, but during dinner you had him engaged in quite civilized conversation."

"And you aren't mad at me anymore." Ian barely controlled the urge to go lie down on the chaise beside her and take her in his arms. Did she have any idea how inviting and tempting she was?

Elizabeth watched him. Conversation hadn't been the only thing on his mind when he had scaled the wall to her bedroom window. She was certain of that . . . and pleased. But she found herself feeling strangely shy. His gentle kiss had stirred her, but she wasn't sure she could trust herself to engage in anything else. He was just too appealing, and the situation was ripe for far more than she was willing to do with a man she had just met.

"Ian, how old are you?" she asked, trying to break the sexual tension that she felt rising between them. "You met Michael at school, but you seem much more mature."

"You mean older?" Again the glint of amusement, warmed by some other emotion.

"I don't mean it negatively," she countered. "There's a sureness and steadiness about you that

I've only seen in men who've found their place in life, who are sure of themselves and their destiny."

Ian ambled over and sat at the foot of the chaise. "That's a bit heavy for midnight conversation, don't you think?"

"Maybe." His thigh was millimeters from her bare feet, and the heat of his skin as well as the tickling from the hair on it wasn't helping her keep her cool. "But I am curious," she added.

"Okay." He leaned back on his hands and looked at the ceiling. "I went to Nebraska when I was nineteen. Five years for the bachelor's and master's. That would have made me—"

"Twenty-four when you hit Harvard."

He smiled and looked at her. "I should have known better than to patronize a financial wizard."

"I'm no wizard, but I do well for my clients. So you were several years older than Michael when you met. What drew you together?"

"You are a persistent lady." He reached over and gently tickled the sole of her foot. Elizabeth jerked back, protesting sharply. But instead of stopping, he took her other foot in his hand and ran his fingers over the arch. "You also have beautiful feet," he said.

His touch didn't help. Elizabeth began to feel a shimmering, delicious twisting deep inside. What she really wanted was for him to release her foot and move up to cover her body with his own. And to cover her lips with his.

"Millennia to develop such a foot," he murmured, running his fingertips over her ankle. "Sheer artistry."

"Why, thank you, sir." She tried to sound sarcastic. "But I thought we were on the subject of your past and meeting my cousin. Not the shape of my toes."

Ian knew he was getting to her. The tiny pulse just behind her anklebone had already increased its rate, and he could see a blush in her cheeks. But he decided to continue playing the game her way... for a while longer.

"You know about freshman hazing," he said. She nodded. "Well," he went on, "if you remember, when Mike first went to Harvard he was tall but thinner than he is now."

"He was a scrawny teenager," she agreed, smiling at the memory. "I remember how surprised I was when I saw him at Christmastime, how much he'd developed."

"Late bloomer. Anyway, he stood out because of his height and was a natural target for the upperclassmen because he looked like a weakling. And you know Mike. He couldn't resist trying some of his jokes on people. He became a marked man."

"That's when you stepped in? Superman to the rescue?"

He shook his head. "I'm not that noble. I have to admit that I hardly noticed him at first. After all, I was in graduate school, and he was only a frosh."

"So...?" She sat up and leaned her elbows on her knees.

"So one day I was plodding across campus to the library, and he happened to be heading in the same direction. We ended up walking up the steps in unison, and I noticed that he was sporting one hell of a shiner. He smiled and said hello, and I, in my usual blunt way, pointed at the eye and asked if the door was still in one piece. He grinned wryly and said sure, all sophomore doors stay in one piece. That's when I figured he was being picked on.

"Instead of going inside, we sat down on the steps and introduced ourselves. We shared our problems and that was the beginning of our friendship."

"So you became his protector, and he taught you social graces?"

"Not exactly." The light in his eyes told her that he was thoroughly enjoying reminiscing with her. "I pulled him out of a few scrapes, but mainly I pushed him into a program of physical training and taught him to defend himself. I couldn't always be at his side, and he wasn't about to stop being himself."

"The irrepressible jokester."

"Right."

"And what did you do in return?"

Ian shifted position so that he was sitting cross-legged in front of Elizabeth, looking directly into her eyes. "Why don't I just give you a simple example?"

"All right." A fluttering started deep inside her.

"Before I met Michael," he said, a wicked gleam in those silver eyes, "*if* I had managed to find the time and nerve to climb up into your bedroom in the dead of night, we would not have spent the past twenty minutes or so talking. Either I would have been out on my ear, or..." He glanced behind him at the bed.

"I get the idea," she said quickly. "But since you met Michael, I imagine you've climbed many a wall with seduction on your mind."

"Curious about my sex life?" The look in his eyes was more intense.

"Of course not," she lied. "I just . . ."

Her words trailed off. Ian was edging forward, looking almost exactly as he had when he'd circled her in the forest. Elizabeth's heart started to beat wildly, but she remained motionless, caught by the sensual shimmer in his eyes. Then their lips met.

This was no brush-kiss! His mouth gently persuaded hers to open, and his body slowly eased hers back on the lounge. She wrapped her arms around his neck, feeling the oak-tree hardness of his back and shoulders and the magical quality of his kiss.

Ian held his weight off her, but let himself indulge in slightly pressing against her and feeling the rounded swells of her breasts against his chest. Her slender thighs lay between his own, and he didn't dare bring their hips into contact. Then she would have every right to declare him no gentleman! But he tasted the sweetness of her mouth and wound his fingers in the silk of her long hair. Heaven . . .

"Elizabeth?" A soft voice calling her name and a quick, furtive rap at the bedroom door brought them both immediately to their feet.

"It's Jennifer," Elizabeth whispered. "She must have seen the light under the door." The knock was repeated, and she thought she detected a strained note in Jennifer's voice when she called her name again. Remembering the sadness she had noticed in the other woman's eyes, she knew she couldn't put her off, no matter how much she wanted to continue kissing Ian. "Just a second, Jen," she called, then whispered to Ian, "I've got to see her."

He looked disappointed, but grinned slyly. "Saved by a knock at the door?"

"I wasn't 'saved' from anything. I was having just as good a time as you were."

"I doubt that." His eyes were unreadable. "But I'll just let myself out the same way I—"

"You will *not*," she whispered, pushing him toward the bathroom. "I don't let men I kiss risk their necks just to keep my reputation. Go hide in the shower stall or something until she's gone. Then you can leave safely through the door." To her relief, he obeyed.

Ian still felt the blood zinging through his veins as he shut the bathroom door behind him and heard Elizabeth let Jennifer into the bedroom. That had been some kiss, and he was disappointed that it had ended all too soon. But she had been responsive, and he knew that tomorrow he would get a chance to get close to her again. For a moment, he gazed around the room, savoring the scent of her that lingered in this private place and noting the neatly arranged toiletries. Then he moved silently to the window, unhooked the screen and let himself out. As he climbed down the wall, he whistled softly to himself.

ELIZABETH LISTENED to the outpouring of sorrow and confusion from Jennifer, and her heart went out to the younger woman. "I love Michael," Jennifer was saying. "I could never love anyone else. I want to have his children. Remember what Robert was saying tonight about heirs?''

Elizabeth nodded. ''I thought that particular remark was meant for me until Michael jumped in, and I could see that you were affected by it, too.''

Jennifer started to cry. Elizabeth reached for the box of Kleenex on the bedside table, handed it to her and put a comforting arm around her shoulders. It was some time before Jennifer cried herself out, but finally she took a deep breath and spoke.

''I'm beginning to believe that we're unable to have children,'' she said. ''And Michael won't take my worries seriously.'' She blushed under her tan. ''He just laughs and says all we have to do is keep on the way we've been doing, and everything will work out.''

''Maybe he's right.''

''Elizabeth...'' Jennifer's tone was angry now. ''I'm actually embarrassed to tell you how often we make love! If I haven't conceived by now, something's definitely wrong.''

Elizabeth considered Jennifer's words. Her cousin-in-law was in fine physical shape because of her tennis playing. She was slender and wiry, and could slam a ball so hard that it literally whistled its way across the net. A separate room had to be cleared out to house the growing number of trophies she had collected. Once Jennifer had even confided to Elizabeth that before Michael had asked her to marry him, she had been considering going pro, but that she preferred home and hearth. Elizabeth found that almost incomprehensible, thinking that any woman with a talent should develop it to the fullest, but she accepted the old-fashioned attitude in Jennifer because she cared so much for Michael's young wife.

"We need to see a professional fertility counselor," Jennifer said, a hard note in her usually soft voice. "I've argued myself blue in the face with Michael, but he just doesn't listen."

"Oh, he's listening, all right. Jennifer, he's changed since I last saw him. He's as jumpy and nervous as a cat. Even the timing of his jokes is off. I knew something was bothering him by the way he spoke and behaved this evening. You're getting through to him. Maybe it's taking time, but you know Michael—when he doesn't want to worry, he just won't. At least not outwardly."

"But we don't have time!" Jennifer threw up her arms. "We need to start a family as soon as possible—neither of us is getting any younger. I don't care if he isn't ready. I want him to face the truth. Infertility on *his* part could be the problem."

"True enough." Elizabeth thought for a moment. "But you can't just drag him to a doctor. He'd have to be willing." She glanced over at the closed bathroom door and hoped that Ian wasn't overhearing this intimate conversation. He'd likely offer to hog-tie Michael and do the dragging!

"Tell you what," she said. "I have a good friend, Sue Fuller, who's a gynecologist. I know she counsels couples on these matters. How about letting me set up an appointment with her for you? She'll do me the favor of working you in as soon as she can. Don't tell Michael—just say you're coming into the city to visit me and do some special shopping. Then, when

Sue gets the results from examining you, you'll have factual ammunition to throw at him. If there is a problem with your body, maybe it can be fixed. If you're fine, then it's his turn."

Jennifer shook her head mournfully. "I just know he wouldn't go in. He has as much pride as any Marlowe, and his ego would be so crushed if he found out he was—"

"Listen." Elizabeth took Jennifer firmly by the shoulders. "Do you or do you not want to solve the problem?"

Jennifer's eyes filled with tears. "I do."

"Then you have to be strong enough to help Michael take the steps necessary. Egos mend, and there are other options to having your own baby."

"I know." Jennifer bowed her head. "But I want *ours*."

"Jennifer, you know life's not going to give you everything you want." She thought back to Ian's description of his years on the farm. "You and I have had it so easy compared to so many other people."

"You're making me ashamed of myself." Jennifer gave a little laugh. "And you're right. I'll just have to accept whatever happens."

"Now that sounds more like the Jennifer I love. Besides, once you have some facts, if you care to, you can share the problem with Robert and Grandmother. Even if Michael is too stubborn to listen to you, I know he'll have a hard time resisting those two. Especially since it's evident how badly Robert wants a grandchild."

Jennifer rolled her eyes, which told Elizabeth that she had been hounded by her father-in-law. *Caught between a rock and a hard place,* Elizabeth thought. *No wonder the poor woman is so upset.*

Then Jennifer squared her small shoulders. "Thanks, Elizabeth. I'm so glad I came up to talk to you." Elizabeth received a hug.

"Now I'd better get back to bed," Jennifer said, standing. "I don't want Michael waking up and finding me gone. By the way, we decided it would be fun to play doubles in the afternoon. Willing?" Her tone and expression were challenging.

Elizabeth groaned. The thought of being on the court with the tennis flash and gigantic, powerful Ian made her cower. She did exercise regularly at an aerobics class, but she wasn't sure she was up to this.

"Chicken," Jennifer teased. "I promise to go easy on you. And Ian volunteered to be on your side. He could probably just hit the ball with his hand, not bother with a racket."

The mental picture sent Elizabeth into peals of laughter. She agreed to the match, declaring it would be worth it just to see Ian in action.

"And if you're really lucky," Jennifer went on in the same teasing tone as she moved toward the door, "you might run into Bill Stockdale. I suppose Adelaide told you that he and Muffy broke up, and gossip hath it that his unrequited affection for you was the cause."

Elizabeth swore. "If I see him and he tries to get friendly, I'll just loose Ian on him."

Jennifer's eyes widened. "You're safe, then. I know Ian likes you from some of the things he said and the way he looked at you when you weren't aware." She opened the door. "Thanks," she said in a voice husky with emotion. "You've helped me so much."

"That's what families are for."

Tears filled Jennifer's eyes, but they didn't spill. "I guess that's right," she said, then left.

Elizabeth expected Ian to emerge from the bathroom—he must have heard the door close. She wondered if she could just send him on his way, or if they would be drawn into another kiss. She hadn't needed Jennifer's assurances that Ian liked her—his caresses had made that plain.

And she had to admit that she liked him, too. Not just because of his looks and sexiness, but because of the things she had learned about him. After a few more moments, she went over and opened the bathroom door herself.

Empty. And the screen was off the wide-open window. That idiot! Climbing walls again. Only this time he didn't have the advantage of the thick ivy, since the vine refused to grow on this side of the mansion. Her heart hammering in her chest, she stood cautiously on the commode and peered down into the darkness. No crumpled form lay sprawled on the grass.

Relief flooded her. She closed the window and sat on the seat for a moment to calm herself. Really, she thought, who was she to be giving out psychological advice when she was such a ninny about heights. Maybe she should give therapy another try.

She walked out of the bathroom, turned off the light, shed her robe and crawled wearily between the sheets. If she was going to survive the game in the afternoon, she had better get plenty of rest, she warned herself.

Her body began to relax in spite of the strains that had been put on it since she arrived at the estate, and she knew that sleep would come soon. As she grew drowsier, she remembered that she had never learned Ian's age. Since she wasn't sure how long it had taken him to get his doctorate, and how many years he had been working, she could only guestimate and put him in his early thirties. The tropical sun had weathered his skin, so it was difficult to tell by looking at his face. His body was certainly that of a man in his prime, though. She ought to do some serious showing off of him at the club. Word would spread that she had a new beau, and even if she never saw Ian again, never showed up with him again, it would start new gossip that would discourage Bill—*if* Adelaide was right about the rumors of his continuing affection for her.

But the thought of not seeing Ian again brought a feeling of emptiness. She liked him, in spite of the differences between them, and she let images of him do whatever they wanted in her fertile imagination while she drifted into sleep.

CHAPTER FOUR

WHEN SHE AWOKE, Elizabeth could tell by the position of the sunlight on the pewter-colored carpet that it was midmorning. She had overslept for hours!

Of course, she reasoned as she showered and hunted up tennis clothing, she had been up half the night, so her laziness was forgivable. Combing out her hair without bothering to dry it, she tucked the long damp strands behind her ears. She ought to cut it short, she thought as she made her way downstairs to sneak a late breakfast from the kitchen. Cutting it would give her a more fashionable, sophisticated look, anyway, but she wasn't sure she could stand to have it short after leaving it long all her life. Decisions, decisions. She headed for the back hall.

"Elizabeth?" Robert's call stopped her. *Caught,* she thought, turning to smile sheepishly at her uncle.

"Good morning," she said cheerfully, watching him approach, concern written all over his face. He was in his Saturday casuals: polo shirt and light-gray slacks. He carried his golf shoes, and she figured that he was on his way to the course.

"Are you ill, Elizabeth?" he asked when he reached her. "Since you went to bed so early, I assumed you had arisen before any of us, but I just learned from Charters that you hadn't even been down for breakfast."

"I was tired, but I just couldn't fall asleep." Not exactly a lie, just not all the truth. "I was on my way to the kitchen for breakfast now." She smiled. "I assume you know about the Great Tennis Match this afternoon."

He seemed to accept her explanation. "I do and approve heartily. When you lived here and used the club's facilities regularly, you had a healthy glow about you this time of year. Now you seem so pale. Well, forgive me again. I know it's your life. I just—"

"You just love me," she interjected, giving him a kiss on the cheek. *And can't stand not running my life like you do your corporations,* she thought. But it was a loving thought, not a bitter one. Robert was the way he was, and she didn't want to change him. She simply did what she felt was right for herself, regardless of his opinion, though she never ignored his advice. Her uncle was a wise man.

Elizabeth asked if he would like to join her for a cup of coffee while she ate, and he agreed, saying he had time before teeing off. They sat in the kitchen as the large, cheerful Swedish woman whose unpronounceable name had led the family to resort to the simple title, Cook, poured coffee for them and started to assemble a breakfast for Elizabeth. In her lilting English, Cook informed Elizabeth that she had been missed by herself and the other people who kept the mansion running. She also commented that she thought Elizabeth looked too thin. Had she been eating properly?

"Not you, too, Cook," Elizabeth replied, laughing. "First my uncle worries about my health, and now you say I'm too skinny. Believe me, I am *fine*."

"Aren't you at least lonely?" Robert asked. "After living among us for so many years, doesn't the solitude ever get to you?"

"I miss you all," she said, including the cook. "But I'm happy and too busy to be lonely. Robert, I have friends, and you know I love my work. Being so near my office gives me more time for both. Think of the hours I used to waste commuting."

"Just promise me one thing," he said, setting down his cup. "No, make that two. First, if you ever need our help, you won't hesitate to call. I know firsthand about Marlowe pride, and I'm afraid that you've got a big dose of it, my dear."

She laughed. "That's the pot calling the kettle black, all right."

His grin was wry. "Maybe so. But I really mean it, Elizabeth. Members of this family are meant to help one another."

"True." She remembered her session with Jennifer last night. "All right, I promise that one. What's next?"

"That you'll plan to come home more often." There was a pleading look in his eyes. "Don't stay away for so many weeks the way you did this summer."

Elizabeth bit her lip. She had deliberately avoided coming back in order to make it perfectly clear to everyone that she had meant it when she moved away. And now that she was learning how much she liked being alone, she shied away from the idea of sharing a lot of her spare time, even with her beloved family. "I'll be back as often as I can," she hedged. "I can't promise any more than that."

"If it's your social life," he offered, "you can bring a houseguest anytime. You know that."

She smiled wickedly. "Even if he's one like Ian?" Robert looked heavenward.

At that moment, the subject of her words, accompanied by Michael, entered the room. The men were dressed handsomely in tennis whites, and Elizabeth felt her heart beat faster at the sight of Ian. The whites showed off his body to perfection and complemented his tanned skin and dark hair.

They greeted Robert and herself, Michael giving her a kiss on the cheek, and Ian looking as if he'd like to do the same, only on her lips. The look in his gray eyes was warm.

Ian resisted embarrassing her by sweeping her into an embrace and kissing her as he had last night. He called bawdily to the cook in her native language, one of several he knew, and received a cheerful scolding in the same vein.

"Food!" Michael thundered. "Feed us, Cook, for we duel in an hour." He scooped up a chair and sat down next to Elizabeth.

"So, older cousin, age making you sleep late?" he asked, grinning.

"I had trouble getting to sleep." She could see that Ian was trying his best to keep a straight face. "*Things* kept bothering me," she added. Ian didn't flinch.

They bantered good-naturedly, Robert even joining in in a more dignified way, while Cook prepared enormous sandwiches for the two younger men. Michael explained that Jennifer was already at the club, practicing.

"Oh, boy." Elizabeth covered her face with her hands. "Ian, if you're not a great player, we're dead."

"I hate to be the one to break the news to you," he said, an amused light in his eyes. "But the last time I played tennis was about seven years ago with an old Britisher in Singapore. I don't even remember how to score."

"We're dead," she moaned.

But dead they weren't. Jennifer gave the three a few minutes to warm up on the backboards, and Elizabeth watched Ian out of the corner of her eye as she worked her ball. He had no style and was awkward, but the man was a natural player, hardly ever muffing a return. Hope began to rise in her.

Ian concentrated on his hand-eye coordination. He had been warned of Jennifer's reputation and had no intention of being whipped badly, especially along with Elizabeth. Every minute he was with her made him feel that there was potential for something special between them. Even though they hadn't touched today, he could sense the delicious tension between them. He wanted to hold her and kiss her, and instinct told him she wanted exactly the same thing. He promised himself he'd make ample opportunity for that later. Swinging at a yellow tennis ball, he sent it careering back to the board, making a loud thump with the power of his serve. His peripheral vision caught a number of people stopping to stare at him.

Their arrival at the club had caused a stir. He was used to attracting attention because of his size, but when he had been introduced to some of Elizabeth's friends, there had been a definite curiosity in their eyes. And his instincts told him that it had little to do with his appearance. He whapped the ball again.

"Court time," Jennifer called. "And for heaven's sake, Ian, don't drive a hole in the backboard. This is a game, not a war."

Ian grinned at her. "Just so you keep that in mind, too, Miz Marlowe, ma'am."

Elizabeth strolled over, and Ian draped his arm across her shoulders. "What do you say, partner? Shall we whip them with mercy or without?" The flowery scent of her perfume mingled with the natural, feminine scent of her, and he inhaled with pleasure.

"Ian," she cautioned, "if we limp our way to a marginally unhumiliating defeat, we'll be doing fantastically."

"How about a kiss for good luck?" He gazed down at her, then covered her lips with his own before she could answer.

Weakness, delicious weakness, flooded her, and Elizabeth felt only regret when he made the kiss a short one. Worried that her arousal had destroyed any possibility of even hitting the ball, she allowed him to lead her to their side of the court.

The two pairs squared off, and she noticed that a small crowd was gathering to watch. *Oh, this is going to be awful,* she mourned inwardly.

But it wasn't; it was fun. Jennifer kept her promise about not playing her usual murderous style, and

Ian proved to be skillful at partnering, giving Elizabeth the ball when the moment was opportune and not trying to overwhelm their opponents with his strength. Michael played antically, frequently making his cousin blow a return because she was laughing too hard. She and Ian actually won one set, though they were defeated in the others. But not by too much, to her surprise.

At the end of the match, Ian literally grabbed another opportunity to get close to his lovely partner. Remembering that the elderly Englishman he had beaten in Singapore had apologized for not being agile enough to leap the net to shake the winner's hand, he scooped Elizabeth up in his arms and cleared the net easily while she screamed at him to put her down before he killed them both.

Her heart racing in fear, and her face flushed from the onlookers' laughter and applause, Elizabeth hissed warning curses into Ian's ear, only delighting him with her range of vocabulary, imagination and the soft caress of her warm breath.

"I had no idea what a cad I was, Lizzie," he teased, lowering her slowly so that her body stayed close to his. They had both perspired during the game, and she seemed even more alluring, angry and sweaty.

"Great game, Ian." Jennifer shook his hand firmly. "And that was quite a feat, getting over the net like that. Elizabeth, you shouldn't be so upset with him."

"I'm not upset," Elizabeth answered icily. "I'm furious. He took a terrible chance—"

"Nonsense," Michael interrupted her. "I've seen Ian do physical feats that would turn your hair white, cousin."

So have I, she thought, remembering the climbing stunt. Ian, it seemed, had a penchant for doing risky things. In spite of her attraction to him, it was probably a good thing she wouldn't be seeing him after tomorrow. The last thing she needed was to become attached to a man who took his own safety so lightly.

"Come on, Elizabeth." Ian touched her shoulder. "I knew I could make it without any trouble or I wouldn't have tried it. You ought to know that I wouldn't do anything to hurt you. Say you forgive me, and let's go buy the winners a drink."

He looked so appealing standing there grinning at her that she just couldn't resist. "All right," she conceded. "But next time please ask before you decide to play Superman with me in your arms."

His eyes warmed. "I'll be sure to do that, Elizabeth," he said, an undercurrent of sensual promise in his words that sent a thrill through her. Yes, indeed, she thought. It was a good thing they wouldn't have a chance to let this get going. There was a distinct possibility that this man could make her lose her romantic objectivity. . . .

The clubhouse was pleasantly cool after the heat of the afternoon sun. Elizabeth stretched, already feeling muscles that would be sore in the morning. "Oh," she commented, "I haven't had a workout like that in a long time. I think I need some time in a Jacuzzi more than I do a drink."

"Bow to tradition," Michael told her. "You lost, and you must pay the price."

Laughing at the atrocious middle-European accent Michael had used, Elizabeth agreed, and the four of them found a table that looked out on the golf course. The greens were emerald in the afternoon sun, and the course was crowded with players. "Maybe we'll see Robert," she said.

"I hope he has a good game," Jennifer commented. "When he does poorly he's an absolute bear."

"Not unlike another little athlete I know," Michael said tauntingly. Jennifer made a face at her husband. Michael returned the favor, and they both started laughing as if at some private joke.

Ian watched, jealousy biting at him. Mike and Jen were still so in love after almost four years of marriage. Oh, he'd seen signs of tension in them both—no relationship was without its problems. But affection didn't seem lacking. He wondered what it would be like to share life and love with one woman. To have a family. But that would mean settling down, giving up his frequent trips to distant, fascinating places. His own childhood, even with differences in outlook between his parents and himself, had been a secure one, and he would give no less to his wife and child. He just wasn't ready.

"You know," he said, turning to Elizabeth, "I never did learn exactly what it is you do in that concrete jungle you seem so fond of. I know it has something to do with finance, but what specifically?"

"Before I answer that," she stated, a challenging note in her voice, "why don't you tell me what you've got against New York?"

"I feel suffocated there."

"I feel stimulated."

"We have a definite environmental disagreement, don't we, Liz?"

Anger flashed in her eyes—thunder in the blue. "Ian, whenever you use that nickname, all I can think of is lizards. I really wish you'd stop."

"Lizards?" He laughed. "I'd never thought of that. Sorry. I have a habit of shortening names automatically. In your case, I'll try to make an exception."

"I'd appreciate it."

A waitress came to their table and took drink orders. It was beer all around.

"What?" Michael asked. "No G and T, Elizabeth? I thought that was all you ever drank after tennis. Have you changed so much I can't predict your drink favorites?"

"People do change, Michael," she said, giving Jennifer a glance. Her cousin-in-law winked at her.

"Let's get back to my question about your profession," Ian interjected. "As a scientist, I'm naturally curious and hate to have a question go unanswered."

Elizabeth shrugged. "I simply analyze the financial market and advise some people how to invest their money so it'll do the best work for them."

"She's being modest," Michael said. "She has her own stable of very wealthy clients who wouldn't invest a dime without her approval. Our Elizabeth seems to have precognition concerning the money market. She's downright uncanny."

Elizabeth blushed at the open compliment. Michael didn't give many of those. "I just keep up with the news, study industry, read the right journals. It's not hard to make choices when you've done your homework."

"You must not have time for anything else." Ian leaned an elbow on the table and regarded her out of smoke-gray eyes. "Somehow I have difficulty picturing you spending all your time nose to the grindstone. New York must be full of guys without much sense if you don't have an active social life."

"I have friends," she replied. "I go out." Smiling, she confessed to being a movie freak. "I'll go see anything, good, bad and indifferent. I love being taken to some exotic place for a few hours."

Ian regarded her as conversation lulled while the waitress served the beer. Her favorite form of entertainment was probably an unconscious replacement for travel, for visiting foreign places, for seeing the real thing. He wondered if anyone had ever pointed this out to her. He decided he'd better wait to do so. He had ruffled her feathers enough today.

"Do you ever take on small-time clients?" he asked. "My financial condition is either feast or famine, depending on grants, royalties and work in the movies. I could use some advice on planning—I tend to spend every cent the minute I get it and then I'm broke until the next windfall."

"That's a terrible way to manage money!" She was genuinely horrified. "You'd better find yourself a manager where you live whom you can trust. I'd be happy to help you, but since you don't live in New York—"

"Just because I don't like it doesn't mean I haven't accepted the necessity of living there for a while."

"You live in Manhattan?" Elizabeth was amazed. She felt a tingle of excitement ... and then a frisson of worry. If he lived there, no doubt they would see each other again, especially if she agreed to help him with his finances.

Ian took a long drink of his beer. A number of emotions had just passed over Elizabeth's face. Clearly, he had her disturbed. Interesting. "I'm in a famine period," he confessesd. "A friend of mine who has a studio apartment on the West Side is letting me live in his place free for a while. He's in Los Angeles working in a movie. Where do you live?"

"Upper East."

"So we're a simple subway ride from each other's front door."

"Isn't that a coincidence," Michael said. The smug expression on his face told Elizabeth all she needed to know. He *had* arranged for Ian and herself to meet this weekend. Had presented them to each other like prize animals!

But he couldn't have been sure that they would hit it off. He couldn't have known that Ian would appeal to her so much, that Ian would be interested enough in her to climb up a wall, for goodness' sake, to talk to her.

Or could he? Michael was known as a master of industrial politics. He knew people. She glanced at Jennifer. Too bad the talent didn't extend to himself, to his own psyche.

"Yes, that is an interesting coincidence," she repeated as sweetly as possible. "And I meant what I said about offering to help you straighten out your finances, Ian.'' That ought to make everyone happy. She gave Michael a suspicious glare. He only smiled back. Ian's eyes were glimmering like quicksilver.

Ian had already reasoned that Michael's invitation had been a setup. At first he had balked, not wanting to be saddled for a whole weekend with a spinster blind date who might turn out to be unpleasant. But when he had arrived in New York weeks ago and had phoned his old friend, he knew that the setup would be worth it just to get a chance to see Michael in his home environment. They could always get together in the city, but Ian had jumped at the opportunity to get away from the crowds and noise for a couple of days. What he hadn't agreed to, now to his regret, was to call Michael's Manhattan-dwelling cousin, who planned to visit the estate the same weekend, and catch a ride with her. Instead, he had chosen the bus as the cheapest form of transportation, and Michael had met him at the depot nearest the Marlowe estate. He planned, however, to ride back with Elizabeth.

"I'll be getting some royalty money in October," he told her. "Until then, I'm nickel and diming it, as usual. I have applied to be a guest lecturer at New York University, Columbia and several smaller colleges, but haven't received notice that they want me yet.''

"But it's a possibility.'' She queried him further and decided that his erratic income would best be budgeted carefully, with small amounts invested in strong, steady money funds and growth stocks. That way he would have enough to live on decently, plus the security of the investments to help him through lean times.

"It must be frightening not knowing when you are going to have money," Jennifer commented. "You were right, Elizabeth. I'm wrong to ever complain—"

"Complain about what?" Michael asked sharply, looking at his wife. Had she, he wondered, confided their private, *very* personal problem to his cousin?

"Oh," Jennifer responded in a cheerful tone, allaying his suspicions, "about anything." She gave her husband a kiss. "I have such a wonderful life."

"So have I, Jennifer," Ian interjected. "Only different from yours. I've been privileged to wake up to the sound of meadowlarks singing at dawn on a spring morning in the Nebraska Sandhills. I've watched a family of mountain gorillas gather food on a misty hillside in Africa." He chuckled. "From a respectful distance and through binoculars, I've seen lionesses stalk zebras, working for the family meal while the king of the pride dozes in the shade, stirring himself only occasionally to scratch."

Elizabeth listened, entranced. What an exciting life he led, if unpredictable. Her imagination soared as it had when she was a child. "I wish I could see some of that," she whispered to herself. If only she wasn't earthbound by her fears...

Ian's sensitive hearing picked up what Jennifer and Michael had not. He reached over and touched Elizabeth's hand, trying to communicate his understanding and sympathy. He also resolved to find some way to help her, if he could. If she was willing to help him, he should only return the favor in some way.

They chatted on for a while, comparing life-styles and experiences. Michael ordered another round of beers and some munchies to accompany them. Elizabeth settled back, relaxed and thoroughly enjoying herself. She put her worries about any future relationship with Ian aside and simply appreciated his company and that of her relatives. They were all, she decided, very compatible.

The lounge was beginning to fill up as club members finished tennis matches and golf rounds. Several times the foursome was interrupted by friends and acquaintances who came over to say hello to Elizabeth. Most, she realized, were also curious about Ian.

One older woman, who was a good friend of her grandmother's but known as a merciless gossip, grilled Ian to the point of rudeness. He handled it well, answering all the woman's pointed questions with a gentle politeness that made Elizabeth admire him all the more. If she was being probed like that, she would have clammed up and given the woman no information at all. But Ian proudly declared his background and occupation. Michael finally saved him by standing and announcing that the beer had done its job, he needed to visit the men's room, and would Ian care to do the same. After the two men had walked off, excusing themselves to the ladies, Adelaide's friend also departed.

"Apparently we aren't interesting," Jennifer whispered, giggling. "All Mrs. Nosiness wanted was the skinny on Ian. In five minutes, everyone in this place is going to know all about him.''

Elizabeth had to agree, and she found that she was more than a little annoyed at the fact. Ian's past had seemed a treasure that belonged only to her, since he had shared it with her under such intimate circumstances. She resented, illogically, that it was soon to be public knowledge.

"Uh-oh!" Jennifer suddenly exclaimed. "Don't look now, but the last person in the world we want to see today has just entered the room."

Elizabeth turned to see who she meant and saw Muffy Turner engaged in conversation with Adelaide's gossipy friend. The young woman's head was lowered, and she was clearly listening intently to what the older woman said.

"Just what we need," Elizabeth moaned, turning back to Jennifer. "Would it be possible to escape through the kitchen?"

"Not without letting the men know where we are," Jennifer said. "No, dear friend, I think you're doomed to a confrontation."

"I think I would almost have preferred Bill."

They waited, tension building. Elizabeth picked up a potato chip and crushed it on her cocktail napkin. She didn't know Muffy well. The woman was younger and ran with a different group of friends than Elizabeth had when she had lived on Long Island. But she doubted, from what she had been told by both Jennifer and Adelaide last night, that Muffy felt much friendliness toward her.

"Here she comes," Jennifer warned.

Elizabeth steeled herself and tried to put on a pleasant expression. But Muffy Turner's first words to her destroyed any chance she had of hanging on to her temper.

CHAPTER FIVE

"I HEAR you've got a new boyfriend, Elizabeth," the brunette said from where she stood beside the table. "Bill wasn't good enough for you, but you must be a real fool to let a country-hick fortune hunter date you!"

Elizabeth felt the explosion building inside her. If she released it, Muffy Turner was liable to be history. Lady or no lady, she had a right to protect the reputation of her friends. And she certainly considered Ian Bradshaw a friend. Jennifer must have seen the steam rising, because she put a restraining hand on Elizabeth's arm.

"Terrific seeing you, too, Muffy," Jennifer cooed. "Were you able to land that job with that ad agency I heard you talking about last weekend?"

Muffy reddened. "They said they'd call," she snapped.

"Don't call us, we'll...and so forth, hmmm?" Jennifer was really twisting the knife, Elizabeth thought. Good. It was giving her time to cool off.

But Muffy returned her venomous attention to Elizabeth. "I don't believe I got an answer, Miss Heartbreaker. Is it true that you've taken up with a man who studies *monkeys* for a living and whose parents are Midwestern *dirt* farmers?"

"My father grew wheat." Ian's huge form loomed behind Muffy. "You know, young lady—the stuff the bread you eat is made of. Or maybe you don't know that. Perhaps you've grown up thinking that it was produced magically for your personal enjoyment."

The brunette whirled to face him, her gasp of surprise audible to Elizabeth, who had to struggle to keep from laughing aloud. Muffy Turner had really dug her own grave this time.

Ian glared down at the obviously embarrassed and confused woman. This was just the kind of snotty snob he had expected Elizabeth to be. Not bad-looking, but compared to *his* lady...

"As for the monkeys, miss, mankind's greed is driving animals out of their natural, God-given habitats. My job is to prepare information that will help provide a place for the remaining ones to live as full a life as possible." The scorn in his voice and on his face was withering, and as Elizabeth watched, Muffy actually seemed to shrink. What, she thought, would he have done if he had overheard himself accused of being a fortune hunter?

"I...I..." Muffy stammered.

"Hi, Muffy." Michael appeared behind Ian. "Ladies, I just ran into Dad. Time for us to head back home. Bye, Muffy. Get that job?"

Wordlessly, Muffy scurried away. Elizabeth finally gave vent to her feelings, laughing first, then getting up to give Ian a hug. "That was wonderful," she told him. "Jennifer will tell you what *I* was nearly ready to do."

"I believe," Jennifer said in an artificially cultured tone, "that Elizabeth would have defended your honor, Ian, in the unladylike manner of decking Miss Turner."

"Then I would have probably stomped on her," Elizabeth added. "Your method was much more civilized." She smiled up at him.

Ian was surprised. He would have expected Elizabeth to exchange insults, perhaps, but for her to physically defend his honor? Her temper must have a shorter fuse than he had yet seen.

As they made their way out of the club to the parking lot, Michael told him a story that confirmed this. Shortly after her parents had been killed, a classmate had made the mistake of taunting Elizabeth about being an orphan and had implied that her dead father had been a poor pilot. The kid was out of school for a week, Michael said. No one, he declared, denounced the good name or honor of anyone his hot-tempered cousin cared about.

The knowledge brought a glow to Ian. Had he really managed to gain her affection already? Certainly their kisses had been passionate, and she had volunteered to help him with his perennial money problems. But to care for him enough to start a physical fight with a catty bitch? No, he really didn't think she would have done that, in spite of what Jennifer said.

When they got to Michael's Rolls, Elizabeth realized that she'd left her racket by the table and excused herself to retrieve it, saying she'd be right back. Hurrying into the clubhouse, she almost bumped into the next to last person she wanted to see, Bill Stockdale.

"What did you do to Muffy?" the blond man demanded, blocking her way. "I saw her just a minute ago, and she was sobbing something about you and your boyfriend insulting her."

"What do you care?" Elizabeth snapped. "You aren't engaged to her anymore." She tried to move past him, but he wouldn't let her.

"You haven't changed a bit, have you?" he accused. "Still riding roughshod over people's feelings."

"Bill, she insulted my friend, not the other way around. And if you don't get out of my way, you're going to be sorry."

"Muffy's a sweet person. She couldn't have—"

"Bill. *Move.*"

He seemed to hear the warning in her voice because he finally stepped aside. Elizabeth stalked through the lounge and retrieved her tennis racket. Nobody else had better cross her today. She felt like a thunderstorm about to break out in fury.

Fortunately the only person who stopped her on the way out of the lounge was Betsy Williams, an old friend who remarked favorably about Ian.

"That's one of the yummiest men I've seen in a long time," the well-proportioned redhead said. "Where in the world have you been hiding him, Elizabeth?"

"Somewhere in the world," she replied. "I just met him yesterday, actually. He's a scientist who does international work." That, she thought, ought to counter any rumors that Ian was a fortune hunter. Betsy's green eyes widened in awe.

"Well, I *am* impressed," she said. Elizabeth explained that Ian had gone to Harvard with Michael, that though there was a difference in their ages, they had become close friends, and that Ian was Michael's houseguest.

"That seems to have changed," Betsy said with an impish smile. "I was playing tennis the same time the four of you were, and I saw that kiss he gave you before the match started, not to mention him leaping the net with you in his arms. I think you have a lot of man on your hands, dear."

Elizabeth chatted for a few more minutes, then told her friend that she was keeping Michael and Jennifer as well as her "lot of man" waiting and had to run.

Unfortunately, in the lobby she "ran" into both Muffy and Bill. It seemed that there had been a renewal of affection between the two because Bill's arm was round Muffy's thin shoulders, while she wept softly into a tissue. He looked outraged.

"You lied to me, Elizabeth Marlowe," he said. "Muffy told me in detail how the man you were with insulted her intelligence and treated her disrespectfully."

"What Ian said to her was far less than what she deserved," Elizabeth retorted. "And I don't care to discuss this any further." She started to move past.

But Bill released Muffy and grabbed Elizabeth's arm with enough force to hurt. "You go get your friend to come in here and apologize or I'll—"

"You'll what?" Ian's deep voice made Elizabeth look toward the doorway. He stood framed in it, afternoon sunlight backlighting him like some avenging hero. At the sight of him, she almost forgot the pain in her arm.

"Go on, mister," he said, ambling slowly toward them. "I'd really like to hear what a cowardly cretin like yourself plans to do when I refuse to withdraw my words. And if you don't release Miss Marlowe, I'm going to take that hand, rip it off and stuff it down your throat."

At that point, Elizabeth swung her racket, hitting Bill squarely on the shins and achieving her freedom. Bill danced around, howling with pain, and Muffy started to scream.

Elizabeth walked calmly up to Ian, put her arm through his and said, "Let's go. I'm tired of wasting time."

Ian let her guide him toward the door. He hated turning his back on a potential enemy, but this was Elizabeth's turf and he would let her orchestrate a dignified exit. Provided, that was, that the man she had hit would let her.

He didn't. Just outside the entrance, Ian felt his shoulder grabbed and a fist graze the side of his head, hurting his ear slightly. Moving quickly, he pushed Elizabeth out of danger and turned to face his opponent.

The blond man was clearly hysterical with rage. He charged, fists flailing, and Ian had no difficulty keeping out of his way. *Let him wear himself out,* he thought. *Then maybe he'll be more reasonable.*

But the damned brunette was standing in the doorway, screaming at the top of her lungs, and a crowd was gathering. Just the kind of embarrassing scene Elizabeth would hate. Ian decided to end the farce.

On the next pass, he caught the other man by the arm, instantly hammerlocking him. He waited a moment until the pain made his opponent stop struggling.

Elizabeth watched, fascinated. Bill was no match for a man Ian's size and strength, but he was large and athletic. That Ian had immobilized him so easily was amazing. She had envisioned a lengthier, bloodier struggle. She saw Ian speak a few words into Bill's ear, then he released him. Elizabeth waited in horror for the fight to start again. Even Muffy had finally shut up.

But Bill just walked away, limping across the parking lot to his car. Muffy hurried after him. They got in his Jaguar and drove off.

"Let's go home, Elizabeth." Ian took her hand and led her toward a wide-eyed Michael and Jennifer.

"What did you say to him? "she whispered. "He was out of control. How did you get him to just leave like that?"

Ian grinned at her. "I simply explained what would happen if he didn't. I guess I got through."

Elizabeth decided she didn't want to know what Ian had promised.

"Great show," Michael said when they reached the car. He slapped Ian on the back. "Stockdale was an idiot to try to mess with you."

Ian laughed. "I think he went for me because the lady whacked him across the shins with her racket. I was just the most acceptable target."

"I told you she's a fighter." Michael opened the doors, and they all got in. When Ian had settled beside her in the back seat, he took Elizabeth's arm and examined the bruise left by Stockdale's grip. It was a darkening purple circle, like an ugly bracelet, and the sight of it made him curse aloud.

"What's the matter?" Jennifer asked. Both she and Michael looked back, then exclaimed in anger as Ian displayed the injured arm.

"It's not that big a deal," Elizabeth insisted. "I'll just wear long sleeves until it fades."

"The man brutalized you," Jennifer declared angrily. "He shouldn't be allowed to get away with that."

"He hasn't," Ian said quietly, cradling her injured arm in his hands. "The hammerlock I gave him will be a memory his arm, back and shoulder muscles will have for quite some time." His voice had a satisfied ring to it.

"I'm just sorry that such a pleasant afternoon had to end on an ugly note," Elizabeth said. "I'm grateful to the three of you. I haven't *played* in far too long."

Ian stroked her arm gently, creating soft shivers of delight. "That's a problem I can help you solve when we get back to the city. I'm an expert when it comes to 'playing.'" The look he gave her promised that the kind of play he had in mind wouldn't be confined to the tennis courts.

When they arrived at the mansion, both Adelaide and Charters met them at the door. Her grandmother's friend had called already, giving Adelaide a completely distorted version of what had happened at the club. Elizabeth immediately straightened out matters with a truthful accounting of the situation. Her story evoked anger from the two older people, but she assured them that Ian's handling of Bill physically and Muffy verbally had been sufficient. "Let's just let the matter drop," she pleaded.

It was dropped until Robert returned home from his golf game. Elizabeth was soaking in a relaxing bath, thinking sensual thoughts about Ian, when there was a knock on her bathroom door. Jennifer told her that her uncle and her rescuer were getting it on verbally and that not even Michael had been able to calm his father's temper.

"He keeps saying that Ian's actions caused a scandal and that Marlowes don't get involved in scandals," she said as Elizabeth, hair up in a towel and a robe around her body, followed her downstairs to the den. She could already hear voices raised in anger.

The three men were standing, Robert and Ian with hostile expressions on their faces and Michael looking helpless.

"It couldn't have been necessary to rough Stockdale up!" Robert was shouting. "Couldn't you have just *reasoned* with him, handled it like—"

"He threw the first punch!" Ian's eyes flashed silver. "If you don't like the way I handled it, then you tell me how you'd have 'reasoned' with the man. He had already hurt Elizabeth badly. What was I to do, according to your code, Mr. Marlowe? Let him have the same fun with me?"

"There's always a peaceful solution!"

"Always, my butt!" Ian strode toward the door, pausing to give Elizabeth a quick kiss. "I'll call you sometime this week. I'm leaving this place. I don't stay where I'm not wanted." And then he was gone.

"Ian!" Elizabeth, Jennifer and Michael chorused. But it was too late. The big man was gone, probably to the guest room to collect his things. Elizabeth turned to Robert.

"Did you even *listen* to his side of the story?" she asked angrily. She pushed up the sleeve of her bathrobe, showing her uncle the dark bruise on her arm. "Does this look like the work of a man who could be reasoned with? Peacefully?"

Robert's face went from red to white. "Stockdale did *that* to you?"

"This is my arm, isn't it?"

"Father, if you weren't so damned concerned about the Marlowe name, maybe you'd realize Ian's behavior was entirely appropriate under the circumstances." Michael took a deep breath, and Elizabeth could tell that he was having just as much trouble controlling his anger as she was. And though tears were running down Jennifer's cheeks, her lips thinned in fury.

Robert seemed to collapse from the inside. He staggered over to a chair and sat. "I heard that Ian spoke rudely to Muffy Turner and then picked a fight with Stockdale because he was Elizabeth's old boyfriend. I admit the stories were conflicting, but that was the gist of it."

Elizabeth folded her arms across her chest. "Do you have any interest in hearing what really happened, from people who are your family and whom you are supposed to be able to trust?" Her uncle nodded slowly.

They each told him their versions, and that they felt Ian had handled matters well.

"Oh, I suppose he could have ignored the slurs Muffy made about his family and his profession, but the man does have some *pride*," Elizabeth said sarcastically.

Robert put his hand to his forehead. "I admit I was wrong. Please go find him and tell him I want to apologize."

"I think you ought to find him," Jennifer said. "You were the one who misjudged him, not us." Elizabeth and Michael agreed.

Robert stood slowly. He barely liked the man. Apologizing to him was going to be very difficult, but he knew his family was right. And somehow he knew Elizabeth's anger wouldn't dissolve until he had made things right with Bradshaw. From her vehement defense of the man, it was clear she felt more than a passing friendship for him, a fact Robert found disquieting. He wanted Elizabeth to marry as much as he wanted almost anything, because he felt her life was lacking as she did not have a loving husband. But Ian Bradshaw would never make her happy, running around the world as he did. Elizabeth's fear of flying was deeply ingrained, and she would be left alone frequently if she chose a man like that. But doing the honorable thing came before his own qualms.

"I'll go to the guest room," he said. "Please wait here for us."

Just then Adelaide came into the den, moving more rapidly than Elizabeth had seen her grandmother do in years. She was highly agitated. "What have you done?" she asked the assembly. "Why has that lovely man left?"

Elizabeth joined the others in clamoring for an explanation. Clutching her fist to her chest, Adelaide sat and told them.

"He came into the library, where Charters and I were deciding whether to polish the floor this week or wait until later in the season when the weather—"

"Grandmother," Elizabeth interrupted, kneeling in front of the older woman. "No details. What did Ian do?"

"He looked like thunder," Adelaide said. "He had his bag, and he asked Charters if he would drive him to the nearest bus depot. He asked politely, but you could tell he was very, very angry." She shook her head and assumed her most serious scolding expression. "I don't know what you children have done," she said, including her own son, Robert, "but a guest has never been driven from this home before." She reached for Elizabeth's arm and held it up so that the bruise was apparent. "Especially not a young man who so gallantly and diplomatically saved Elizabeth and defended his own family's name." Her lips thinned. "I promise you this, by tomorrow the neighborhood of Crystal Cove is going to know the truth!"

Elizabeth knew it would. Adelaide would start at church, then spend some time at the club. Those she couldn't catch at either of the two main social places would be getting phone calls. Adelaide was a determined lady, and when she made up her mind to defend a person, that person was defended.

"Did Charters agree to drive him?" Robert asked.

"If he had asked *me*, I would have done it." Adelaide squared her shoulders. "I consider myself a fairly brave person, but Dr. Bradshaw is formidable at his best. At his worst... Well, anyway, I gave Charters permission, and they took off."

"Michael, Robert," Elizabeth said, "drive as quickly as you can to the depot—the one he arrived at yesterday. I'd go, but I don't want to waste the time dressing."

"I'll go, too," Jennifer volunteered. The three of them left at a run.

Elizabeth moved to the chair facing her grandmother. She sat and waited for the older woman to speak.

"You're taken with this young man, aren't you," Adelaide stated.

"I haven't known him long enough to be sure."

Her grandmother's eyes suddenly sparkled, and she looked years younger. "Sometimes it happens at the first meeting. The magic starts, a romance follows, and finally true love."

"You grew up in a much more romantic age, Grandmother." Elizabeth unwound her towel and started to dry her hair. "A woman lived only to find the man of her dreams. I expect much more from life than that."

"And you've already achieved it. You're a success, young lady. And before you are thirty. But you must think about a family. You nearly *are* thirty, after all."

"Women have children later in life." The old argument, Elizabeth thought. But she was too worried about whether they would catch up with Ian in time to waste mental energy sidestepping her old disagreement with Adelaide. They went at it from all angles until she was ready to scream with impatience. Just when she was about to snap, Charters appeared in the doorway.

"No one seems to be home but yourselves, ladies. Will you be taking dinner in the small dining room?" he asked calmly.

"Charters!" Elizabeth jumped up, aware of the bizarre sight she made in her robe with her hair flying every which way. "Where is he? Did they find him? Is he coming back?"

"I assume you mean the good, but furious, Dr. Bradshaw."

"Of course she does!" Adelaide declared in an impatient tone she rarely used with the family servants.

"He was very angry, and I did nothing to dissuade him from leaving. He was quite decent to me, but declared that he was taking the first vehicle out of the station, no matter what the destination." Charters cleared his throat and looked straight ahead. "I believe his parting words were, quote, 'I hope I never see this stinking place again.' Unquote."

"Oh, dear." Adelaide put her hand to her mouth.

Despondently, Elizabeth left the room, ignoring Charters's questions regarding dinner. Ian was gone, and she would never see him again. That knowledge made her feel horribly empty, and she knew food would do nothing for that kind of hunger.

She managed enough energy to fix her hair and dress in jeans and a pullover. Maybe, she told herself, it was just as well because of all of the misgivings she had entertained about getting involved with him in the first place. She had only known him for one day, after all. The affection she had begun to feel would fade, and someday he would be just an interesting memory. But deep inside, her heart whispered that she was wrong.

The trio returned empty-handed and depressed. Dinner was finally served, but it was a quiet affair. Gloomy, almost as if someone dear had died. Several times during the evening, Michael had tried dialing the phone number Ian had given him, but there was no answer.

Robert apologized again to everyone and declared that he intended to write Ian a letter of formal apology the next day. Elizabeth wondered if that would do any good.

She and Michael, Jennifer and Adelaide played cards while Robert sat gloomily in his chair, seeming to read a book, but the pages turned very slowly. Finally, he closed the tome with a snap and declared that he was heading for bed. The others followed soon after.

Elizabeth lay sleepless for a while, thinking of the excitement of the night before when Ian had entered her room in such an unconventional fashion. She *missed* him, she realized. But because the day had been full of emotional and physical strain, she soon fell asleep.

On Sunday everyone tried to avoid mentioning Ian. They dutifully went to church, sitting together in the Marlowe family pew. After the service, Elizabeth left right away in her own car, explaining to her family that she didn't care to answer the questions of curious neighbors. They all said they understood, but that they would remain for a while to help clear Ian's name.

Back at the mansion, Elizabeth tried once more to reach him, but received no answer to the ringing telephone. Not certain of how financially strapped Ian was, she worried that he had allowed his temper to take him too far away to get back to his temporary home. To take her mind off him, she started to pack for the return trip to the city after lunch. She had no intention of waiting until later when the tunnels and bridges would be tightly packed.

But leaving was as wrenching as ever. Jennifer cried and hugged her tightly, whispering thanks for her help and advice. Michael gave her a hug and brotherly kiss and told her not to worry about Ian. He was certain to be in touch with her and probably himself. Elizabeth remained skeptical. Robert was especially difficult to say goodbye to, because she knew how badly he felt about his part in driving Ian away. Adelaide, on the other hand, seemed oddly contented. She, too, was confident that Ian would once again be a guest in the Marlowe home, and she told Elizabeth that the mutual attraction she had noted between them gave her this feeling. Elizabeth dismissed her grandmother's words as hopelessly romantic and unrealistic. Pride and anger could destroy a budding friendship like hers and Ian's.

Charters carried her luggage to her car and told her with uncharacteristic concern in his voice to take care. She gave his stiff and proper figure a hug and assured him she would do just that.

Music from her radio on the drive into Manhattan deepened her gloomy mood. Every song seemed to be about lost love. Finally, she switched to a rock station. If the singing was about love, at least she couldn't understand the words.

Her building boasted a parking garage with an armed security guard as attendant. He recognized her, raised the door and waved her in.

Elizabeth's apartment felt like a dear old friend who was suddenly keeping distant from her. She unpacked, checked through her mail and then wandered aimlessly into the kitchen to think about dinner. As she took eggs out for an omelet, the phone rang.

She dropped one of the eggs, swore and answered the phone in a snappish tone. Ian Bradshaw's cheerful voice replied, "Thought I was supposed to be the guy who was ticked off." His words were slurred. "Care to tell me why you're mad?"

"Ian!" She dropped another egg. "Where are you?"

"Bar on the corner of C'lumbus and Seventy-fifth. Wanna come see you."

Oh, no, she thought. He had been drinking. She didn't want him on the streets alone in that condition. He'd be an easy target for muggers...or worse.

"You stay put!" she ordered. "I'm going to catch a taxi and come get you. It'll be quicker than getting my car. Don't you move, Ian Bradshaw! And don't you have one more drop to drink!" She hung up to the sound of his inebriated chuckling.

CHAPTER SIX

IT TOOK ABOUT fifteen minutes by taxi to get from Elizabeth's Upper East Side apartment to Ian's bar. After she had hailed the vehicle, she realized that Ian had neglected to name the establishment. The cabbie made her even more nervous by giving her a long look and suggesting in the brutally frank manner of many New York taxi drivers that she was out of her mind for going to a bar on Columbus Avenue.

"A high-class lady like you oughta hit the places on your side of town," he muttered. "Leave the working-class bars to stiffs like us."

Elizabeth had countered haughtily that she was meeting a client, and did he know which bar was on that particular corner. He did, and continuing to mutter to himself about people staying in their own territory, he drove her there. Slowly. Elizabeth looked out at the passing scene, but her thoughts were on Ian Bradshaw.

Lord only knew what had actually happened to him between the time he had left the depot near Crystal Cove and when he had phoned her. And then there was the mystery of why he had phoned at all. His anger had seemed so great that she had assumed he would stay away from her for a long time in spite of his hurried kiss and promise.

The cabbie took her past Central Park on Fifty-ninth and then up Columbus to the corner Ian had specified. A part of town that Elizabeth had always associated with artists and actors was also, she now realized, a neighborhood that housed countless families of working people. It was crowded to the point of giving *her* claustrophobia; she could imagine what it did to a man used to wide-open spaces. She paid the surly driver, tipping a bit generously in the hopes that he would treat his next passenger a shade more politely, and entered the bar.

She was out of place. In the designer dress and jacket that she had worn to church that morning, she looked as though she had been dropped in from another century. The men and women who filled the smoky interior clearly labored with their hands and bodies for a living. Not, as she did, with her brains and social connections. She almost turned and fled from the stares.

"Lizzie, over here." Ian's deep voice drew her attention to a darker area to her left. Following his call, she moved until she spotted him, sitting alone in the farthest booth from the entrance, his back to the wall. A can of beer sat on the table in front of him.

"This place isn't exactly your style," he said, grinning and rising to take her hand. "You look like a chinchilla that wandered into a group of musk-rats."

She gripped his hand and pushed, making him sit so that she could slide in beside him. "Never mind about me," she snapped. "Why are you drinking? Why do you want to see me?"

In the bar's dim golden light, she could see a glint of amusement in his eyes. "Do you really care?" he asked.

"Of course I care." She spoke the words more loudly. "Where in the world have you been, anyway? We called and called, and you were never home. Where did you go?"

"We?"

"Michael and I. Robert wants to apologize."

His expression hardened. "He does? Why?"

"Because he finally calmed down and let us tell him the truth about what happened."

"But he wouldn't listen to it from the likes of *me*."

"Ian, don't be as stubborn as he was. He's genuinely contrite. He knows he wronged you, and the entire family is making sure that the whole neighborhood knows the true story, as well."

"I'm sure they'll believe that a stranger, an outsider to their little society, was in the right and that one of their own was the villain." He picked up the can of beer and drained it, then signaled to the waitress for another.

"How many of those things have you had, Ian?" Her concern for him was growing.

"A few," he said evasively. "Want one?"

"No, I want to know about your activities and whereabouts for the past twenty-four hours."

He gave her a strange look. "You aren't my keeper, Elizabeth."

"You called me," she countered. "If it wasn't to ask for help, then why—"

He cut off her question with a kiss, holding her face so that she couldn't free herself, even when catcalls and cheers of approval resounded from nearby tables. At first she kept her lips tightly shut, infuriated that he would do this in such a public place. Then the magic swept over her, and she was weakened by the passion of his caress in spite of her anger. She relaxed, and he released her.

"That's why I called," he said softly, looking into her eyes. "You've been on my mind every waking moment and most of my dreaming ones. I think, Miss Marlowe, that I'm addicted to you. I called because I needed a fix."

"That's very flattering," she said in as cold a tone as she could muster. "But I don't believe a word of it. You called because you've managed to get yourself into some kind of trouble, and you want me to help you. Well, I'm willing to do that, Ian, but you're going to have to cut out this nonsense and tell me the truth."

Ian regarded her beautiful, angry face and ran his hand up and down the icy metal sides of his beer can. He had to admit that he was a bit buzzed, and that he had called her entirely on impulse. But he also wondered if his words weren't closer to the truth than he cared them to be. When he had stormed out of the Marlowes', he had fully intended to wait several days, maybe even weeks, before contacting her. But the pay telephone on the bar's wall had drawn him like a magnet. Just the way she did.

"Ian, quit staring and tell me what happened." Her voice whipped him out of his reverie. At a nearby pool table, the crack of a well-struck ball brought rowdy shouts from the players.

He looked around. The bar was a favorite of his because it gave him a chance to observe his fellow creatures at uninhibited recreation, and because it was near the one-room garret that his friend was letting him use. But as the evening progressed, the crowd was becoming a little too uninhibited, and Ian realized this was no place to discuss personal matters. Because of his size, he had been left to himself in the past, but Elizabeth's beauty was enough bait to draw some of the bolder men eventually, and the last thing he wanted was to become embroiled in another fight over her. The first had caused enough trouble, and he didn't want her to get the impression that he was pugnacious.

"Let's get out of here," he said, "and go to your place."

If getting him out this bar would stop him from drinking and get him to be truthful with her, Elizabeth thought, then well and good. "Let's go," she said, rising. Ian followed.

But when she finally closed her apartment door, strong arms went around her from behind and warm lips started tasting her neck and earlobe. She pushed futilely at his forearms. "Ian, stop it. You promised!"

"And I don't lie." Another nibble, and he released her. "You're just irresistible, that's all."

"Ian!" She put her hands on her hips. "The whole story. Now!"

He hicupped, but walked steadily over to her peach-colored sofa. Sitting, he patted the cushion beside him. She stood firm.

mation and material he had about his finances.
Then, to Elizabeth's astonishment and slight disappointment, he left after giving her only one tender
kiss, saying he'd see her tomorrow and thanks for the
dinner. They made a good team in the kitchen, he
added before closing the door. Elizabeth pondered
the remark, his behavior and the entire situation between them before she finally fell asleep that night.

First thing the next morning, she called her gynecologist, Sue Fuller, and got an appointment for
Jennifer on Wednesday afternoon. Then she tele-
phoned the estate to tell Michael that Ian was all
right. He howled with laughter when she filled him
in on the details, and passed her to Jennifer.

"Wednesday afternoon," Elizabeth said. "Sue
can see you then. She usually takes the afternoon off,
so fitting you in was no problem." Jennifer whispered her thanks, then in a normal tone said she
would love to come into town on Wednesday and do
some shopping. They would meet at Elizabeth's office around eleven.

An hour later, Elizabeth's office greeted her in a
friendlier manner than her apartment had, and she
wondered if the negative vibes she had felt the night
before had been because she wasn't sure she'd ever
see Ian again. Since he was coming to her office this
very afternoon...

Nonsense, she told herself as she greeted her secretary and had the young woman add Ian's name to
her list of clients.

"He's not going to be a very large account,
Nancy," she explained. "So don't worry about a

great deal of extra paperwork. He's really just a friend I'm doing a favor for."

"Is he cute?" the curly-haired blonde asked teasingly.

Elizabeth shrugged. "Judge for yourself."

The morning passed quickly for Elizabeth. Two clients to meet with. Letters to answer. Market news to study. Calls to make and return. Her happiness, she decided, was not due to Ian's impending arrival, but to her pleasure at being back to work at the job she loved.

She lost track of time after lunch. About three o'clock, Nancy knocked on the door, entered, shut it and leaned back against it, both hands pressed to her heart.

"He's *gorgeous*," she moaned. "If he's just your friend, you've lost your female mind."

"I met him Friday." Elizabeth kept her tone cool, but inside she was as excited as Nancy seemed to be.

"Don't you believe in love at first sight? I do. And I think I just experienced it."

A surprising pang of jealousy shot through Elizabeth. "Don't be silly, Nancy. Besides, the way we first met, love was hardly an issue. Please show Dr. Bradshaw in."

"*Doctor?* He can examine me anytime!"

"Nancy," she said, her tone warning. The secretary scurried out of the office.

When Ian entered, Elizabeth could see why Nancy had been so smitten. Dressed in a go-to-hell style all his own—sweater, tweed sport coat, jeans and boots—he made a dashing figure. And he was smiling broadly. "I got a job," he announced.

Impulsively Elizabeth stood and came around the desk to give him a congratulatory kiss. "That's wonderful," she said. "Where?"

"Bali."

Her heart sank. He was leaving. Her disappointment must have shown, because he put his hand under her chin and lifted her face to look at him. "I want you to go with me."

She couldn't believe her ears. Was he out of his mind?

"Ian," she said, "we hardly know each other. And not only does the idea of a plane flight that long make me break out in hives, but I have responsibilities here. I can't just pick up and take off the way you can."

"I understand all that," he replied, still holding her in a loose embrace. "But the job won't start for weeks—more than a month. We'll have plenty of time to get to know each other, and Miss Marlowe, it might be good for you to try a flight like that. As I understand it, your parents were killed in a small private plane. Once you get up in one of those wide-bodied overseas monsters, you're hardly aware you're—"

"Don't say it!" She cut off the word with her hand. "I can't bear to even think it."

He tightened his embrace and kissed her throat. "Look, I know it seems impulsive of me, and maybe we won't even like each other by then, so you won't need to worry. But why not, for once in your carefully organized, structured life, take a chance? We can always cancel your reservations at the last minute."

She sighed, thinking that the way her body was reacting to his caresses, it was highly unlikely that they would not be friends, or even more than that, in a month's time. "What kind of a job is it?" she asked.

"Film consulting. They're using Bali as the site, but it's a story about some American teenagers who survive a..."

"Survive a what?"

"Oh, I forget. Anyway, they end up wandering through the wilds of Africa, and the director needs someone to oversee the animal aspects of the plot."

Elizabeth arched an eyebrow. "The kids survive a plane crash, don't they?"

Ian shrugged and grinned sheepishly. "I just didn't want to make you think about it again."

She pushed away from him. "Let's get something straight right now, Ian. I don't care for being lied to. Or for being sheltered and overprotected. It was one of the main reasons I left my home. If we are going to have any kind of a relationship, please be open and honest with me and let me handle my own problems." She turned and walked back to her desk. "Now, let's get down to business."

Feeling a bit annoyed at his act of kindness being called a lie, Ian reached into his inner jacket pocket and took out the envelope containing his financial records. He handed it to her and sat in one of the two chairs in front of her desk.

He studied Elizabeth as she studied the information. Maybe he had made a mistake by impulsively inviting her on the trip. They really didn't know all that much about each other. Maybe she would turn out to be too much like her uncle for his tastes. Maybe he should call Bill Jordan, the director who had hired him, and tell him he wasn't bringing a female companion, after all.

But she had felt so soft and warm in his arms, and he loved the way a tiny crinkle appeared between her honey-colored brows as she studied his papers. Well, they did have time, since shooting wasn't scheduled to begin until after Halloween. Jordan was a superstitious man, and he wanted All Souls' Day over before he made the picture. By then, Ian figured he would know how he really felt about the woman sitting across from him.

He looked around the room. It was tidy, like her apartment. Her degree hung on one wall, but there was also a collection of watercolors on the wood paneling that he found interesting. One and all showed scenes from wild and exotic places. More unconscious longings?

"Ian." He turned to look back at the most beautiful sight in the room. "You've hopelessly mismanaged your finances. And I'm not trying to insult you. You are simply a babe in the world of money."

"That's why I'm here." He spread his hands in a gesture of appeal. "Help me, Elizabeth."

They spent more than an hour reviewing possibilities. First, she declared, he would have to open a bank account and get a line of credit established. Since he could expect royalty checks by the end of October and was leaving town just at that time, it would be wise for him to borrow a small sum from her, in addition to what was left from his gambling winnings, then take out a bank loan and acquire some low-key, secure investments, paying back both the bank and herself when he returned, quite a bit richer, from the consulting job.

"Please say 'when *we* return,'" he interrupted. "Think positive."

She frowned and then smiled. What could it hurt? "All right, when we return. How's that?"

"How's dinner?" He smiled seductively. "Just you and me in a small, intimate Italian place I know."

She looked wary. "Intimate the way your bar was?"

"I warned you . . ."

"You told me you had— Never mind. Let's get back to business." She shook her head as if in exasperation.

Ian got up and went around the desk to loom over her. "Elizabeth, I trust you. Any decision you make is fine with me. I couldn't care less about my money. I always seem to get some when I absolutely need it. What does matter to me is whether or not I get the pleasure of your company this evening."

His words were so vehement that she was momentarily startled into speechlessness.

Her hesitation brought back his doubts. Had he misread her actions? Was she really just a beautiful cold fish who only wanted his business, not his affection? When she finally agreed to dinner with a smile, he felt a heavy load lift from his heart.

"You'll love the place," he said, bending and kissing her lightly. "What say I pick you up around seven?"

"Only if you'll agree to go Dutch." She patted the papers on the desk. "You are going to have to be very stingy for the next few weeks, my handsome friend."

"Dutch!" He straightened. "No way. I don't even like the idea of borrowing money from you. When I ask a woman out, *I* pay."

"Ian, this is the eighties. It's all right not to be old-fashioned about dating expenses. As your friend as well as your adviser, I can't in good conscience let you throw away your money on me."

"I'm not throwing it away." He put his hands on his hips. "I'm investing in our relationship."

She couldn't think of a rebuttal to that one.

IAN TOOK THE SUBWAY back to his neighborhood, returned to his room to get ready for the date and found a special delivery letter in his box. The envelope was made from elegant, creamy paper, and the return address had Robert Marlowe's name on it. Why on earth would the man who had treated him so badly be writing him a letter? Opening it, he discovered a carefully worded apology.

The contents stunned him, and he considered them as he showered and dressed. Marlowe had a great deal of pride, just as he did, and Ian realized what it must have cost the man to write that letter. He was still angry, but in the face of this apology, he knew he would have to start dealing with that emotion. And it also gave him more hope for himself and Elizabeth. It took depth of character and guts for Marlowe to do what he had done. If Elizabeth had the same traits, as he suspected from what he knew of her so far, then things might work between them. She might even decide to go to Bali. He imagined her sunbathing in a scrap of a bathing suit on one of the golden beaches south of the capital city of Denpasar, and he wondered if he could wait until seven to see her again.

But he did, and it was worth it. She greeted him at the door with a welcoming smile, ready to go, her open coat already on over a silky slip of an aqua dress, her purse on her arm.

"You look beautiful," he said, kissing her ear so as not to smudge her makeup. That was for later in the evening.

"So do you," she replied, openly admiring his suit. "For a man who cares nothing about money, in that business suit you could pass for a rather large stockbroker."

"Heaven forbid!"

The restaurant was on Mulberry Street in Little Italy. The plump owner recognized Ian immediately and whisked them past others waiting for seating to a relatively private table. All the while he and Ian spoke in rapid Italian. Elizabeth knew she was the subject of much of the conversation, and she also wondered just how many languages her escort knew. So far she'd counted three.

They placed no order, but wine and food started arriving almost immediately. "I made prior arrangements," Ian explained. "I eat here often, and I know what the specialties are. I guarantee you'll never be able to eat everything. Generosity is the byword here."

"For a country boy, you've managed to make yourself pretty much at home in the city," she replied. "You have your neighborhood bar, and you're obviously in with the owner of this place." *The chameleon,* she thought. *Even if he doesn't say he cares for it, he has adapted to the urban life.*

He shrugged. "It's only sensible to make the best of things. Although I'd prefer to be elsewhere, I had the offer of a free place to live." He reached across the table and took her hand. "And I had the opportunity to meet you." There was no mistaking the affection in his eyes.

"Ian, you do think about all of the differences between us, don't you?"

He smiled, the skin at the corners of his silvery eyes crinkling. "I prefer to dwell on the positive. We have more in common than is apparent, Miss Marlowe."

"Such as?" Her curiosity was aroused. Besides the sexual attraction and the respect she felt growing between them, she could think of nothing else that could hold them together.

"For one thing," Ian explained, "we've both defied our families and made our lives what *we* wanted them to be." Elizabeth conceded him the point.

"We're both successful at what we do."

"But," she reminded him, "our professions are molded to entirely different worlds. Mine to the city and yours to . . . goodness knows where."

Reluctantly Ian gave her that point. They continued to talk and laugh as they ate. Time passed, and eventually Elizabeth glanced down at her watch.

"I hate to act like Cinderella," she said. "But tomorrow is a working day, and if I don't get at least a few hours sleep, I could mess a deal for a client."

"Since I am now a client, I'd hate for that to happen." Ian signaled for the check. "Tomorrow night?"

"Dinner at my place," she said quickly, not wanting him to take her out again and spend his small cash reserve. His pleased look told her she had done the right thing.

They kissed lingeringly outside her door, but Ian bade her good-night without trying to come inside. Tomorrow, he decided, would be soon enough to try heavier romancing.

He returned to his building feeling thoroughly satisfied with the way their relationship was going. But alarm coursed through him when he saw that the door to his room was slightly open. So far he had been left alone by the human predators of the city, but evidently his luck had run out. Well, if the thief was still inside, he thought, he was going to regret having invaded this territory for the rest of his life. Crouching, Ian opened the door slowly and crept into the room.

CHAPTER SEVEN

BUT NO THIEF AWAITED HIM. Instead, Ian straightened and shut the door behind him as he gazed, stunned, at the inebriated figure of Michael. Sprawled on the couch that folded out into Ian's bed, a half-empty bottle of Scotch in his hand, his friend waved weakly. "Hi, buddy," he said, his words slurred.

Ian kicked out the desk chair and sat with his arms resting on the back. "What's the matter, Mike?" he asked.

"Landlady let me in." Michael gestured toward the door with the bottle. "Told her I was your long-lost brother."

"In a way you are. Now why the unexpected visit and sodden condition? Why aren't you home, sleeping with Jennifer?"

Michael tried to rise, but couldn't. He slumped farther down on the couch. "Sleeping with Jennifer's the problem, ol' friend."

"Explain."

Michael did. Ian listened with growing sympathy as the man talked about his dilemma. How desperately Jennifer wanted children, his own fears and insecurities, and the fight between them that had driven him into the city to seek out the one man he felt close enough to to unburden himself.

"Course," he admitted, staring at the now three-quarters-empty bottle, "I had to get plastered to share this with you. Ian, I'm goin' nuts. I wanna have kids, and I don' wanna. I wanna make her happy, but I don't know about being a father. It spooks me, friend." He paused and took another swallow of Scotch. "An' what if I'm not *able*," he added, his features screwing up as if he was struggling to keep from crying. "My dad would give his left arm for an heir of Marlowe blood. Adoption wouldn't make him happy, even if Jen and I could live with it." He frowned at the bottle. "But, by damn, I don't feel like I can't make a baby. I just wanna keep on loving her and believing that when the time is right, she'll get pregnant!"

Michael's pain was so deep that Ian felt himself beginning to hurt along with him. He racked his brain trying to come up with words that could help Michael, but nothing surfaced. Then the phone rang.

"Ian." It was Elizabeth. "I got a frantic call from Jennifer. Michael found out from her that I'd arranged for infertility testing for her on Wednesday, and they had a terrrible row. He stormed out of the house hours ago. Do you have any idea where—"

"I know exactly where. Your cousin is currently seated on my sofa bed, drinking himself into oblivion. Tell Jen that I'll nursemaid him and not to worry."

"Oh, Ian, you're a lifesaver! Thank you, thank you. I'm really grateful."

"I'll remind you about that tomorrow night, Miss Marlowe, ma'am." He smiled as he heard her blow a kiss to him before hanging up.

Ian turned back to Michael, but the younger man was unconscious. *Just as well,* Ian thought as he took the nearly empty bottle from slack fingers. Tomorrow was going to be a physical nightmare for Michael to add to his emotional one. He arranged his friend as comfortably as possible, and then got his sleeping bag from the back of the closet. He had bedded down in far less comfortable places than the floor of a New York apartment, and he didn't resent Michael's intrusion at all. In fact, he was flattered that the other man still considered him such a close friend after all these years. He hoped he could help.

The next morning Michael remained in the apartment's tiny bathroom for quite some time before emerging white faced and red eyed. Ian forced coffee, toast and aspirin in that order down him and then suggested that he lie down for a while.

"No," Michael said. "I need to get home. Jennifer will be worried sick, not to mention Robert. But I'd better phone them first, and then I'll call my office. Think I'll take my very first sick day."

Ian busied himself in the small alcove that served as a kitchen, so that he wouldn't be eavesdropping on Michael's calls, but when he heard Michael talking to Robert he asked to speak to the older man. With a puzzled look on his face, Michael handed him the receiver.

"This is Ian Bradshaw, Mr. Marlowe. I received your letter yesterday afternoon."

He heard the man clear his throat after a moment's hesitation. "I meant every word," he said. "I was very much in the wrong. You are welcome to be a guest at the estate anytime, and in addition I must thank you for caring for my fool of a son."

"He has a problem, Mr. Marlowe. One I think you should discuss with him father to son."

"Thank you again." His voice was a little stiff, and Ian knew that even though he had apologized, the older man wasn't any fonder of him and probably resented the fact that Michael had turned to him for help. Elizabeth's uncle was going to be a difficult person to get along with. For a number of reasons.

He patched Michael up as best he could before sending him on his way, encouraging him to talk openly with his family about the problem. Keeping it bottled inside, he declared, was what had led to the "bottle." Michael agreed, but sounded reluctant, and Ian wondered if his advice would be taken.

He phoned Elizabeth's office and got her on the line after dodging a bit of verbal flirtation from her secretary. The young woman had openly admired him yesterday, but Ian had only one lady on his mind these days. He told that lady that her cousin was on his way home and that he thought Michael might need some professional counseling.

"The need seems to run in the youngest Marlowes, doesn't it?" she replied wryly.

"You said it, I didn't."

After they had finished talking, Ian showered, dressed and went university touring to see if any of his contacts had decided to take him up on his offer to guest lecture. It wouldn't bring in much money, but it would enable him to wine and dine Lizzie more often.

Pleasantly surprised, he found half a dozen professors who were eager to put him to work. He structured a schedule that wouldn't keep him overly busy and then returned to the apartment to start drawing up the lectures that his friends had asked for... and to await the hour when he would once more be in the delicious presence of Elizabeth Marlowe.

ELIZABETH HURRIED through the afternoon's work, leaving earlier than her usual six o'clock to grocery shop and prepare both the dinner and herself for an intimate evening with Ian. Her feelings for him were even warmer since he had been so kind to Michael. A man who proved to be such a good and loyal friend just might turn out to be the kind of man she would enjoy a more serious romance with than she'd ever had. It was too bad, she reflected as she prepared game hens with wild rice, that their professions and habitat preferences were so different. Without those barriers, things might even get *very* serious between them.

Elizabeth chastised herself for even entertaining such thoughts. She hadn't known the man for a week, for goodness' sake. She was just beginning to enjoy complete freedom for the first time in her life, and it was no time to be thinking of settling on one man. Not even a man like Ian.

But when he arrived carrying roses and looking fantastically sexy in a beige jacket and brown trousers, she forgot her resolve and reservations.

"They're lovely," she said, taking the flowers and giving him a kiss. "But do you mind if I scold you for spending the money?"

"Not to worry." He gave her a wide grin. "I landed a bunch of lecturing gigs this afternoon that'll bring in a few hundred a week. I can afford to blow a little of it, can't I, Miss Moneymatters?"

"I suppose so," she conceded, putting the flowers in a cut-glass vase and setting them on the coffee table. The blooms had a peachy tinge to them that went well with her couch, and she wondered if Ian had deliberately chosen them for their color. When asked, he merely smiled.

"Well, then, Dr. Bradshaw," she said teasingly, "at least tell me about your lectures. Where will they be and what will they be about?"

Ian widened his eyes and leered at her. "Sex," he whispered huskily. "Within the next few weeks hundreds of innocent young New York university students are going to be shocked to learn that they aren't the only ones who enjoy the activity. Animals get it on, too, you know."

"Ian, are you serious?" Elizabeth laughed. "I never know when you're kidding or not."

"Actually," he said, sobering, "that's only a part of what I'm going to say. I have a chance to instill in a small group of urban youth the same desire I have to preserve what we can of our fellow planet dwellers. If I get even one person to feel the way I do, I'll count my lectures a success."

"Ever the crusader," she said, moving over to take his hand. "Dinner's almost ready. Would you like a drink first?"

"Wine will be fine."

During the meal, which she served on her dining room table, having created a romantic atmosphere with candlelight, he regaled her with intriguing facts about the creatures he studied. She learned that males of some species actually court the female of their choice by bringing small gifts. "Food, of course," he said, dismembering the game hen with skill. "But sometimes shiny bits of stone, flower petals, anything that's eye-catching."

"Like the roses?" she teased. "Or dinner last night?"

He looked at her, his expression both sensual and amused. "You have my number, lady. I'm caught in my own verbal trap."

"On the other hand," she said, wanting to continue a conversation she found interesting, "don't the males just sometimes jump the first available female?"

"Sometimes, but don't compare it to rape in human society. Only orangutans, of the higher level of mammals, share that bad trait with us."

"I would think lions—"

Ian laughed. "Oh, no, not a male lion. The female has a more violent temper. If the male tried anything she didn't like—especially if she was the highest ranking lady in the pride—she'd pin his ears but good."

"Fascinating." She studied him by the candlelight. So was he, she thought. Such a mind, such a sense of humor, such an attractive personality. Such a sexy man!

He chuckled. "People really have such odd ideas about lions. In his prime, if he has a large enough harem, about all a big male does is mate, eat and sleep. Quite a life."

"But it's over when a younger lion beats him up, isn't it?"

He nodded. "But we all age, and he did have his place in the sun."

"That's very philosophical." She took a sip of wine. "And reminds me, I never did learn how old you are."

"I'm thirty-four. Want to check my teeth?"

They chattered and bantered through the end of the meal, which Ian declared scrumptious. Afterward, he removed his jacket and tie, rolled up his sleeves and insisted on helping her clean up. He was not, he declared, a freeloading lion, letting his female do all the work. Elizabeth laughed and said that she doubted if lionesses did dishes.

The dishes done, they returned to the living room, and Elizabeth felt her pulse start to speed up. "I do want to thank you again," she said, feeling a growing nervousness, "for what you did for Michael. And for getting me to think about trying therapy again for my own problem. It's been many years, and I might be mature enough now for a doctor to help me."

"Why don't we go sit on the couch, and you can show me just how thankful and mature you are." Seduction was back in his eyes.

"Well, get right to the point!" she exclaimed, suddenly annoyed at his directness.

"See!" He laughed. "Never come on to a lioness unless she's in the mood." He put his hands on both sides of her face. "Let's see what I can do to put you in the mood," he murmured, and his lips touched hers.

Gently, softly, teasingly, warming her with the sensation. Elizabeth sighed. She might as well relax. She wanted to touch and kiss him so badly that it almost hurt; there was no sense in pretending otherwise.

Ian felt her give in, felt his own immediate arousal at the touch and taste of her. *Keep it under control,* he warned himself. *The lady will be kissed and caressed tonight, but nothing more. Give her time to come to you with no reservations, and it will be well worth the wait.*

But after he had led her to the couch and had experienced more of Elizabeth Marlowe, he wasn't sure just how far his control would stretch. Her body was lithe, her curves firm but womanly soft. When he cupped a breast, she accepted the move, even pressing herself against his palm eagerly. And her kisses! Tender fire!

Elizabeth knew she was tempting fate, but she couldn't seem to stop her reaction to him. Everything about him excited her. Never had a man been able to ignite her passion like this, and though she found it irresistible, she was also alarmed by it. She had no control at all!

Fortunately, Ian seemed to. Although he kissed her deeply, tantalizing her with his lips and tongue, his mouth never went farther than her throat. And though his hands caressed her body, raising her blood pressure considerably, they didn't touch the overheated skin beneath her dress. It was as if he were exploring, learning her for future, more intense, loving.

And she was doing the same. Her hands caressed his body, and she was amazed once more by the solidness of him. His arms, chest, back and abdomen were rock hard. She didn't dare check the condition below his belt, but every so often, as they moved, she would brush up against the unmistakable sign that he was as aroused as she was. His self-control won her admiration.

Eventually he slowed the pace of his kisses and caresses, pausing now and then to look into her eyes. His gaze made her shiver. It was as if he were giving her soul the same loving treatment he had lavished on her body.

"You're the most beautiful, sensual woman I've ever met," he said, knowing the words were true and not legal lover's lies. He'd known women all around the world, but none could compare with Elizabeth. At his words, she lost her look of soft passion and smiled wryly.

"You don't have a touch of Irish in you?" she asked. "That sounded like sweet blarney to me."

"I know." He cradled her against his chest. "But whatever you think, I know that I meant it."

She nestled in his arms, thinking how secure he made her feel, how unusually... womanly. She wished she could stay this way all night.

But soon, to her disappointment, he released her and stood. "It's nearing pumpkin time," he declared, stretching. "And I know my Cinderella has a big day tomorrow with Jennifer coming in. It really isn't any of my business, but if you feel she won't mind, could you tell me how things go?''

"Of course."

"And dinner? This time my treat?"

"Oh, Ian, I have a dinner engagement with an important client. One I really can't afford to break."

He felt a surge of jealousy, which he quickly squashed. She was, after all, a businesswoman and had obligations. "I have to admit disappointment. Will you call me?" She agreed.

They lingered at the door before he left, enjoying a short reenactment of their earlier pleasures, then he was gone. As she prepared for bed, Elizabeth felt the same eerie emptiness that had gripped her when she had thought he was out of her life for good. But she put it down to unfulfilled desire. Certainly, there had been plenty of that this evening. On both sides.

It took quite a while for Elizabeth to fall asleep. Images of Ian and remembered sensations kept tormenting her with sweet promises.

The next morning, however, she did her best to put him out of her thoughts and concentrate on cramming a day's work into a few hours so that she would be free for Jennifer. After Michael's behavior Monday night, she was certain the younger woman would need some sympathetic hand-holding.

Nothing was further from the truth. Jennifer arrived at her office precisely at noon, head held high. "If Michael won't face his problems," she said firmly, "I love him enough to *make* him face them." She explained that he had learned about her upcoming visit to the doctor because she'd decided not to keep her plans a secret. It was, she declared, open season on honesty from now on. Elizabeth was a little stunned by her attitude, since she seemed an entirely different woman than the weeping wife who had poured out her story a few nights ago. But then, she reasoned, this was more like the Jennifer who played killer tennis, showing no mercy to a worthy opponent. And in Michael, she certainly had a worthy competitor in life, as well as a partner. The only reason Elizabeth accompanied her to Sue Fuller's office after they had enjoyed a pleasant lunch together, was to ask her physician friend what her recommendations would be for therapy for her height phobia. Jennifer, it was clear, did not need handholding anymore. She had the bit in her teeth and was off and running!

Elizabeth relaxed in Sue's waiting room while Jennifer was being examined. She had brought a briefcase filled with material she needed to show her client at dinner, but decided that a period of rest was probably more important, since she hadn't done too well along that line last night. When Sue, a tall salt-and-pepper haired woman, and Jennifer reappeared, Elizabeth was almost dozing.

"See what happens to workaholics when you give them a few minutes' break," Sue teased as Elizabeth stifled a yawn.

"I'm not a workaholic," she countered. "Just . . . busy."

"When you don't need to be," Jennifer interjected. "Even I don't understand why you work so hard when you've got a fortune of your own from your inheritance."

"I thought we came here because of *your* problems, not mine." The subject was making Elizabeth testy, partly because there was some truth in their words.

"It would seem that Jennifer has no problem," Sue announced. "I need to run a few more tests to be sure, but all the plumbing is in the right place and looks normal. If you'd like, Jennifer, I'll set up an appointment for your husband with a colleague of mine, and then we'll know for sure if the difficulty is physical. From there, you'll have a number of options, including counseling."

"Speaking of which—" Elizabeth rose "—I need to ask a favor of you," she told the physician.

Elizabeth glanced at Jennifer. She wasn't sure she could talk freely with another person around, even one as dear as Jennifer.

"Go on into Sue's office." Jennifer made shooing motions. "I understand that some things are private, no matter how close a relative is." Her smile told Elizabeth that she wasn't offended.

When they settled in Sue's conservative office, Elizabeth found herself trembling. This was going to be tougher than she'd thought.

"You…you know my…problem with high places and f-flying," she said. Sue nodded.

"Well, I've decided to…to try to do something about it again. Af-after all, I am almost th-thirty years old, and it's pretty silly for a gr-grown woman not to be able to even think about get…getting on an airplane without suffering from the jitters like I am right now!" The last words came out firmly. She saw a spark of approval in Sue's brown eyes.

"Did Jennifer's boldness trigger this?" she asked. "Or is your need to finally be healed due to something else? It would help me advise you if I knew."

Elizabeth haltingly explained about Ian, her feelings, the trip. "He's the catalyst," she said. "Without him, I would probably have gone on living with this thing. But he speaks so enticingly of other places that I...I think I want to see them."

"With him?"

"I've only known him a very short time."

"Think you need any professional counseling from *my* specialization?" Sue smiled.

Elizabeth blushed, but shook her head. "We aren't *that* serious," she said, thinking of the romantic activities they had indulged in the night before. Maybe she should... But no. That would be an open admission to herself that she would be going to bed with him, and she intended to do that only with a man she loved. Her feelings about Ian were still too unclear...

"I'd recommend that you skip an analyst this time, Elizabeth," Sue said. "I have an acquaintance who's not an M.D., but has a degree in psychology. And she's a phobia specialist." Another smile, this one amused. "When you meet her, you'll understand why she chose to focus only on crippling fears."

"Give me her name. I'll make an appointment."

"Let me do it for you. I can get you in sooner."

After they left Sue's suite, Elizabeth and Jennifer went to a quiet bar on Second Avenue and sipped wine while they conspired on the matter of getting Michael to agree to see the doctor.

"He ran to Ian when he needed someone to talk to," Elizabeth pointed out. "And I'm willing to bet Ian could be very persuasive if Michael balks and you need help."

Jennifer laughed. "I can just see it. We arrive at the doctor's office, Michael tied and trussed like a side of beef, Ian carrying him under one arm." Elizabeth joined in her laughter, though she wondered if the humorous picture foreshadowed reality. She hoped Michael was more mature than that.

"Anyway," Jennifer added, sobering. "The jury's still out on me. Sue won't know for certain until the test results come in."

"Chin up. Sue's an uncannily accurate diagnostician."

Jennifer took a sip of her wine, then looked directly at Elizabeth, a smile on her face. "How are things going between you and Ian *really*?" she asked in a teasing tone. Elizabeth had told her a little at lunch, piquing her curiosity. "And I don't mean the stuff about the roses and dinner. Is this the big romance you've been waiting all your life for?"

"Don't be so nosy." Elizabeth grinned to take the sting out of her words. But she had no intention of letting Jennifer know exactly what was going on. She wasn't even sure herself.

"Does he kiss well?" Jennifer seemed determined to tease.

Elizabeth decided to play. "Fabulously," she replied, looking heavenward.

"And . . . ?"

"He's obviously been around." Elizabeth glanced at her watch. "Oh, I had no idea it was so late. I've got to run to make my dinner date with my client."

"Not Ian?"

"Unfortunately, no." She gave Jennifer a kiss on the cheek and wished her luck with Michael, promising to help if needed.

Dinner with her client was a success. The elderly gentleman, who had made his fortune in shipping, gave her the go-ahead on several investments that would bring her large commissions. And she enjoyed the man's company, listening to him reminisce about making money in the good old days when honest hard work earned an honest buck. He had been one of the shrewdest of his peers and had probably bent a rule or two here and there, but Elizabeth listened to the half truths without comment. His efforts had employed many people during a time when jobs were scarce, and had boosted the country's economy by exporting American goods for sale abroad.

It was nearly eleven when she returned to her apartment. On the hallway floor in front of her door was a small box. Plain, brown and wrapped with twine. She picked it up and shook it. Something rattled.

What in the world...? she wondered, unlocking her door and taking the box inside. Who would leave a package, unprotected, outside her door? Even though security in her building was tight, there was always the possibility that one of her neighbors might not be entirely trustworthy. She set the box on the table in the small entryway, put her briefcase and purse on the coffee table and shrugged out of her coat.

When she opened the strange package and saw the contents, she burst out laughing. No note accompanied the pieces of colored glass and polished pebbles, but she knew who they were from. Despite the lateness of the hour, she dialed his number to thank him for his "courting" gift.

But he didn't answer. Disappointed, she hung up. Maybe he was at that bar near his place. Maybe even on a date with another woman. Not green-eyed-monster time, she cautioned herself, but a feeling of jealousy rose, anyway. The idea of Ian kissing and touching another— The telephone's ring interrupted her gloomy musings.

"Elizabeth!" Ian's deep voice sounded relieved. "I've been calling for hours. Where have you... Never mind. I need your help. I'm in jail."

"I don't believe you, and thanks for the darling little collection of—"

"I'm *serious*, Elizabeth. I'm in the Central Park pokey. You've got to come down and bail me out. I don't know anyone else to call on."

"Ian, if this is another one of your tricks..."

"Want to talk to a cop?"

"Yes, I do."

She waited for a moment, and then listened with growing horror as a man who called himself Sergeant Wilson explained that Ian had no identification, and in order for him to be freed on bail, a person with good standing in the community would have to vouch for him. He knew of the Marlowe family and told her that her word in person would be enough. Elizabeth said hurriedly that she would be right down. It wasn't until she was outside, the doorman hailing a cab for her, that she realized she hadn't asked what the charges against him were.

CHAPTER EIGHT

THE TAXI PULLED UP to the ominous, fortresslike building, and Elizabeth got out. She paid the cabbie without taking her eyes off the station. Just looking at it was intimidating, and she wondered and worried about what Ian could have done to get himself in such a dreadful place.

Inside she was directed to where Sergeant Wilson sat behind an old, scratched desk. When she introduced herself, he stood and shook her hand, a sign of respect she doubted many who waited before this desk received.

"The charge against him is battery," the slightly overweight sergeant explained. "But he's filed countercharges against the other man. If you'll come with me, Ms Marlowe, I think we can work something out. The incident was minor, over a silly issue, and the courts are clogged enough as it is. We like to resolve these things on the spot whenever possible. The fact that your friend had no ID was what really forced the officer at the scene to arrest them both and bring them down. The other man's wife insisted on coming, too. She's waiting in another room with the cause of the altercation."

"May I ask what it was?" She had her suspicions.

"A mutt," the policeman said. "Your friend accused this guy of mistreating his little yappy mutt. According to witnesses, the guy took enough offense at the animal lover to take a swing at him. Really stupid, considering the size of your friend."

"Only in New York," Elizabeth said, sighing. "And only Ian Bradshaw."

"Yeah. That's the big guy's name, all right. Said he was a doctor of animals or something. Never seen a guy so mad about a dumb little pooch."

"Dr. Bradshaw *is* an unusual man," Elizabeth agreed.

He led her to a room where a uniformed officer was keeping watch over two prisoners. They sat on opposite sides of a long table, and both were handcuffed…and glaring at each other. The officer smiled at Elizabeth and touched the brim of his cap.

"Elizabeth!" Ian started to rise, but the officer put a restraining hand on his shoulder. "You should have seen what this jerk was doing to the poor dog," Ian went on, ignoring the police.

"It's my damn dog, you big ape!" the other man, a thin fellow half Ian's size, yelled. "You got no right telling me how to treat my own dog."

Ian glared at the sergeant. "If he'd been dragging a kid around like that, all unkempt and undernourished, wouldn't I have been in the right to complain?"

Sergeant Wilson looked at Elizabeth. "Any suggestions?" he asked.

"Yes." She pointed at the thin man. "Do you really want the dog? Would you be willing to take a hundred dollars for it in exchange for dropping the charges against Ian?''

"I'm not dropping any charges against *him*!'' Ian shouted. "He deserves punishment for the way—''

"Ian, shut up!'' Elizabeth looked at the other man.

"You'd give me a hundred for a lousy mutt?'' he asked. She nodded. "Lady,'' he said, "you got a deal. Just lemme see the cash.'' She fished a one-hundred-dollar bill from her purse and put it on the table in front of him. Then she turned to Ian.

"Take the dog, drop the charges,'' she said sternly. He held her gaze for a moment, looking stubborn. But then he nodded. "*If* this creep promises never to own another animal.'' The thin man agreed readily.

When Elizabeth saw the dog, she immediately understood why a person with Ian's beliefs and temperament would act the way he had. The puppy was mangy and its little ribs could be seen through its straggly white coat. The sour-faced woman gave the dog up gladly when she learned they had been given so much money for it, and Elizabeth watched as the puppy made yippy little sounds of joy and licked Ian's face. Such tenderness came over Ian's rugged features that tears stung her eyes.

"I think you have a pet,'' she said. "Love at first sight if I've ever seen it.''

He looked at her, his own eyes bright with gratitude. "Thanks, Lizzie. I'll pay back—''

"No you won't. Consider it a gift.''

They left the station, the puppy resting contentedly in Ian's arms, a condition Elizabeth could well understand. She knew the feeling of security he gave. Then an unpleasant thought occurred to her.

"We should have called for a cab inside," she said. "It can be dangerous in Central Park at night, waiting for a taxi to come by."

"Don't fret. You've got me and Spike here to protect you."

"Spike?" She started to laugh. "Isn't that kind of a tough name for such a little thing?" She patted the small furry head.

"Got to give him something to live up to," Ian said, and waved down a cab to take them home.

DURING THE NEXT FEW WEEKS, Elizabeth witnessed two miracles. First, under the knowledgeable care of Ian, Spike flourished like a wilting flower given proper sun and water. Only in Spike's case, it was Ian's love that really made the difference. Rarely did the man go anywhere without his little pet tagging along. The animal filled out, his fur shone and his dark eyes gleamed with energy and life and doggy adoration for his new owner. Watching Ian with his pet, Elizabeth grew more and more certain that the man was capable of deep, nurturing love.

The other miracle involved Michael. Jennifer's tests came up normal, and she told Elizabeth that though Michael had not been happy about it, he did go to be tested himself. The results were encouraging. In light of the couple having no physical problems, Sue Fuller had advised them to relax for a while and see if Michael hadn't been correct in his original opinion that they should simply let nature take its course. Pressure off, Michael reverted to his old, lovable self, and Elizabeth could tell that Jennifer had decided to accept the situation as it was. At least, she had confided, for a while.

Since Ian and Robert had mended their fences to an extent, Elizabeth and Ian and, of course, Spike, had taken to spending short weekends at the estate, leaving the city on Saturday and returning on Sunday. Elizabeth had several reasons for the visits: she wanted to monitor Jennifer and Michael's situation; she wanted her family to get to know Ian better, since her feelings for him grew stronger daily; and she wanted them to be prepared for the possibility that he would become her lover.

Ian clearly loved the chance to get out of the confines of the inner city. He would loose his pet from its leash and the two of them, along with Elizabeth, would spend hours walking in the woods of the Marlowe estate. Spike was ecstatic on these weekends, sniffing scents beyond the range of his human companions and then bounding off in search of new discoveries. While he frisked, Elizabeth and Ian made discoveries of their own.

The days had chilled then warmed as Indian summer gave the land a last taste of comfortable weather before winter set in.

One mild Saturday, after lunching with Adelaide and Robert, Ian, Elizabeth and Spike headed out into the woods. Ian wore jeans and a sweater; Elizabeth, slacks and a turtleneck. When he leaned against a tree and pulled her against him for a long kiss, it almost felt as if no clothes separated their bodies.

"Mmm," Ian murmured, nuzzling her neck and enjoying the sweet scent of her flowery perfume. "You have got to be the best thing that's happened in my life since I was born, Miss Marlowe."

"That's a serious statement, Dr. Bradshaw," she replied teasingly. "Are you sure you mean it?"

Sunlight, falling through a gap in the pine trees, gleamed on his black hair and made his eyes glow. At least she thought that was the cause of the warmth she saw in the silvery depths.

"I mean it, ma'am. And I'm also quite serious about still wanting you to make the trip with me. I need a firm commitment soon."

Elizabeth looked away. She had chickened out of her appointment with Sue's phobia specialist the week before, pleading that with her life already complicated by her romance with Ian and an increasing workload as the Street moved out of the late-summer doldrums into full financial swing, she simply didn't have the time or energy to deal with her fears. Ian hadn't been pleased, but said that he understood it would take a long time to overcome something that had been a part of her for so many years. He had not, however, taken back his invitation to travel to Bali with him. In fact, he had increased pressure recently by leaving travel brochures around her apartment when he visited. The pictures and descriptions, she had to admit, were inviting. If only they could go by *boat*. But that was out of the question because of the time factor. She could afford to be away from her office for the two weeks Ian would be needed on location. Nancy was capable of handling minor situations, and if a major crisis came up, she could always use the overseas telephone. A cruise, however, would take months.

"I've been doing some reading about problems like yours," Ian said, putting his hand under her chin and lifting her head so that she had to face him. "Some experts suggest that gradual exposure to the object of fear will sometimes help desensitize the sufferer."

"The key word is 'sometimes.'"

"Elizabeth, you're a brave person. I've come to know you well over the past weeks. We've been companions for almost a month, and though I can't speak for you, I know I haven't been the least bit interested in seeing another person socially. I *care* about you, I want your company in Bali, and I want to help you get over this thing." He paused. "And I believe you long to get over it, too. I think that deep down you have a spirit that would love adventuring, traveling to exotic places."

"Oh, no, not me." She lifted her hands from his shoulders and shook her head vigorously. "I like it right here. At home."

Ian sighed inwardly. Part of her problem was her own damn stubbornness. She refused to face the truth. Her love of movies—they had been to dozens already; the pictures on the walls of her office and apartment; even her choice of leisure reading material—*National Geographic*, fiction and nonfiction about high adventure. All of it pointed to an inward yearning. But would she admit it? No way.

"You're lying to yourself, you know," he told her, rising frustration making him less careful than usual with his words. He had been letting his affection for her get in the way of helping her. Well, no longer, he vowed.

She pushed away, angry. "I know myself, Ian. I'm not some animal you can observe and analyze."

"I didn't mean to imply that. But sometimes a person hides the truth from their own consciousness in order to avoid facing facts. Elizabeth, you've had the worst experience a child can have—losing your beloved parents. Don't you think that there might be facets of yourself you don't understand or won't face?"

"I have *been* to analysts! They didn't think I was crazy!"

"I'm not saying that," he said, feeling helpless. "I just feel strongly that I can help—"

"I don't need your help or anyone else's!"

Ian watched with a sinking heart as she stalked away, her shoes making crunching sounds on the carpet of pine needles and fallen leaves. *Let her cool off,* he told himself. *Then bring it up again. It's going to take persistence to get through to her.*

Spike reappeared, small pink tongue hanging out as he panted from running. Mission: squirrel chasing, Ian thought. He sat on the ground, his back against a tree. Spike jumped into his lap, and he absently stroked the dog's now silky hair while he pondered the problem of Elizabeth Marlowe.

He didn't have to take her with him. It was only a two-week job. In fact, he didn't have to do it himself, but he needed the money. His salary would carry him for quite some time. His friend's job in Hollywood wouldn't last forever, and eventually he'd have to find a place of his own and pay for it. And nothing in New York was cheap. Besides, he wanted to go. He had been in Bali before and loved the opulent scenery and gentle people. And lately, a longing for his old free life had consumed him. He knew he had to get away from the city, or he'd go nuts. The crowds, the pollution, the impersonality of it all. He *hated* it. In fact, Elizabeth was the city's one redeeming factor. A lovely flower in a concrete and steel slag heap. Face it, he told himself, he had itchy feet. It was time for him to be on the move again. She might be a flower, but she was also an anchor, however compelling. Dammit, he wanted to share Bali with her so much! Maybe he should consider drugging and kidnapping.

The sound of footsteps interrupted his musings. "Hi, buddy." Michael appeared through the trees. "I saw Elizabeth go storming into the house. Lovers' quarrel?" He sat down next to Ian.

"Sort of." He needed to talk, and Mike knew Elizabeth well. Maybe he could help. Ian filled his friend in on most of the details.

"Mind a personal question?" Michael asked when he was finished. "Are you two...you know, *really* close romantically now?"

Ian shook his head. "She's not ready. I like her a lot, Mike. More than any other woman I've known. I intend to be very, very careful in my treatment of her."

"Sounds suspiciously like more than 'like.' Maybe that's part of your problem."

"*I* don't have the problem, Mike. She's the one who can't fly." Spike whined as his master's voice rose, and Ian patted him soothingly to calm him.

"What about this little guy?" Michael added a pat of his own. "He can't go with you. You plan to board him?"

"No. I asked Jennifer if she would baby-sit him. He likes her, and she's fond of him. I think it'll work."

Michael let out a long sigh. "Maybe I ought to get her a pet of her own. It might take her mind off this kid thing."

"Sounds like you still have a problem."

"Not like before. Since we know there's nothing wrong, she's not after me all the time to see a doctor. Our love's as strong as ever. But I know she wants a baby so badly."

"And you?" Ian asked, remembering his friend's inebriated confession. "Have you come to terms with your own ambivalences?"

Michael waggled his hand. "One day I wish she would get pregnant, the next I'm glad she isn't. I think about it a lot, trying to work out my own feelings. It isn't easy."

"If you want a suggestion," Ian offered, an inspiration hitting him, "I'd recommend taking Jen off for a second honeymoon somewhere remote and private. You two seem happy here, but face it, the estate's a glass bowl. You never know when you're going to run into a relative or a servant. It's kind of comparable to a chimp clan, everyone living all over everyone else."

"God, don't ever let Robert hear you say something like that." Michael laughed. "He'd blow his cork."

"I do seem to have that effect on him," Ian said, remembering that when Spike had first met Robert, the pup had been piddling on the boxwood bushes that lined the driveway. Robert had been frostily polite, informing Ian that animal urine turned the bushes brown and would he please have his beast perform his functions back in the trees. Ian had agreed just as frostily, but when Robert had bent to pat Spike when the dog had run over to sniff his shoes, he felt himself warm toward the man slightly.

"But anyway," he went on, "chimps are promiscuous within the clan—no comparison meant here— but my point is that when a couple go off by themselves for a while, conception almost always occurs, whereas it doesn't usually from the casual contacts."

Michael leaned his head back against the tree trunk. "I like the idea of a secluded vacation. I haven't taken off since I started with the company."

"Go for it!" Ian slapped his friend's shoulder.

ELIZABETH PACED the library. Her emotions were in turmoil. He had no business trying to pry into her mind like that! No business at all. They were still merely friends, after all, not committed lovers.

But she had to admit that his behavior and some of what he had said indicated a concern about her that could be a reflection of deep feelings. Deeper than just the romantic friendship she thought they shared. Had Ian fallen in love with her?

"There you are, dear." Adelaide entered the library. "I just received a telephone call and got the most interesting bit of news. You'll never guess."

Elizabeth smiled. Adelaide did love local gossip so, and it pleased her to see her grandmother excited about the latest tidbit. "Must be good news," she hazarded.

"*Very* good news." Adelaide clasped her hands together. "Bill Stockdale and Muffy are engaged again. And everyone is giving you and Ian the credit for their reunion."

"That's wonderful." They deserved each other, Elizabeth thought wickedly.

"We're having dinner at the club tonight," Adelaide went on. "Perhaps we'll see the happy couple there."

Hopefully they wouldn't, Elizabeth thought.

"Well, dear, I'm off to call some more people," Adelaide told her. "It's so wonderful to be able to spread good news." She gave Elizabeth a wistful look. "I only wish I was spreading it about you and Ian."

"A month!" Elizabeth flared, remembering how angry she was at Ian. "I've known the man less than a month. I love you, Grandmother, but if you start matchmaking, I'll really be angry."

Adelaide just laughed. "I don't think I have to matchmake with you two. I think it's already been done." She pointed toward heaven. Then, giggling, she left the room.

Annoyed, angry and confused by her feelings, Elizabeth started to pace again. She caught sight of Jennifer heading toward the greenhouse, a flower basket and shears in her hands. Feeling the need to talk to a discreet and understanding friend, Elizabeth hurriedly followed.

The air in the greenhouse was at least twenty degrees warmer than that outside. She received a smiling greeting from her cousin-in-law.

"You look," Jennifer said as she began to snip blooms, "as if you have something bothering you. Did you come here to talk?"

"Very intuitive." Elizabeth sat on the workbench by the potting table and launched into her tale. Jennifer listened without comment until she was finished.

"Go," Jennifer told her. "He's trying to help you, and you both love each other. I don't understand why you haven't lured him to bed yet...or why he hasn't seduced you. For two highly intelligent people, you're handling your relationship like a pair of dodo birds."

Her words shocked Elizabeth into silence. She could form no rebuke as she had with Adelaide. The mention of love coming from Jennifer had the ring of reality. Was she really self-deceived? And if so, could Ian be right about her avoiding her fears? Did she actually have a hidden yen to travel, expressing it in her favorite forms of entertainment and choices of art? Ian hadn't brought those up, but she was willing to bet that was where he had come up with his analysis.

"Love's a funny thing," Jennifer went on, ignoring her silence. "When I met Michael, I was ready to fall in love, so I knew almost immediately that this was the man of my dreams. But you're so adamantly set on living your life single that you wouldn't know love if it came up and bit you on the nose." She snipped another blossom.

"Jennifer!" This was so unlike the gentle woman she thought she knew. "How can you presume to know what's between Ian and myself?"

Jennifer grinned. "You just finished telling me an earful. And it doesn't take a genius to recognize two lovebirds."

"Great. First we are dodos. Now it's lovebirds." Elizabeth rested her elbows on the potting table and groaned. "Maybe I could think clearly if he wasn't ramming this trip down my throat."

"I doubt it." Jennifer put down the shears and came over to sit beside her. "Remember that until I came bawling to you with my problem, I was just running in circles, driving myself and Michael crazy. You cannot depend on yourself for everything, Elizabeth. You said it yourself. That's what families are for. To help each other get through this puzzle called life."

Elizabeth felt close to tears. "I can't love him," she whispered. "He goes all over the world, and *I cannot get on a plane.*"

"Try." Jennifer shook her shoulder encouragingly.

"Remember the talk I had with Sue after she was finished with you?" Jennifer nodded. "Well, I asked her help in getting counseling. She even arranged for an appointment."

"And?"

"I canceled." Elizabeth put her head in her hands. "If I can't even make myself go for professional help, how can I possibly expect to get on a plane?"

"Believe in yourself. That's what I'm trying to do." Jennifer stood, gesturing to emphasize her point. "Every single day when I first look into the mirror I tell myself, 'Mrs. Michael Marlowe, you will be holding your own baby in less than a year.' Some days I believe, some days I don't. But I'm going to keep at it!"

Her determination showed all over her, and Elizabeth felt ashamed. She had secretly thought that she was the stronger woman, since she had sought out an independent life, but now she faced the truth. Jennifer Marlowe had more guts than she ever would . . . unless she quit whining and forced herself to change. "I know what I'll do," she said. "I'll start cutting out pictures of planes from magazines and taping them up in places where I'll be forced to look at them daily."

"That's the spirit! A positive step."

Elizabeth discussed further ideas for rehabilitating herself with Jennifer while the other woman finished her task of gathering flowers. She also decided to give Ian the shock of his life when they arrived back in the city. She would come on to him so sensually that he wouldn't be able to resist her. Then perhaps they could speak openly about their real feelings. And, experiencing a twisting fear, Elizabeth told herself that she would agree to go on the trip with him. If their love was a true one, she would have to start adapting to his way of life. The big question in her mind was would he be willing to meet her halfway.

She followed Jennifer out of the greenhouse, but paused when she heard a faint strange noise. "What's that?" she asked. "More of Michael and Ian's jungle noises?"

"No." Jennifer looked concerned. "I think it's someone screaming."

IAN TOSSED a small twig and Spike retrieved it, dropping it by his hand, the dog's wagging tail indicating he wanted more of the game.

"That's one cute pup," Michael said. "You know, you never did tell me how you got him."

Ian had avoided recounting the tale in front of all the Marlowes, knowing his session with the police wouldn't be something Robert would approve of, but now he told Michael the whole story, swearing his friend to secrecy. Michael roared with laughter.

"That's one hell of a way to acquire a pet," he said, wiping tears of mirth from his eyes.

Ian started to reply, then stiffened. "Listen," he said, putting his hand on Michael's arm. "Do you hear a strange sound?" Spike's ears, he noted, were perked. Then the little dog ran barking in the direction of the mansion. "It's a woman screaming!" Ian was on his feet and running, not glancing back to see if Michael was behind him. If something had happened to Elizabeth... His chest constricted, and he increased speed.

CHAPTER NINE

ELIZABETH RAN right behind Jennifer into the house. The screams were coming from the general direction of the kitchen. Could Cook have injured herself? Or Adelaide? She and Jennifer rounded a corner and barely avoided colliding with Ian, who was dashing toward the kitchen from another direction.

"Thank God you're both all right!" Ian exclaimed, pulling the two women to him, but giving Elizabeth a quick kiss. Spike bounced around at their feet, barking excitedly.

"Where's Michael?" Jennifer asked. "I thought he said he was going out to visit with you."

Ian looked behind him. No sign of his friend. And the screams had stopped, replaced by the most creative round of curses he had ever heard in the Swedish language. "Hear that?" he said. "I think Michael may have taken off in the other direction."

"I don't understand." Jennifer looked concerned. Cook was yelling, so she must have been the one who'd been screaming. In any case, why hadn't Michael followed Ian?

Ian gave both women a rueful look. "You can't understand what she's saying, but I'm willing to bet that Mike will be served nothing but gruel for at least a month." He led the way to the kitchen.

The sight that met Elizabeth's eyes made her want to burst into laughter. Cook was covered in flour from blond head to feet. She was yelling and wielding a wicked-looking cleaver, but the object of her ire was clearly no longer a menace, if indeed it ever had been. Lying on the floor along with the overturned flour bin was the chopped-up remains of what Elizabeth tentatively identified as a taxidermic snake. Clear on the other side of the room lay the open-jawed, wickedly fanged head. Cook had probably removed that with her first blow, Elizabeth decided.

Ian crossed the room to the flour-covered woman, speaking soothingly in Swedish. His first sentence reassured her that he had nothing to do with the situation. Proclaiming his innocence in the sincerest of terms seemed vital, considering the cleaver.

"What the devil's going on?" Robert appeared in the doorway, followed closely by a worried Adelaide. The elderly woman peered around the doorjamb, her thin hands clutched to her chest. "My God," Robert went on. "Bradshaw, if you're in any way responsible for this mess...!"

"He's not, Dad." Michael entered the room from the back door. When he saw Cook still brandishing the cleaver, he paled. "Ian, I'd counted on you to disarm her for me," he said.

Ian politely asked Cook to lay down the weapon. "If you only carry out your threat to feed him chopped earthworms, it'll be revenge enough," he added in English. Looking triumphantly indignant, the large woman set the cleaver on the butcher's block.

"Michael, what did you do?" Jennifer asked, her tone scolding. "We heard her screaming all the way from the greenhouse. I think this time you really have gone too far." Robert, Adelaide, Elizabeth *and* Cook echoed her sentiments.

Ian moved to one side. This was a family matter, one in which he had no business interfering, except to keep Michael from being turned into chopped herring by the furious Swede. Spike was sniffing the severed head of the snake, a cobra. Ian signaled his pet to return to him. Spike obeyed immediately.

Michael fell to his knees in front of his family and the angry Cook. "I confess to putting the stuffed cobra in the flour bin," he said. "But in case no one else remembered, today is Cook's birthday, and I didn't want her to feel neglected." He rose, dusting flour from the knees of his slacks. "Another token of my esteem for your incredible services," he said, reaching into his pocket and taking out a small box. Handing it to the now astounded Cook, he added, "I bet you can even make earthworms tasty."

Cook slowly opened the box, gasping when she saw the contents. Taking it out, she displayed a beautiful diamond pendant. Then, talking in rapid Swedish, she gave Michael a floury hug.

Elizabeth moved over to Ian's side. "I take it he's forgiven," she murmured, touching his hand.

"Forgiven, scolded and has promised that no worms will be forthcoming." He took her hand in his.

Robert noticed the gesture. The growing affection between Elizabeth and the big ethologist had not met with his approval, but he knew there was nothing he could or would do to stop it. She was a grown woman, he reminded himself for the thousandth time. And he was certain that the differences in their backgrounds and goals would eventually drive them apart, anyway. He would just endure and bide his time. After he and the rest of the family had proclaimed Michael's act a bit overdone, but typical of his wacky brand of thoughtfulness, he retired to his study to read and work until it was time to leave for dinner at the club.

ELIZABETH STROLLED at Ian's side along the golf-cart path. They had both opted for a walk instead of dessert, but it wasn't the exercise that concerned her. When they were far enough away from the clubhouse not to be seen, she reached for his hand.

"I want to apologize for this afternoon," she said. "You were right, and I've been too blind to see it."

"No apology needed." He lifted her hand and kissed it. "I've been pushing too hard. You had a right to blow up."

"I'm going with you to Bali."

Ian stopped dead in his tracks. "Would you mind repeating what you just said?" he asked, facing her.

"I don't have time for lengthy therapy, so I've come up with a few ideas of my own to help me get on the plane. I'll ask Sue if she'll prescribe a heavy-duty tranquilizer, and I *will* make it."

Ian stared at her. There was more in her eyes than determination, though that was what he heard plainly in her voice. He wished he could see her better in the twilight, but at least the course was cleared of players, and they were alone. What he believed he saw in her eyes was love—love for him. Why else would she have decided to put herself through what was bound to be an agonizing experience? Wonder filled him, and he remembered Michael's subtle question about the depth of his feelings for her. Suddenly, he knew.

"I love you, Elizabeth," he whispered, drawing her close for a kiss. "I don't mean because you've decided to go. I just realized it now, but I've loved you for weeks."

"I only realized I felt the same way this afternoon after our argument," she murmured, running her fingers through the softness of his hair. "It took a number of figurative sledgehammers to pound it into my thick head, but I love you, Ian."

His embrace tightened. "We'll work it out, Lizzie," he whispered, his voice husky with emotion. "This is a fine, true love, and we'll make it work."

His kiss was passionate, almost overwhelming. She gave in to it completely, letting him feed the flames of her growing desire with his caress.

Later they returned to the dining room, holding hands openly. Elizabeth realized that their mussed appearance was going to make it apparent to one and all what they had been up to in the darkness, but she was too happy to care.

"My, my," Michael declared teasingly. "I think we were doing more than walking off dinner, weren't we?"

"*You* weren't there," Elizabeth countered, taking the seat Ian held out for her. "So how would you know what we were doing?"

Michael was about to reply, mischief in his eyes, but Adelaide stood and waved to a couple across the room, calling to them to come over. Elizabeth closed her eyes. It was Bill and Muffy. She knew the couple wouldn't refuse an invitation from one of the matriarchs of Crystal Cove. She opened her eyes, seeing the obvious reluctance on their faces. But they came.

In contrast to Elizabeth and Ian's rumpled looks, Bill and Muffy were impeccably attired and coiffured. They accepted the Marlowes' congratulations with perfect politeness. "I suppose we owe it in part to you, Dr. Bradshaw," Muffy said in a sugary tone. "If it hadn't been for our little...clash, Bill and I might never have rediscovered our affection for each other."

Ian grinned. "Well, I guess I know how you feel," he drawled, his deep voice almost a purr. "I just found out tonight that Elizabeth and I are in love."

Elizabeth swallowed hard. She hadn't expected him to make an announcement. Glancing around the table, she witnessed mixed reactions. The only truly negative one was from Robert.

"How nice," Muffy replied. Turning to Elizabeth, she asked, "And have you two set a date yet?"

Shoot from the hip, Elizabeth told herself. *Might as well let it all come out now.* "The only 'date' we've set is one early in November. I'll be flying to Bali with Ian. He's consulting for a film company there, and I haven't taken a day's vacation since I opened my office four years ago."

"Bali!" Robert exploded. "Elizabeth, you can't do that!"

"I promise to send postcards," she said in a placating manner.

"I thought you couldn't fly," Bill accused. He had been eyeing Ian warily, clearly thinking about what had happened in September. "Remember that day I tried to get you to go flying over the Sound with me? I thought you'd faint on the spot."

Elizabeth lifted her chin. "I'm going to overcome my fear," she stated.

Later, when they'd returned to the mansion, Robert ordered Ian and Elizabeth to his office. There he lectured them sternly, saying he understood they were both adults, but that there were certain social rules one simply did not break.

"Like telling the world that you and your... lover are going on an overseas trip together!" he blurted.

Elizabeth watched her uncle fume and knew that he was really just concerned about her. She hoped Ian understood, as well.

"Mr. Marlowe," Ian replied coolly, "you know that no one can keep a secret for long around this place. It's as open and gossipy a community as I've ever seen, and I've seen my share. Personal secrets were better kept in my hometown in Nebraska than they are here."

"Tell me, then," Robert snapped, "what do you think your parents would say if they knew that their son was taking a young woman along with him?"

"When my folks meet Elizabeth, which they will sometime, I know they will heartily approve of my choice."

Robert paled. "Then you are marrying?"

"No," Elizabeth interrupted hurriedly. "We each have our own lives to lead. Being in love doesn't make it necessary that we marry... just be happy. Besides, you know how I feel about my career. A family wouldn't fit in."

Robert sagged against the desk. "I just want you to be happy, Elizabeth. And after all these years, I cannot imagine your wanting to fly."

Ian put his arm around Elizabeth. "I promise you, sir, that she's going to be one of the happiest, most contented women in the world. I intend to do everything I can to help her overcome her anxiety. She's strong willed, as you well know, and working together, we can, I'm sure, get rid of this phobia."

"If she comes to any harm because of you, Bradshaw, I'll hound you until you'll wish you never heard the name Marlowe."

Ian grinned. "I'm sure you'd do just that, sir."

"Will you two kindly shake hands," Elizabeth pleaded. "It's very uncomfortable for me to have the two men I love best at each other's throat."

Ian's hand shot out immediately. Robert was more hesitant, but he complied.

"Thanks." Elizabeth kissed them both. "Now I'm taking myself off to bed. I'll see both of you wonderful men in the morning."

"Darling," Robert asked, "would you please send Charters in with two glasses and some brandy. I don't know about this young man, but this old one could use a nightcap. Ian?"

"I'd be delighted."

Elizabeth left to find Charters, her heart singing with joy.

ON THE WAY BACK to Manhattan the next afternoon, Elizabeth tried to get Ian to tell her how his private session with Robert went, but he just smiled and said that it went fine. He also said it was important to him that Robert learned to trust him with his adopted daughter. Then he moved on to a more personal topic.

"Since we've come out of the closet about our mutual love, Elizabeth—" he rubbed the nape of her neck seductively "—how do you feel about more complete physical expression of that love?"

She started to laugh. "I was planning on seducing you tonight."

Ian stroked Spike, who was sitting on his lap. "Since we have all Spike's stuff, and there's no question of 'your place or mine,' since mine has walls so thin I can hear my neighbors snoring at night, we'd better plan on your apartment, love." She agreed, warming at his term of endearment. Everything was going to be fine.

They stopped in Chinatown to pick up takeout, not feeling like cooking. Spike whined and strained to get at the package of food as Elizabeth drove them uptown, but a reprimanding word from Ian soon had him sitting quietly again.

"You have really done wonders with that dog," she complimented him. "I don't know when I've seen a healthier, better trained animal."

"The secret's teaching with love as the motivation," he replied, gazing at her with longing in his silver eyes. "Love works wonders with any sentient creature."

"Including flight-fearing blondes?"

"Especially," he stated, promise in his word.

They shared the exotic meal, and Ian promised to take her to a restaurant in SoHo that served Balinese food later in the week. "Their *rijstaffel* will help prepare you for the meals you'll be enjoying soon."

"What's ri...whatever you said?"

"It's really a feast comprising many different dishes. The word is Dutch and literally translated means 'rice table.' Rice is the base, but some of the hottest, spiciest and tastiest dishes I've ever had were served at *rijstaffel*s."

Laughing, she asked help in learning to pronounce the exotic word. By the time she had it down, dinner was over, and Ian was looking at her with expectation. Almost, she thought, nerves beginning to tingle with a combination of anticipation and anxiety, the same way he'd stared at her in the woods when he had stalked her.

"I—I'll just take a shower and change," she said, rising from the table. His hand closed over her wrist gently.

"If you're getting cold feet, darling, we can wait. I won't force you in *any* way." The tenderness of his touch and expression melted her.

"Who needs to shower," she whispered. She sank into his lap, wrapped her arms around his neck and gave him a simmering kiss.

"You're sure?" Ian felt that if she wasn't, he would literally burst. He loved her and wanted to make her a part of himself so badly that it was agony.

"I'm sure," she declared, unbuttoning the top of his shirt and running her hands over the soft skin of his muscular chest. This was the first time she had touched him without the interference of clothing. The sensation brought a sound of appreciation from her.

Ian's passion flared. Her touch and low moan told him that she was emotionally ready. He was emotionally *and* physically ready, but he intended to arouse her to the boiling point. He had waited this long, and he was determined to make her experience as ecstatic as possible.

Slowly, he undid the front of her blouse, kissing her soft throat as his hands found the naked skin beneath the silky material. Again she uttered a sound of contentment. He cupped a breast, pleased to discover the peak hardened.

Elizabeth squirmed with pleasure, Ian's caresses arousing her all the more because she knew he loved her. On the way back from the estate she had realized that he had already made concessions to her way of life. And even though she couldn't extract a bit of information about the talk he'd had with Robert the night before, she had noted that her uncle had treated Ian more civilly than ever this morning. Then Ian undid her bra, and the sensation of his lips teasing and tasting her nakedness drove all logical thoughts from her mind. She twisted her fingers in his hair and threw her head back in ecstasy.

Ian shrugged out of his shirt and tossed it on the carpet, commanding Spike to lie down on it and to stay. His scent would comfort the dog, and the command would keep him from bothering them. He thanked his stars that he'd had the foresight to take Spike for a duty walk before starting dinner. Getting up after lovemaking to walk the dog would hardly have been a romantic way to begin their love affair. He scooped up the lady on his lap and carried her to the bedroom.

It was the first time he had been in the room and was relieved to find she owned a king-size bed. He kissed her lightly. "Did you buy this one especially for me?" he teased. "You have no idea how frustrating it is for a guy my size to sleep comfortably on a regular bed."

"Especially when you have a female companion?"

"You're the only female I ever want in bed with me," he declared, the look in his eyes convincing her that he meant it. She rewarded him with a deep, lingering kiss.

He didn't ask her preference about lights. Ian was determined to view her loveliness openly. Setting her down, he felt the breath catch in his throat at the sight of her perfect breasts, naked and framed by the lavender silk of her bra and blouse. He leaned down to enjoy them.

Elizabeth felt a fire start deep inside her, an ache that was delicious and painful at the same time. Ian's naked upper torso was magnificent, his tanned skin golden, his body hair sprinkled in an attractive pattern that fanned out over his wide chest and then arrowed down over his flat abdomen. As he caressed and kissed her breasts, she tried to tug his belt loose.

"Not yet, honey," he cautioned. "I couldn't depend on my control, and I want to savor every sweet inch of you first."

"Savor!" she shouted. "But don't take too long about it. Ian, I *want* you!"

He chuckled and moved his lips lower, teasing her stomach. "I figured you'd be noisy about this," he murmured. Elizabeth whacked his broad back with her palm in reproach, but as his fingers worked her slacks away from her body and his mouth made bolder discoveries, she could only caress him lovingly and prove his point by ecstatic exclamations.

Finally, she was completely naked, and Ian eased back to gaze at her. "You're beautiful *everywhere*," he whispered, gently touching the golden triangle between her thighs. She arched to his fingers.

"Please, Ian," she implored. "I can't wait any longer!" She reached for his belt buckle, and this time he didn't stop her.

Once he was naked, Elizabeth marveled at the total male beauty of him. No idealized Greek god could be any more perfect or desirable. Her hands instinctively knew how to give him pleasure, and soon he was caught by a passion as wild as her own.

He entered her slowly, carefully, until he had filled her completely. Then they lay still for a moment, gazing into each other's eyes.

"I love you so," he said and began to move.

Elizabeth thought the sensations that coursed through her body would drive her delightfully insane. Forgetting everything except the man in her arms, she wrapped herself around him. "I love you, Ian," she whispered. "I'll always love you."

Her admission increased his ardor, and Ian's heart filled with a brand-new emotion. She was his woman. From that moment, he knew there could never be another.

Show her, he told himself, straining for control. Her sweet, hot wetness was driving him to the brink, as was her beautiful, writhing body. Stopping his own pleasure for a moment, he rolled over so that she was on top of him, her long thighs straddling his body.

"Take your pleasure, ma'am," he said, smiling and reaching to touch her. She gasped with ecstasy and began to move on him.

With his hands loving her so skillfully, it took only a few moments for a throbbing release to pour through her. Elizabeth pushed herself down on him as far as she could, the primitive sounds of passion and pleasure coming from her throat surprising her. For a moment the sensations were so intense that she had to close her eyes. When she opened them, he was grinning up at her.

"That's one," he said.

"You mean . . . you didn't . . . ?"

He shook his head. "Let's try it another way now."

Time passed slowly, deliciously. Ian took her to realms of sexual fulfillment Elizabeth never dreamed existed. His strength and prowess were beyond anything she had imagined a man capable of. It was like being at the mercy of a force determined only to give her delight. And her body claimed each moment greedily.

As she began another shuddering climb to the heights of ecstasy, Ian knew he had to join her. Burying himself deeply in her, he clasped her body to his and allowed himself to experience the wonder of union with his love. The joy of it brought him a release unlike any he had ever felt. He had been planning to tease Elizabeth about her cries of passion, but now he was doing the same, making the sounds that lovers had made through the ages when carried beyond the bounds of reason by their love. Gradually the madness of desire left him, and he was left, sated satisfied and sweaty, locked in her arms.

Elizabeth held her man, feeling the throbbing in her slowly fading into a warm, pleasantly achy sensation. "I know I won't be able to walk for a week," she said softly, stroking his back. "And I don't think I'll need to keep going to exercise class, if this is your idea of normal lovemaking."

Ian groaned and rolled over, taking the weight of his body off her. "This *was* special," he admitted. "I doubt if I'm capable of this every night of the week." Then he grinned at her wickedly. "But I'm willing to try."

Elizabeth stroked his cheek. "Then I'd better take my doctor friend up on her offer for pills. According to my biological calendar, we were safe tonight, but the last thing this woman needs is an unplanned pregnancy."

Ian kept a smile on his face and nodded, but her words brought a strange sadness to him. He hadn't really thought about it before, but the oneness he had felt with her during their lovemaking was a *mating*. A commitment that went beyond a simple love affair. Her declaration back at the estate had made it clear to him that she didn't want marriage, though he had discussed the possibility with Robert when they had shared brandy after she left. He had admitted to the older man that with all the differences in their ways of life, marriage seemed a very remote concept for Elizabeth and himself. But now he wondered. Was it what *he* wanted, even if she didn't? And by marriage, he meant family. Children. The kind of home he had enjoyed as a boy in spite of the discrepancies between his parents' outlook on life and his own.

Boy, oh, boy, he thought. *What have you gotten yourself into this time, Bradshaw?* He had fallen for a woman who would never agree to his old-fashioned terms and ideas. The image of Lizzie Marlowe barefoot and pregnant, content with hearth and home, was one he could hardly conjure up.

But when he did, it made his heart ache with the sweetness of it.

Elizabeth got up and turned off the lights. She sensed that something she had said bothered him, but she couldn't put her finger on the exact words. Mentally, she shrugged. Maybe he was just tired. He ought to be exhausted. She certainly was!

But when she climbed back into bed to snuggle next to him, the warmth of his body and the security of his embracing arms drove all doubts from her mind. This was where she belonged, and she would do anything necessary to stay here. Gradually, she fell asleep.

Ian lay awake for a while longer, tossing ideas around in his head the way Spike tossed old socks.

Making Elizabeth change her mind about her lifestyle was going to take some careful planning...if he decided that was the way he really wanted to go. His heart cried out immediately that it was, but his brain told him to wait. It was much too early in their relationship to be thinking permanency. They weren't even living together yet, for pete's sake!

But his gut feelings had seldom failed him in the past. He fell into a troubled sleep, haunted by the problem of how to rearrange both of their lives so that they could meld as they should.

CHAPTER TEN

TERROR GRIPPED ELIZABETH. Smothering, wrenching horror. She was falling, falling through blackness toward an invisible finality. She was doomed and would never see Ian again! The pain of that knowledge almost surpassed the panic she felt at falling. She screamed in agony and awoke to find herself alone in bed. A nightmare, she realized, but she couldn't stop herself from sobbing and shivering.

"Elizabeth!" Ian ran into the room, followed by Spike. The dog trailed his leash, and Ian was fully dressed. "What's the matter?" he asked, alarmed.

"Just...just a nightmare." She huddled under the covers, unable to move. He lay beside her and gathered her into his arms. Almost immediately that special sense of security came over her, and her uncontrollable physical reactions subsided. She clung to him.

"What kind of nightmare?" he asked gently, stroking her tear-streaked face with the backs of his fingers. He had a pretty good idea what it had been about, but he hoped she would be able to talk about it.

She shook her head. "I'll be all right in a minute," she said, her voice almost normal. "What time is it? You didn't let me oversleep, did you?"

"It's only seven," he replied, feeling a surge of disappointment at her reticence. "Don't worry, punctual Miss Marlowe. You won't disgrace yourself by being late for work." He kissed her soundly and then ordered her to shower and dress while he fixed breakfast. She collected the shreds of her dignity and complied.

Ian noted that she was subdued at breakfast, and he began to wonder if her mood was a result of the nightmare or the dramatic steps their relationship had taken in the past couple of days. Not willing to stew, he asked.

"I love you," she told him, brightening. "Last night was the most wonderful one of my life. What frightened me so much in the dream was the idea that I might lose you."

"How?" he pressed. *By dying in a plane crash,* he decided privately.

"Only...a sense of loss." She smiled, hoping to fool him. She was determined that he not know the truth. She would conquer her fears. She loved him enough to do it.

Ian accepted the extra key to her apartment and watched her leave for work without pressing her further. He just gave her a loving kiss and, after she had left, set out himself with a grim sense of purpose.

The librarians at the central research library were used to seeing him, since he visited the institution regularly, but he noted a few raised eyebrows when he headed for the psychology section instead of ethology. Gathering every tome he could locate dealing with phobias and anxiety, he settled in to study. Spike, allowed in by special permission, dozed at his feet.

ELIZABETH FOUND it hard to concentrate on business, and that was unusual for her. Being in love, she decided, was confusing. She had forced herself to dismiss thoughts of the nightmare and the moment when she would have to prove her love by boarding the dreaded conveyance that would take her to a strange land. She could only pray that the security Ian gave her would also give her the strength to make it.

During her lunch break, she made herself go to the newsstand around the corner and buy several travel magazines. The photograph of a Concorde on one of the covers made her too nauseated to consider eating, but she took them all back to her office and forced herself to flip through the pages.

That afternoon, she phoned Sue and asked for a prescription for birth-control pills.

When she arrived home, Ian was already there, and a delicious aroma filled the apartment. "Ian," she said in a scolding tone, putting her arms around him, "you don't have to cook for me."

"I wanted to, love. I like to, and it's seldom I have a chance to work in a kitchen as finely appointed as yours." He kissed her tenderly. "Let's chow down," he said. "Then I want to talk to you about something."

Curious, but not worried, Elizabeth joined him in a meal that set her taste buds tingling. He explained that it was a mild curry with a lentil side dish, a meal he'd developed a taste for while spending some time in India. One of the few advantages, he declared, of New York was that the ingredients for most foreign foods were readily available.

"I can't believe I actually heard you speak positively of the city," she teased. "No small miracle."

"Attitudes can change," he said with a cryptic look on his face. "And that brings me to the subject I wanted to discuss."

"And that is?"

"Elizabeth," he said, standing and starting to clear the table, "I don't believe you should try to go to Bali with me. I don't think you're ready."

Momentarily dazed, she stared at him.

"I've spent the day doing research," he continued. "I'm afraid the experience would be too traumatic now. Maybe later, after you've been to therapy, tried short trips—"

"I'm going!"

"After you stop having nightmares about it!" he shouted.

She pushed her chair back so hard that it crashed to the floor. Spike started barking. Stalking across the room, she picked up her briefcase and dumped the contents on the coffee table. The travel magazines tumbled out with the other papers. Ian was amazed.

"I may never stop having nightmares," she said, lifting her chin and giving him that haughty Marlowe glare. "I may never make it to therapy. But I am going on this trip with you if it kills me."

"Lizzie." He put down the dishes and went over to embrace her. "I love you too much to let you risk your emotional and physical health just because I selfishly want you by my side for ten days. Until I started reading about it, I didn't realize how deeply aviaphobia could affect its victims." He thought of the statistics he had found on psychological scarring, even actual death from terror. He wouldn't risk her to anything like that. He would do this job, but afterward he would look for permanent work in the city. One of the many zoos would surely have a position for someone with his qualifications. Hell, he could even teach, if it came to that. Do some more writing. There were many possibilities.

Elizabeth leaned her head against his chest, listening to the pounding of his heart. His concern was out of love, she knew, but she *had* to try. Days ago, she would have jumped at the opportunity to get out of the trip. But not now.

"Ian," she said, lifting her head to look at him. "I understand that you're trying to do what's best, but I have to do this. You give me a sense of security that I've never felt before. I believe that with you by my side, I can succeed."

For a moment he gazed down at her. Beneath the love in her eyes was that indomitable spirit that was part of her inner beauty. The strength he admired so much. He kissed her tenderly.

"All right, love," he said. "But we're going to load you with enough tranqs to knock out an elephant. You're going to be higher than the plane the entire trip.''

Laughing and covering up her feelings of anxiety, she hugged him and teased him until he scooped her up and carried her off to the bedroom.

IN SPITE OF HER BRAVE WORDS Elizabeth didn't sleep a wink the night before the flight. Not even Ian's nearness brought her comfort. Tomorrow she would find out the kind of stuff she was made of. The flight had now grown to be an obsession with her, and she suspected that even if it wasn't for Ian, even if he disappeared in the morning, she would get on that plane just to see if she had the courage.

At dawn they rose and took a cab to the airport. She had been reluctant to leave her Mercedes to the mercies of Kennedy's parking lot for ten full days. The time of day, she decided as they entered the Brooklyn Tunnel, was most appropriate. Dawn. Execution time.

Ian could almost *feel* her dark thoughts, but he counseled himself to silence, putting his arm around her shoulders and sitting as close to her as possible.

''You two off honeymooning?'' the cabbie asked.

''Business trip,'' Ian answered. To fill the silence that was beginning to get on his nerves, as well, he regaled the driver with stories about the country they were headed for. Hearing about the delights that awaited the end of their plane ride just might ease Elizabeth, he reasoned.

Elizabeth clutched her purse. Within it was the supply of tranquilizers Sue had prescribed. She hated the idea of relying on medication and had resisted this morning when Ian had tried to get her to take one. But as they neared Kennedy, she began to wish she'd been less stubborn.

Inside the terminal, however, she felt better. Ian took them through the process of checking in, and soon they were in the waiting area. He left her for a moment, returning with a paper cup filled with water.

"Pill," he commanded. "And I mean business this time." He grinned. "What would it do to your sense of dignity if I had to force-feed the thing to you?"

She nodded. "You're right. I feel as if a thousand insects are crawling over me, and I'm so jumpy that when that man over there snapped his newspaper open, I almost screamed."

"But, love, you're here," he said encouragingly. "You made it this far. You'll make it the rest of the way." She took the pill. He sat down, holding her hand tightly.

When the call came to board, Elizabeth thought she would be sick on the spot. But she managed to stand on shaky legs and let Ian guide her through the boarding tunnel. As they entered the airplane, she looked straight ahead, knowing that if she let her eyes see anything but the chairs, she couldn't count on her reaction.

They were in first class. Ian explained to her that Bill Jordan was generous, and since the flight would be a long one, first would be far more comfortable. He suggested that she hook on the plastic earphones and tune into one of the musical offerings, close her eyes and try to forget where she was. She complied, but the death grip she had on his hand told him she was suffering terribly. His heart went out to her, and he wondered again if he had been right to let her convince him to bring her along.

When the plane began to taxi for takeoff, Elizabeth started to pant and her hand became slick with sweat. A stewardess appeared to ask if anything was wrong.

"She's afraid of flying," Ian explained. "If you'll bend the rules a little and let me raise the armrest between us, I think I can help her handle it better." The stewardess quickly gave her permission.

"It's going to be all right, love," Ian murmured. He lifted the barrier between them, loosened his seat belt, wrapped his arms around her and kissed her until they were airborne. When he released her, her head fell onto his shoulder. The tranquilizer had finally taken effect. Lizzie Marlowe was zonked. He signaled the stewardess and asked for a blanket and pillow.

"Does your kiss always have that effect on her?" the pretty Oriental woman asked. She was smiling, teasing.

"It would be a tragedy, since I love her so much," he replied. Then he explained that Elizabeth was tranquilized and asked for dispensation for occasional odd behavior. "I'll turn inside out to get her through this trip with as little stress as possible," he said. The stewardess nodded understandingly.

He tucked Elizabeth in, propped her feet on the soft-sided bag he had brought on board and removed her shoes. The longer she slept, he thought, the better. He took out the script for the film and began to go over it again, making more notes in the margins.

She awoke after they had been in the air for about six hours. Still groggy, she mumbled a request for his help to get to the bathroom. He signaled for the same stewardess and explained that once inside the toilet, she would probably need further help and that there was no way a man his size could get in there with her.

When she emerged, Elizabeth looked a bit perkier. She thanked the other woman and made her way back to her seat on legs that seemed steadier.

"You're right," she said in a cheerful tone. "I don't feel like I'm in a you-know-what. This is so big, and the sailing's so smooth." She smiled triumphantly. "You may make a world traveler of me yet, Dr. Bradshaw."

But she hadn't counted on the three plane changes they had to make to get to Bali. Amsterdam, Bangkok and one more in Jakarta. Ian's care and the pills helped, but by the time the Garuda Line plane, much smaller than the jet that had taken them out of Kennedy, landed near Denpasar, she was in mental fragments.

"It's hopeless, Ian. I may be stuck here the rest of my life," she lamented as they were driven the few miles into the city in a car sent by the film director.

"You'll make it back," he declared. "The first time has to be the worst. Now you know that you won't end up in a disaster just because you put a few miles between yourself and the ground."

"I wish you hadn't put it quite that graphically."

She tried to enjoy the next ten days without dwelling on thoughts of the return flights. Bali was beautiful, and she took advantage of the many tours offered since Ian was gone during the day, working with the film crew up in the hills. Shopping was an adventure, and she spent far more than she had planned, picking out exotic gifts for her family and friends. When Ian returned in the evenings, they would go out to one of the many restaurants, some in the luxurious hotels of the southeast beach area outside Denpasar, and some that Ian had discovered on his own the last time he'd been in Bali. He wasn't as fluent in the local language as he was in others, but he spoke enough to get by. And the fact that he attempted at all seemed to delight the natives; Elizabeth and Ian received excellent service wherever they went.

And the nights were heaven. Ian was dark from his days in the tropical sunshine, and Elizabeth thought he grew more handsome all the time. His accounts of the film crew's exploits were delightfully funny.

"When we were shooting just outside the sacred forest—you know the one, Sangeh. You toured it the other day."

She remembered vividly. The forest teemed with "sacred" monkeys who were bolder than any New York organ grinder's beggar. She'd had the sense to keep her distance, but others on her tour hadn't been as wise, and she guessed that Ian was going to describe the same things she had seen.

But his experience had been slightly different. One of the crew had been foolish enough to try eating a sandwich while they were setting up, and literally hundreds of the animals charged him, demanding shares of the meal. Even after the terrified man had dropped the food and run for dear life, several of the bold beasts had chased him for almost half a mile.

"I had to make threatening sounds in their lingo to get them to leave him alone," he added. "None were willing to take me on, and after that, they kept to themselves. But you can bet your boots nobody ate a morsel until we left the area."

Elizabeth laughed until his kiss silenced her, and they began the passionate explorations that preceded every night's sleep.

She saw little of the film crew, since they were busy all day, and Ian monopolized her every night. But the people she did meet briefly seemed pleasant and interesting, and she could understand why he enjoyed working with them. In fact, when she thought about it, she realized that she had liked all his friends that she had met. She began to wonder what his parents were like. Would they approve of her relationship with their son, or would they have old-fashioned values and think her a "loose woman" for all practical purposes living with a man she wasn't married to? Ian still retained his digs on the West Side, but since they had become lovers, he spent little time there except during the day when she was at work. Would they get along as well, she wondered, if they shared one roof permanently?

Elizabeth sent her family a number of postcards, detailing accounts of her adventures but not mentioning her dread of the return trip. Bali had so many new sights, sounds and smells that it was easy to write card after card. The music that seemed to be everywhere, the lush green countryside, the lovely people with their colorful dress. Although she experienced the occasional moment of homesickness, she was enjoying the time away from her familiar surroundings—except when she thought of how she'd be getting home.

A few days before they were scheduled to return, she began to lose her appetite. She had to force herself to leave the hotel room and she limited her activities to lying on the beach, reading and trying to take her mind off the flight.

Ian noticed the symptoms, and he did everything he could to fill her evenings so that she would sleep through the night. But with a sinking feeling, he observed her anxiety increase. She would start at the slightest sudden sound, a sheen of perspiration appearing on her face. She was slow to enter conversations with his fellow workers. He took her to see the Barong Play, a storytelling dance that she had expressed a great deal of interest in earlier. But at the colorful, exciting production, she barely paid attention. Afterward she only commented in monosyllables.

And her lovemaking had changed. She began acting like a woman with a split personality: one moment seemingly indifferent to his attentions, and the next, wild with passion. He despaired. It hurt so to know that he had been the cause of her pain.

Elizabeth struggled with herself. She had made it here; she could surely make it back. She had no choice, anyway.

But her nights were agony, filled as they were with recurring nightmares that left her panting and sweaty, her heart racing. Ian comforted her as best he could, but even his nearness wasn't enough to keep her from sinking into the torment her imagination inflicted on her.

The night before they were to leave, Elizabeth didn't sleep a wink. When Ian woke and saw the weariness etched on her smooth skin, he knew it would be a battle to help his love get through the flights. "Come on, sweetness," he said, kissing her unresponsive lips. "Let's take a shower together. We have time."

"Ian," she whispered, tears sliding down her face, "I don't think I can even get out of bed. I feel as if I'm actually paralyzed."

He stared at her and was immediately convinced she was serious. He reached for the telephone. The film crew had brought along a physician to care for any member who might succumb to the strange environment. He got the man on the line and explained the problem. "She made it here by the skin of her teeth," he told the doctor when he arrived at the room, bag in hand. "But I don't know how to deal with her condition now."

Elizabeth was aware that she was being discussed, but she could only lie helplessly, cursing the disorder that was now literally crippling her. With all her will, she wanted to get up and act like a normal human being. She had made it here, she told herself again and again. She *could* make it back. She was Elizabeth Marlowe, and she could do anything she set her mind to.

Except make herself move.

The doctor came over and sat on the bed near her feet. He was young, she noted. Sandy hair, tanned and handsome. Dressed in slacks and a Hawaiian shirt. Very Hollywood. He spoke to her soothingly for a few moments, then turned to Ian.

"I have only one suggestion," he said. "If you're willing to put up with the inconvenience, I can give her a shot of a heavy-duty sedative. You'll have to haul her around like a piece of luggage, but—"

"I'll do it!" Ian declared. The doctor started to open his case.

"No!" Elizabeth struggled to sit up, clutching the sheet to her chin. The indignity of being physically out of control in public was just too much. "I'll make it without medicine. Thank you very much for your time, Doctor, but I think now I have the resolve necessary."

The man studied her for a moment. "You're certain, Miss Marlowe?" he asked. "Because there is a danger in undergoing too much stress."

"Elizabeth," Ian added, "don't let your pride put you in danger. I'm willing to—"

"No." She kept her voice calm with great effort. "I'm not even going to take those things Sue gave me. I'm no coward who needs a chemical crutch."

"Miss Marlowe, suffering from a phobia doesn't make you a coward. Millions of people experience different kinds of fears. It's all part of being human."

Ian watched with relief as she smiled for the first time in twenty-four hours. "Thanks," she told the physician. "You're very kind. But I'll make it. I'll be fine." Deep inside, she knew that was the biggest lie she had ever told.

But somehow she found the resources to keep up her act. Even Ian seemed convinced, although he continued to watch her closely.

Getting on the small Garuda plane was dicey, but she made it. Ian's closeness now seemed to be having its old, soothing effect. She white-knuckled the landing in Jakarta, but her legs weren't shaking too badly when they boarded the Thai liner forty-five minutes later. She took her seat, buckled in and gripped Ian's hand.

Ian looked out the window, concern building in him. They had been lucky in Bali—the monsoon season had been delayed, and rain had fallen sparsely. But a look at the darkening sky told him that they might be heading into stormy weather. And that meant turbulence. He glanced at Elizabeth.

Her eyes were shut, her breathing was steady. Even her hold on his hand wasn't the usual death grip. He wondered if she had spent a completely sleepless night and had finally conked out. He hoped fervently that was the case.

But Elizabeth was playing possum. She had noted the sky herself and knew they were in for it. She swore, however, that she wouldn't make a scene, that she would maintain control over her fear.

The next hours were worse than any nightmare. The plane heaved and bucked its way to Bangkok, and she kept from screaming a number of times only by biting her lips. Ian's love and concern was so strong that it was almost a tangible force. When they finally landed, she told him so.

"Ian, when we get back to New York, the first thing I'm going to do after I call my family is get on the phone and reset my appointment with that therapist. I love you too much not to try and get over this thing. Or at least get to a point where I can deal with it."

Ian stroked her hair. "I wouldn't put you through this again for anything, love. Don't worry. I plan to make some changes so that I don't have to fly so frequently." He told her of his decision to seek work in the city.

"But you hate it so there! Except for worrying about me, you've been right in your element on this job. I've seen an enthusiasm in you these past two weeks that I never have before. You love this. You shouldn't have to give it up just because of me. Tell me, exactly how much traveling are you used to doing?"

Ian hesitated. "Until I met you, I traveled as much as I could. Maybe seven, eight times in a good year. But I *can* and *will* cut that. I only do it so much because—"

"Because it's your life! Don't patronize me, Ian. I know how free you feel away from civilization. Somehow, I'll learn to be able to go with you without all this . . . this craziness. I love you too much to let this come between us any longer. I can manage my job long distance. It isn't as if I need the money, anyway."

"But you love your work, and I don't intend to force you to give it up."

"I'm not going to be giving up anything that I don't want to." Her eyes flashed fire. "And you shouldn't have to, either!"

"No argument. I love you, Lizzie. I want to be with you."

His words haunted her for the duration of their journey. She did doze fitfully on the long flights, but when they finally landed at Kennedy, she realized that she had hardly slept at all in two days. Shaking with weariness and weakness, she made it off the plane with Ian's assistance. But when he left her side to retrieve their luggage, Elizabeth Marlowe fainted dead away.

CHAPTER ELEVEN

SHE WOKE UP in a room that seemed completely white. Even the sunlight streaming in the window looked bleached. Elizabeth raised one arm and touched her forehead, struggling to remember.

"Lizzie!" Ian's face appeared in her slightly blurred line of vision. Then Sue's.

"How are you feeling?" Sue asked. The physician gently pulled back one of Elizabeth's eyelids and peered at the orb.

"I'll feel a whole lot better if one of you will kindly tell me what in the world happened and where in the hell I am," Elizabeth replied. Ian looked terrible—red eyed, unshaven, new lines etched into his face. What had gone on? She could only remember feeling dizzy just after he had left to get the baggage.

"You cratered," Ian said. "Passed out from—"

"Ian!" Sue interrupted. "I'm the doctor. Do you mind?"

Ian gestured with his hand, indicating that Sue had the stage. Elizabeth sensed that all was not harmonious between the two of them. She tried to sit up, but found she was as weak as a limp rag. Her vision clearer now, she could see that she was in a hospital bed.

"Elizabeth," Sue said in a soothing professional tone, "you were exhausted from fighting your fears and from lack of sleep. You fainted in the airport. Since then, you've emerged from a light coma to normal sleep. You're going to be fine."

"Coma!" Ian yelled. "You didn't tell me—"

"Will you shut up, Bradshaw," Sue snapped.

"But I had a right to know..."

"You are no relation. You have no rights."

"I'm her lover, dammit. That gives me every right!"

Elizabeth managed to rise up on one elbow. "Will you two get off your high horses and just tell me the facts," she said as loudly as she could. The combatants turned back to her. Ian gathered her into his arms.

"Love," he whispered, his voice husky. "I was so scared. I thought I might have killed you." His unshaven cheeks rasped against hers.

"And the stress might have, if she weren't in such good health otherwise," Sue commented sternly. "Elizabeth, when you asked for the tranquilizers, why didn't you tell me you were planning a journey of such length? I would have strongly warned you against such a long period of anxiety."

"I tried to talk her out of it," Ian said defensively. "I told you that a hundred times, Doctor." He released Elizabeth, laying her down gently, but continuing to hold her hand.

Sue ran her fingers through her graying hair. "And I've told you the same number of times that you should have insisted, Dr. Bradshaw. Elizabeth could have had a complete breakdown."

"Sue," Elizabeth interjected, "don't talk as if I wasn't in the room. Whatever arguments you and Ian have had are pointless. *I* chose to go. I love Ian, and I intend to beat this thing so that I can go other places with him."

"Not until you're cured!" The statement came in chorus. Elizabeth nodded meekly.

After she learned all the details, she understood why they were almost at each other's throat. She had been unconscious two full days. According to Ian, who had never left her side the entire time, her family had been in to visit, but had taken Sue's advice that staying around the hospital would do no good. Michael and Jennifer were staying in her apartment with Spike, and Robert and Adelaide phoned hourly. But Ian had refused to leave. According to Sue, the hospital administrator had even considered calling the police, but Ian had declared that he would raise such a stink that the intimidated man had decided against the action.

"Just what you need, stupid," Elizabeth said in a loving tone. "More trouble with the police." She stroked his scratchy cheek and chin. Sue had left them alone after giving Elizabeth a thorough going-over and declaring her fit enough, but warning against any undue excitement. She had turned to look sternly at Ian, who was slouched sullenly in the chair in the corner of the room. Ian had retorted that Sue needn't worry—he wasn't so sex crazed that he had to ravage Elizabeth on her sickbed. Sue's raised eyebrow indicated that she wasn't sure.

"I couldn't leave you," Ian whispered, kissing her palm. "I felt...felt so responsible, so frightened that

I'd lose you." A desperate look came into his gray eyes. "Elizabeth—" he took her hand in both of his "—marry me, please. I know now that I can't face life without you by my side."

She stared at him. The proposal undoubtedly was the result of his emotional turmoil and lack of sleep. For such a huge man, he suddenly looked very vulnerable, and she thought she could see tears in his eyes.

"I . . . Ian," she stammered. "I'll think about it, I promise." Seeing that look on his face, she couldn't bring herself to refuse him outright, no matter what she thought, how she felt. Later, when he was more in control of himself, they could discuss the impossibility of such a union. But not now.

She loved him. There was no doubt about that. But the idea of marriage gave her qualms both rational and irrational. Would she ever conquer her fear of flying? No matter how hard she tried, how determined she was, it was possible she wouldn't succeed. And marriage brought with it the problem of children. Like Michael, she wondered if she'd be able to handle the responsibility of raising them. And if Ian was away a good deal of the time, she would have to be the primary nurturer. She wasn't certain she could take that, wasn't certain she had that kind of love within herself. Ian would want children, just as Jennifer did. They were both that kind of people. She fought to keep the tears that burned in her from welling up. She remembered what it had been like to be small and helpless . . . and alone.

Ian's heart filled with joy. He hadn't expected such a positive response. "Elizabeth Marlowe Bradshaw," he whispered, ducking his head for a moment, fighting the tears that threatened to spill from his eyes for the first time in decades. "It sounds almost as beautiful as the lady who would be graced by the name," he added.

Elizabeth was saved from a response by the ringing of the telephone on the bed table. Ian picked it up.

"Yes," he said, a wide grin on his face. "She's fine. Want to talk to her?"

It was Robert. Elizabeth listened to him pour out his expressions of anxiety for her and delight that she was all right. Then came the diatribe against Ian.

"If it wasn't for him," Robert said angrily, "you would never have been subjected to such stress. Elizabeth, I want you to seriously consider breaking off your relationship with that man."

Her temper flared. "I just agreed to consider *marrying* him," she blurted, regretting the words the instant she had said them. Robert gasped, and Ian gave a whoop of sheer happiness. *Oh, Elizabeth,* she scolded herself. *Now you've done it! Backing out is going to be even harder now.*

"This seems to be my day for getting surprising news," Robert said, his tone indicating that he was upset, but not too greatly. "At least you're recovering physically, even if your good sense is still suffering. And we just learned today that in approximately eight months, Jennifer will have a child. I'm going to be a grandfather, Elizabeth."

"Oh, Robert! That's wonderful." She covered the mouthpiece. "Jennifer's pregnant," she told Ian. His smile grew even wider.

"Ask Robert if by any chance they snuck off somewhere for a while together." Elizabeth did.

"Odd you should bring that up," her uncle replied. "Michael did take a long weekend away from the office.... He and Jennifer drove to a place somewhere up in Vermont. He wouldn't even leave us a number to call."

"Did they?" Ian asked her. She nodded. "Tell him that was my idea. And I'm willing to bet that's when it happened."

She relayed Ian's comments to her uncle. "Why would he think *that* caused Jennifer's condition?"

"Darned if I know," Elizabeth replied. "Do you want to ask him yourself?"

Ian took the receiver and proceeded to explain his theory of couple-solitude. Robert Marlowe was definitely not taken with the comparison of the Marlowe household to a clan of chimps, but the man was so happy to finally be looking forward to a grandchild that he didn't react as negatively as Michael had predicted. Ian was determined to use anything to get on Elizabeth's uncle's good side, since he was now almost certain that one day he would be a member of the family.

While she listened to Ian explain, Elizabeth stewed. At first, Ian had seemed to be the kind of man who would fit her life plans perfectly. Now he was clearly going traditional on her.

"Yes, sir, I'll tell her," he said, then hung up. "They're coming in to visit you this evening," he said. "I suppose I'd better run back to my place and clean up." He ran his hand over the stubble on his face. "I kept forgetting to ask Mike to bring me a razor, and I've ticked off everyone around here so much by refusing to budge that I didn't think they'd take kindly to my asking them." He jerked a thumb in the direction of the bathroom. "I did shower."

"Thank goodness for small favors," she said, laughing.

After Ian had left, promising to return as soon as possible, she thought about her predicament. Her only hope was to keep coming up with excuses. She loved him and didn't want to hurt him. Eventually he might grow discouraged and drop the issue of matrimony. Although when she considered his temperament she wondered if that was likely. Ian was as determined and stubborn as she.

She turned her thoughts to a more relaxing subject, since she could feel herself tensing too much. Happiness for Jennifer flooded her, along with thankfulness that she wasn't carrying a child. A nurse bearing a meal tray interrupted her musings.

"Well, I see the bear has left," she said, glancing around the room. "Someone told me they'd seen him lumbering down the hall. He hasn't left your side, Miss Marlowe, and it interfered with our ability to care for you." She set the tray down on a narrow table at the foot of the bed.

Elizabeth eyed the woman. Mid-thirties, she decided. Too thin, but fairly pretty with short curly brown hair like Jennifer's. But unlike her cousin-in-law, this woman had a sour expression. "I'm certain that Dr. Bradshaw wouldn't deliberately interfere," she said. "He's far too intelligent to keep you professionals from doing your job."

The nurse pressed a button that raised the head of the bed. "It was more his *presence*," she admitted. "We were all worried that if we made a mistake, he'd rip us apart." Her expression softened. "The man really is devoted to you, Miss Marlowe. I only wish my own husband cared as much.... Well, never mind." She rolled the table up to Elizabeth. "Here's some nourishment. I imagine you're starving."

Elizabeth suddenly realized she was. With a final warning not to try to get out of bed without calling for help, the nurse departed. Elizabeth forgot all her table manners and tore into the meal.

When she had finished, she felt restored. Ignoring the nurse's orders, she eased herself out of bed and used the bathroom. She felt fine and decided to demand release as soon as Sue came back.

Jennifer arrived first. She looked radiant, and Elizabeth hugged her, saying how happy she was about the baby. "How's Michael taking the prospect of fatherhood?" she asked.

Jennifer's expression changed. She picked up the case of personal items and clothing that she had brought Elizabeth and set it on the small bureau. "I don't really know," she admitted. "One day he seems fine, the next he's moody. Depressed."

"Michael? Depressed?"

Jennifer sighed and went over to sit in the chair. "It's very uncharacteristic of him, I know. Even the jokes have stopped. I hope he comes to terms with his feelings before the baby arrives." She patted her stomach and smiled. "I shouldn't worry. This miracle happened. Why shouldn't I expect another one?"

Then she began to query Elizabeth about the trip and her collapse.

To Elizabeth's surprise, she had no difficulty talking about her journey or her fears. Perhaps the experience, including her collapse, had purged her somewhat. She and Jennifer were laughing over one of Ian's stories when Sue came into the room.

"I thought I told you to take it easy," she said, the smile on her face belying the scolding. "But I see you've heard the good news about Jennifer. And I'm overjoyed to note that Dr. Overprotective has finally taken his big carcass out of here."

"Sue, he felt responsible. He loves me. He usually gets his own way. I don't understand why everyone is so put out at him. Personally, I'm flattered that he cared enough to stay."

"I agree," Jennifer joined in defending Ian. "His depth of love and loyalty are rare in people these days. Even his little dog has been pining for him. Any man who can draw that kind of affection from a dog *has* to have a good soul."

"Well, whatever the condition of his soul," Sue muttered, "he was a damned nuisance. Always questioning me as if I didn't know my business. And he nearly drove the neurologists nuts. I thought one of them was going to take a swing at him."

Elizabeth chuckled. "It would have been an action he'd have seriously regretted."

"Your friend does know how to throw all that muscular weight around, figuratively speaking," Sue replied. "I can imagine he's impressive in the literal sense, as well."

"Sue, I want to go home," Elizabeth said abruptly, changing the subject.

"Maybe tomorrow. I want to keep you under observation for at least twenty-four hours now that you've recovered consciousness. My colleagues in neurology agree."

"But I feel fine," Elizabeth protested.

"Feeling and being can be two separate things." Sue looked at Jennifer. "Would you mind waiting in the hall while I give our stubborn friend a once-over?" Jennifer said she had errands and would return later.

"It would have been nice," Sue commented as she did the routine blood pressure check, "if your gigantic lover had been as cooperative."

"Ian's just cut from a different bolt of cloth from most of us."

"You can say that again."

When the exam was over, Sue did declare Elizabeth in apparently good shape. "But you gave us all a good scare. I've made another appointment for you with Jane for treatment of your fears, and if you don't keep this one—"

"She'll keep it." Ian's deep voice reverberated in the small room. "I'll drag her there in chains if I have to." He grinned at Elizabeth. "Hi, love. I grabbed a few Z's after I cleaned up. That's why I took a while getting back." He came over and kissed her. Elizabeth noticed that he wore a heavy jacket, and he seemed to have gained some wiggly weight around his midsection.

"It's too bad you didn't sleep the rest of the day and night away, Dr. Bradshaw," Sue said acidly. "She needs as much rest as possible."

"Sue, I've been asleep the past two days. If you make me rest anymore, I'm liable to go crazy from boredom." Elizabeth glanced at the protuding front of Ian's jacket. He hadn't!

But he had. A muffled yelp forced Ian to unzip his coat. Spike leaped out onto the bed to give Elizabeth an ecstatic doggy welcome. She laughed and hugged the small ball of fur while he licked her face.

Ian faced Sue Fuller. She was livid. He folded his arms over his chest, waiting for the storm. She let him have it, full force, and when she had run out of steam, he merely pointed to the bed.

Elizabeth had decided to ignore the fight. She was lying back with Spike cradled on her chest, enjoying his welcome and stroking his silky fur. He had lost a bit of weight during their absence, but otherwise looked fine. Now she really felt as if she had returned to her old life.

Ian cocked an eyebrow at the irate physician. If Elizabeth wasn't the perfect picture of a relaxed, happy woman, then he'd never seen one. Bringing Spike had been a calculated risk, he knew, and undoubtedly against every rule in the book. But since his reunion with his pet a few hours ago, he couldn't bear to let the little animal out of his sight. He had bathed him carefully, making certain that he was as germ free as any human visitor—probably more so. And Elizabeth's reaction justified his stunt, he decided.

Sue Fuller sighed. "One day, Dr. Bradshaw, always getting your own way is going to land you in a pile of trouble even you can't talk your way out of. And I hope I'm there to witness the event."

"I'm sure with relish." Ian winked at her.

"Cut it out, you two," Elizabeth interjected. "I'm supposed to avoid stress, and having two people I care about fight in front of me isn't helping."

Sue blushed. "I should be going, since I have other patients to visit. You take it easy, Elizabeth." She glared at Ian. "I'm going to shut the door and tell the nurses to knock before entering. When they do, hide the mutt. I could go before the board for allowing an infraction like this." Ian promised to obey her order.

When she left, he shrugged out of his jacket and pulled the chair close to the bed. Then he leaned over and gave Elizabeth the kiss she deserved for being who she was—the woman he would soon marry.

"I have a job," he murmured, nuzzling her neck. "A bona fide nine-to-fiver with a modest but regular paycheck twice a month."

Elizabeth felt a twinge of uneasiness. Nine-to-five was not Ian's style. It was like hearing an eagle announce he wanted to be caged. But she smiled. "Where?" she asked.

"Jefferson Zoo. They've just finished renovations and were looking for an ethology graduate to help set up the exhibits. When I walked in they hired me on the spot, overqualifications and all." He grinned. "I noticed two of my books on the shelf in the director's office."

"How flattering. If he's a fan of yours that might be one reason you landed the position so easily."

A shadow crossed his face. "Probably. I did take a look around, though, and they can use all the help they can get. I know everyone there loves animals and means well, but a zoo still is a kind of prison for any wild thing."

"Including yourself?" she challenged.

He took her hand. "Love, you know I'll do anything to be near you. And now we can get married as soon as possible. Maybe even next week." There was an eagerness in his eyes that made her heart sink. Thinking quickly, she came up with a logical excuse.

"Ian, a Marlowe wedding is like a coronation. It takes months and months of planning and preparation. With Jennifer pregnant now, she's going to need help and attention. It just wouldn't be fair to my family. Maybe after the baby comes..."

The disappointment on his face cut through her, but then he smiled. "Okay, you know the situation better than I do and can judge better. I'm getting impetuous again and I'm pushing you. Sorry." When she kissed him tears of guilt welled behind her closed lids.

Ian lingered, telling her about his plans for his job. The more she listened, the more convinced she became that he was fooling himself in thinking that he would be happy at the zoo. She thought back to the night when he had described the kind of fauna reserve that he dreamed of creating, and she knew in her heart that was the sort of work he should be engaged in. Not designing artificial environments behind barred walls. Concern for him filled her, and she worried that if he did actually accomplish a miracle and break down her defenses against marriage, he wouldn't be happy. He'd be stuck in a crowded city that he had declared from the beginning he didn't like, and he'd be chained to a job that wasted his talents and aspirations.

She loved him. Maybe the best thing to do would be to lose him. Turn him free from his emotional attachment to her and let him get on with his life as he had been planning it before they had met that fateful night.

But her whole being ached at the thought. She was too selfish in her love for him. Her need for his company, his unique personality, his tenderness. No, she couldn't imagine herself walking away.

Several times, Ian had to duck into the bathroom with Spike when nurses entered the room. The first one was the woman who had brought her the meal and had been so openly critical of Ian. She eyed the jacket thrown over the back of the chair, the closed bathroom door, tightened her lips, but said nothing. The next interloper brought another meal tray, and they were nearly caught. Apparently the smell of food reached Spike, and he released a small yelp that was quickly stifled. The nurse looked startled.

"Did you hear a dog bark?" she asked Elizabeth.

"No," Elizabeth lied. "It must have been my stomach growling." She looked up with round, innocent eyes. The woman seemed to believe her and left without further questions. After the door had closed firmly, Elizabeth called to Ian that the coast was clear.

"Whew," he said as he came out, Spike held in one arm, his little muzzle wrapped in Ian's huge hand. "I guess I'd better go. Spike must be hungry, and that'll mean a stroll with pooper-scooper in hand."

The room seemed gloomy and empty after he left, and Elizabeth had to force herself to eat.

Shortly after dinner, Robert and Adelaide arrived, accompanied by Michael and Jennifer. With so many in her small room, it was difficult for Elizabeth to read her cousin's emotions. He acted jovial and relieved that she was restored to health, but not once did he mention the baby.

Everyone else did. "Imagine," Adelaide cooed, "I'll be a great-grandmother. What a wonderful title!"

"If you don't slow down with all your shopping and planning," Robert chided her, "you'll more likely end up like Elizabeth. A victim of stress."

He was solicitous toward Elizabeth, insisting that she return to the estate while she made full recovery. Her insistence that she *had* recovered launched another Marlowe "discussion," which was interrupted by the entrance of Ian, sans Spike.

"I thought she wasn't to be upset," he said, glaring at Robert. "I could hear the lot of you all the way down the hall. The nurses were headed this way, but I told them it was a family matter, and I would handle it."

He looked as if he could handle anything, Elizabeth thought. Without the bulge Spike made in his leather aviator jacket, his booted, blue-jeaned body had an extra formidability about it. His presence made the room seem jammed, wall to wall.

"We were simply talking about Elizabeth moving back to the estate," Robert snapped at him. "It's only logical that she have people around who can watch over her."

"I don't need—" she began.

"She's got me," Ian said quietly. "Elizabeth, Jennifer and I talked about this, and we think I should move into your place permanently—if you agree, of course. I'll carry my share of the rent and food." The look in his gray eyes warned her not to challenge this publicly.

Adelaide gasped. "Jennifer, I would never have thought that you would suggest an immoral thing like that!"

"It's not immoral, Mrs. Marlowe," Ian said, coming around to kneel on the floor in front of the elderly woman's chair. "I love Elizabeth, and after Jen has the baby, we're getting married. There's no reason why I shouldn't start cherishing her now."

Elizabeth groaned inwardly. The room became a cacophony of cries, some glad and some angry—those from Robert. She closed her eyes. Then she felt Ian's arms go around her.

"Are you all right, love?" Concern and adoration filled his voice and eyes. She reached up and touched his cheek.

"I'm just a bit tired," she admitted. She looked around. "I love every one of you dear people," she said. "But I am going to stay at my place in the city, and I want Ian to move in." *He might as well,* she thought. *It's already practically his place, too.* She could argue with him about the rent later. There was no way he could afford even a tenth of what it cost her to live on the second floor, close to precious terra firma.

A round of good-nights followed her speech. Michael was subdued, Jennifer cheerful, Adelaide elated and Robert... Robert was clearly suffering from a turmoil of emotions. He gave her an extra hug, and she saw moisture in his eyes. Ian lingered.

"I won't push my luck by trying to spend another night here," he said. "I start work tomorrow, and moving my junk will take a little time, but I'll be by whenever I can." He kissed her deeply, and she returned the caress with all the love she felt for him. As soon as he was gone, the emptiness returned.

It wasn't long before her mind was taken off her loneliness by the appearance of a tall man with a prominent nose and a slight foreign accent who introduced himself as Dr. Lebeau, her neurologist. He was accompanied by a nurse, and the two of them gave Elizabeth another checkup.

"If anyone else pokes and prods me," she complained, "I may have another attack. I feel fine and want out of here."

The doctor smiled. "I think you can plan on that tomorrow, young lady. After the therapist visits you."

"Therapist? I thought—"

"Dr. Fuller said she did not trust you to keep the appointment after you're released, so she arranged for Dr. Duggin to see you in the morning."

"Very conniving of her."

"Perhaps," he agreed. "But she is your friend as well as your physician. Maybe she does know best, eh?"

Elizabeth reluctantly admitted that was probably the truth, and when the neurologist left, she settled in for a night's sleep tormented by concerns about Ian and curiosity about this new complication in her life, Dr. Duggin.

CHAPTER TWELVE

IN THE MORNING, Ian stopped by early to wish Elizabeth luck in getting sprung from the hospital. He was dressed in work gloves, khakis, boots and his heavy jacket, but also sported a handsome brown-and-gold striped tie.

"I'm going to be messing in a bunch of muck," he explained, "getting those cages ready." He slipped the tie between buttonholes and under his shirt. "But the tie distinguishes me from a laborer. Just a touch of class, you see."

She laughed. "Dr. Bradshaw, I believe you have a streak of vanity in you. Couldn't a common laborer wear a tie, too?"

"Wouldn't think to." He kissed her lovingly. "God, I hope they let you out of here today. I can hardly control myself. Do you realize how long it's been?"

"Not yet a week," she teased. "And I don't feel the least bit sorry for you, you big lug. Do you know what they've been doing to me in this place?"

"I watched, remember?" His expression revealed sorrow. "I cried inside for your loss of dignity, even though you were unconscious."

She threw her arms around him, feeling more love for him than ever. No one had ever loved and respected her this deeply. Not even her own family. Unable to speak above a whisper because of her emotions, she told him how she felt. Ian answered with a passionate kiss.

Elizabeth pulled him onto the bed, relishing the feel of his weight on her, inhaling the spicy-leathery-musky aroma of him and tasting the sweetness of his lips. His arms tightened around her.

Ian drank her in as though he had never kissed her before. He could tell that she had lost weight, but her breasts pushed tantalizingly against his chest, and he could feel them peaking even through the material of her gown and his shirt. Overcome by his desire, he cupped one, teasing it. She made soft sounds of pleasure. He began to slide his hand down to her stomach.

"Excuse me." A knock and a timid female voice brought him rolling off of the bed. Ian straightened his clothes, and Elizabeth regained her dignity almost immediately, though there were bright spots of color on her cheeks. A tiny redheaded pixie of a woman stood in the doorway, an impish expression on her delicate features. "I know this is the right room," she said, her voice more bold now. "But I wasn't aware that Miss Marlowe needed sex therapy, too."

"Too?" Puzzled, Ian looked at Elizabeth. She was clearly doing her best not to laugh.

"I think you must be Dr. Duggin," she said. "Come in and meet my *good* friend, Dr. Bradshaw."

"Ian," he said, taking the tiny proffered hand. What, he wondered, was another physician doing messing with his Elizabeth? Was there something wrong that he didn't know about?

He listened as Elizabeth and the doctor explained that Sue had upped the first therapy session. "So you're the psychologist who's the phobia specialist," he said, trying to keep disbelief out of his voice. "I certainly hope you can help her." He touched Elizabeth's shoulder affectionately.

"Ian," Dr. Duggin said, "I think I know what you're both thinking. How can a squirt like me who looks as if she'd faint if one of you said 'Boo' help patients with problems like Miss Marlowe's?" Her green eyes shone mischievously. "Well, not only am I fully trained, but I started life scared of almost *everything*. To my patients, I can honestly say 'I've been where you are. I *understand*.'"

Somehow her confession made Ian feel infinitely better. He thanked Dr. Duggin, gave Elizabeth a chaste kiss on the cheek and declared that he had to get going. "Don't want to be late for my first day on the job."

"What about Spike?" Elizabeth asked, suddenly thinking of Ian's beloved pet. "Is Jennifer baby-sitting?"

"I forgot to tell you—Spike's part of the deal I got from my boss. He'll have to be leashed, of course, to abide by city ordinances and for his own safety. Don't want his curiosity taking him into the wrong cage. He'd make a quick snack for a panther or a Bengal ... See you this evening, love." He shut the door behind him, wondering how he was going to feel after this day was over and praying that the diminutive doctor would be able to help Elizabeth.

Spike was waiting downstairs with the receptionist Ian had charmed into watching his pet. Thanking her, he scooped up his dog and headed for the zoo.

Back in her room, Elizabeth waited for the inevitable question from the psychologist. "I'm sorry I interrupted you," the woman said, pulling the chair closer to the bed. "You two certainly seemed to be enjoying yourselves."

"We're very much in love," Elizabeth admitted. "And Ian tends to follow his impulses. Since I met him, I've found myself in the most extraordinary situations."

"So I understand." Dr. Duggin frowned. "Since Sue is your personal friend as well as your physician, she did tell me a bit about you, but she seemed reluctant to talk about your friend. He's a doctor?"

"Of ethology." Elizabeth explained Ian's specialty, the job he had taken at the zoo and why she so desperately needed help. "He has to travel, and I want to be able to go with him without blowing my cork again."

"Why don't we start at the very beginning, Miss Marlowe." The doctor took out a notepad.

"Call me Elizabeth, please."

A wide smile. "And I'm Jane, Elizabeth."

AT QUARTER TO FIVE, Ian let the pair of cheetahs into their new home through a tunnel that led from the holding pen to the viewing cages. He leaned on his shovel and watched carefully as the two cats sniffed and explored. Occasionally one or the other would gaze at him, reproach apparent in the golden eyes.

Ian sighed. "I did the best I could, friends. It's cramped, indoors and not much of a litter box, but give me that it beats plain concrete, okay?" One of the cats snarled at him. He turned away, feeling slightly sick. George Crown, the zoo director, was standing right behind him.

"Good Lord, Dr. Bradshaw," the smaller rotund man said. "You've done a magnificent job. And in just one day, too."

"The occupants don't seem too happy with it." Ian kicked a bit of dirt and savanna grass off his boot.

"Oh, they'll adjust." Crown beamed. "It looks so real. You've created an exact duplicate of the environment. The public will love it."

Forget the public, Ian thought bitterly. *What about the cats?* He gathered up his equipment and Spike and headed for the supply room while Crown was still carrying on about the cage.

His mood didn't improve when he arrived at Elizabeth's apartment and found it empty. A pile of his belongings lay in the middle of the living room, demonstrating that Jennifer had kept her promise to move his things. Tomorrow he would have to let the landlord know he was no longer living in the old place. He ought to call his friend in Los Angeles, too, but he didn't feel like it right now. What he felt like doing was pouring out his frustrations to Elizabeth.

But he couldn't do that. If she knew that he was unhappy at his job, it might reduce her chances of getting help from the Elf, as he had come to think of Dr. Duggin. She didn't need any more worries. Besides, his attitude was based on only one day's work.

Maybe he'd get used to it. Maybe... but maybe not. He put Spike down and watched the dog scamper over to sniff his belongings.

"Yes, this is home now, boy," he said, his attitude brightening a bit. A shower and change and some food were next on the agenda. Then to the hospital...with an artificially optimistic report about his first day on the job.

A FEW MINUTES before five, Elizabeth hung up the telephone. After her first session with Jane Duggin, she had been too shaken to leave the hospital by herself and had decided to wait until Ian could escort her home. She had not, however, been too shaken to call her office, ask Nancy to bring over all her mail and to conduct a few hours' business by phone.

She lay back and considered what the psychologist had suggested.

Flying lessons.

Elizabeth sighed deeply. The young woman was a professional, and if Sue trusted her, then she felt she should, too. But to learn to *fly* herself? She grew queasy at the thought.

It was the ultimate solution, Jane had told her. Several therapy sessions might be needed before she'd be ready to take her first lesson, but Jane was firm on the issue. Elizabeth's first assignment was to go to the library and get all the reading material she could on modern air travel. Immerse herself, the doctor had said. Knowledge conquers unreasonable fear.

Well, that much made sense to Elizabeth. She could manage to read a few pages in the evenings about the subject. Another sigh, then she got out of bed to shower and dress.

Sue arrived before Ian. "How did the session with Jane go?" she asked, eyeing her patient carefully.

Elizabeth shrugged. "I became a bit unnerved talking about it, but I guess she knows what she's doing." She sat on the edge of the bed and ran a brush through her long hair.

"You still don't look very chipper," Sue commented. "I don't want you going back to your office until next week." She took a small bottle from her bag. "In the meantime...these are very mild tranquilizers. I want you to take one the moment you feel anxiety. About anything," she emphasized.

Elizabeth started to protest, but found she just didn't have the emotional energy. She was, she realized, still not her old self. And she wondered if she ever would be again.

Ian entered the room, and just the sight of him made her feel better. "They told me down at the nurses' station that you'd been discharged." He nodded to Sue, but came directly over to Elizabeth and took her hand. "Let's go home, love."

"Not so fast, lover boy." Sue planted herself in front of the door, her arms folded across her chest. "You and I need to discuss some ground rules."

Ian felt his temper rise. On top of a crummy day, he didn't need this. "What kind of rules?" he snapped.

"Elizabeth has been through a terrible experience," Sue said in a calm tone, ignoring his rudeness. "For the next few days she needs as tranquil an environment as possible."

"So? I plan to give it to her."

"That's precisely what you will *not* do. Sleeping with you means physical exertion, a type of stress, and it could cause her a number of problems, so keep it platonic, young man."

"Sue!" Elizabeth stood. "I can't believe you brought this up without talking to me about it first. Ian and I are both intelligent adults who—"

The doctor's smile was warm. "Who, dear Elizabeth, are so insanely in love that you've ignored common sense. Common sense dictated that you should have gone through Jane's therapy before attempting a flight. I have no objections to what you do in private later, but for now, please, both of you, take my cautioning words to heart."

Ian felt his spirits drop to his boots. She was right. She was the doctor. But tonight he needed to be close to his love. For her sake, however, his bed would be the couch until further notice. "All right," he agreed. "We'll follow your orders, Dr. Fuller." Elizabeth squeezed his hand.

When they arrived at the apartment, Ian fixed her a simple meal of soup and a sandwich. Neither of them spoke much, and though she felt the warmth of his love unabated, Elizabeth sensed that more was bothering him than the short period of enforced celibacy. When she asked him about his work, he replied only in short sentences. He was not, she deduced, exactly thrilled with his new position.

Spike seemed the only one in a good mood. He welcomed her with unrestrained enthusiasm, and then ran over to Ian as if to prove where his deepest loyalty lay.

After supper, Ian made Elizabeth sit, feet propped on an ottoman while he went about the business of putting away his belongings. It didn't take long, since he didn't have much. Then he sat in a chair opposite her, knowing that if he came too close, he would lose his resolve to obey the doctor's command.

"So how did the session with the Elf go?" he asked.

"Elf?" She started to laugh, feeling at ease for the first time in hours. "You mean Dr. Duggin?"

"One and the same."

"Oh, I don't know." She shrugged. "It's still too early for me to be able to tell. I have to admit some of her ideas sound a little far out. But others I think I can handle. Maybe with time—"

"And love." His gray eyes were slits, but she could see the desire smoldering in them. Really, it was so unfair to deny him . . . and her.

"Ian, maybe Sue was overreacting. I know you rubbed her the wrong way from the start by staying so close to me. Maybe we could bend her rules . . ."

"No, we're doing it by the book, Elizabeth." He scowled. "You ought to know how much this is costing me, but I'd do anything to keep from harming you."

"I love you, Ian." The emotion welled up, filling her until it hurt.

"And I love you. Let's get ready for bed." His tone was gruff.

Sleep came fitfully for her, alone in her big bed. She had snatches of the recurring nightmare about falling, but it was another fantasy that kept filling her mind.

Flying.

She would soar like a bird, free from any fears or fetters of body or mind. It was after one of those visions that she awoke with a start, alarmed by the drastic changes in her dreams. Was all this leading to a kind of insanity? Unable to help herself, she got out of bed and went into the living room.

Ian was sound asleep in a tangle of sheets and blankets on the couch. Lying on his stomach, one arm was dangling to the floor. On his cast-off shirt beside the couch lay Spike, who looked up when she entered. She signaled him to silence.

Waking Ian would be selfish. He had worked hard all day at a job she was certain he disliked. He needed his rest. Collecting a blanket and a pillow from the bedroom, she made a little nest for herself on the floor by his head. She had to have the comfort of his nearness, even if he wasn't aware of her.

Ian awoke first, well before dawn had become day. The living room was filled with a soft pearly light that came in through the curtained windows. He rolled over and stretched, and was thinking unhappily of the day before him when a soft moan reached his ears.

He sat up, staring down in amazement at Elizabeth, sleeping in a sitting position next to him on the floor, her back to the sofa. Spike was curled up in her lap, also asleep. What in the hell...?

Ian rose carefully, moving with the quiet stealth he'd learned from years in the wild. Then he gently gathered the two of them in his arms and laid them on the couch, covering them with his blanket, but leaving Spike a breathing hole. Shaking his head in wonder, he went into the bathroom to shower.

Why had she come to him? he mused as the hot water splashed over his body. If she had needed something, why hadn't she wakened him? He shampooed his hair vigorously, knowing that the work ahead was going to make him filthy. He might as well get as clean as possible before that happened. He was assigned the two lions today. Seeing his favorite felines caged was going to hurt even more than seeing the cheetahs trapped.

He really didn't think this was going to work. He frowned at his reflection in the mirror as he shaved. He would have to find a job that didn't pain him so much if he was going to be a decent lover and husband to her. He could control his moodiness and temper only so long, and then he knew she would catch on and demand an explanation. Lizzie was no dummy, and that made his charade impossible for any extended period of time.

He also needed to know more about what had gone on between her and the Elf. He hadn't pressed for information, but she hadn't offered any, either. Was it possible that they really couldn't have a future together?

No, dammit. He'd find *some* way to beat their problems. All his life he had thought he was meant to be a loner, an unmated, though hardly chaste, male. But with Elizabeth, he wanted all of the things he had thought he didn't need: lasting love, commitment, marriage, children, growing old together. Dammit! He hit the sink with his fist.

A bark from Spike outside the bathroom door brought him out of his reverie. He opened the door, commanding the little animal to be silent and assuring him that breakfast and the morning potty walk were to come shortly. Glancing into the living room, he saw that Elizabeth slept on. Her night must have been rough for her not to have been disturbed by now. His concern and curiosity flared.

But he decided to let nature take its course. She needed sleep, she was getting sleep, and his questions and worries would just have to be shelved. He dressed, fixed a meal for himself, fed Spike, walked him, and when he returned to find her still unconscious, he wrote her a loving note and left for work, taking his pet with him.

WHEN ELIZABETH AWOKE, it was late morning. She shielded her eyes from the sunlight and experienced a moment of disorientation until she remembered the need she'd had the night before for Ian's comforting nearness. He must have awakened, found her and put her on the couch, covering her with his own blanket. A wave of affection swept through her.

She found his note on the coffee table, read it, and the feeling of affection became love. The note was whimsical, endearing and funny.

How fortunate I am to have not one but two dear pets who sleep by my side at night. Hope you rested well, love. See you as soon after five as I can make it. Don't worry about cooking. I'll pick something up.

Love, Ian.

She put the note in a drawer in her desk where she kept personal items. Then she ate a hearty breakfast, readied herself for the day and headed for the nearest lending library. It didn't take her long to collect a pile of literature on airplanes and the history of flight. Loaded with the volumes, she headed home for a day of study. She logged in once with Nancy to check on the office, but the rest of the day she immersed herself in the books.

IAN FOUND some small pleasure in the fact that the pair of lions seemed to like his re-creation of the African plains better than the surly cheetahs had yesterday. The male sniffed the caged area once, then flopped down to snooze in the soft grass. The female took a while longer to adjust, but soon she was scratching her chin against the trunk of a tree—the only one the cage had room for. That's better, he thought. If they had rejected his offering, he would have quit on the spot.

George Crown was once again elated, even to the point of calling in the rest of the staff to view Ian's handiwork. One of the young animal handlers, a pretty biologist whose name Ian couldn't remember, asked him why in the world was he wasting his time at a city zoo.

"You should be out supervising the construction of an open park," she said. "Someplace where the animals don't have to live caged up."

"I have a domestic situation to consider," he replied, feeling a sting from her words. "This is the best I can manage for the time being." The biologist began to protest, but he silenced her with an icy look.

Her words, however, triggered a new line of thought. He considered it on the subway ride home. If Elizabeth could be persuaded to move from New York, he might find a job at an open park, or at least at a zoo where the climate would allow year-round outdoor living. Like San Diego, or Taronga Park Zoo in Sydney. No, he thought, Taronga was out unless the Elf could really come up with a magic brew to heal Elizabeth. By the time he reached the apartment, after picking up some deli food, he felt frustrated, irritated. And horny as all hell.

Elizabeth was reading when he came in. She was surrounded by books, and from the strained look on her face when she smiled at him in greeting, he concluded that the subject matter had not been to her liking. He put Spike down and walked over to give her a kiss.

"What are you studying so diligently?" he asked, stroking her hair. Closer now, he could see that she was upset. A small muscle at the corner of her right eye jumped continually, and the usually clear whites of her eyes were marred by red. Puffiness underneath told him that she had been crying.

"Airplanes," she replied. "Elf's orders."

Ian put the bag of food on the coffee table and knelt. "It hasn't gone down easily, has it, love?" he said. "Maybe you should just forget the whole thing."

"No!" She struck the arm of her chair, just as he had hit the sink that morning. "I'm going to lick this, Ian. I've lived like a frightened rabbit for too long." Her delicate jaw was set.

"You? A rabbit?" Ian laughed and stood, pulling her into his arms. "You're the strongest, toughest, most ornery woman I know. That's one of the reasons I love you.''

She started to cry, and he kissed her. Kissed her as lovingly and tenderly as he could. Her body felt so fragile in his arms, and he wondered if she had eaten anything that day. Another question to put on the list he had for her.

But fragile or not, Elizabeth Marlowe was the one he held, and his reaction to her was overwhelmingly powerful. A surge of desire swept through him, and the kiss became less tender and more passionate.

She felt the change. They *needed* each other, she thought. This idea of Sue's was wrong. Her actions last night had been an indication. Ian's closeness was necessary to her, and that closeness should take its natural course. Tomorrow, she would call and complain... if they made it through tonight.

Ian was barely able to pull himself back from the brink. Torturing images of the two of them ripping each other's clothes off and making love on the carpet flashed through his mind. But remembering Sue's warnings, he controlled himself.

"Whew!" he said, releasing her and turning away for a moment to recover. "When Ol' Doc Fuller finally gives us the go-ahead, Lizzie, you are going to be loved until your beautiful blue eyes cross."

"That kiss almost crossed them." She put a hand on his arm, and he felt her fingers tremble. "Let's eat, lover. I'm famished."

While they ate, they indulged in a mutual grilling. Elizabeth probed him about his work, and he questioned her about her emotional state. His distaste for his job became apparent to her, and her jitteriness was obvious to him. The food tasted like cardboard to them both.

Spike, on the other hand, gobbled up the left-overs as if they were ambrosia. When Ian got ready to take him for a walk, Elizabeth elected to go along. "I've been sitting and reading all day," she declared. "I could use the exercise."

"Want to be the scooper?" he asked, mischief in his eyes. Laughing, she agreed to do the job.

The evening was chilly, but Elizabeth felt better for the fresh air. Reading the books had been agony, but she had persevered without resorting to one of Sue's pills to get her through the day. Several people who lived in the area were walking their dogs, and she cuddled close to Ian, feeling proud to be in the company of such a handsome, imposing man.

They must make a sight, though, she mused. Little Spike alongside his enormous owner. Then around the corner came the exact opposite: a small, elderly woman with a huge Doberman.

It was hate at first sight. The Doberman and Spike started to bark fiercely at each other, and the larger dog jerked away from his frail owner, lunging at Spike.

Ian jumped into action immediately. He scooped up his pet and handed him to Elizabeth, giving her a gentle shove back out of danger. Then he attacked the Doberman.

Elizabeth had never witnessed such a sight. Ian grabbed the animal in such a way that he avoided the snapping jaws. He threw the dog onto its back and, glaring directly into its eyes, began to snarl and growl. In moments, the beast was whimpering and trying to lick Ian's hand. He glared at it for a minute longer, then stood and handed the leash to the startled owner.

"If you can't control your dog," he said sternly, "hire a kid who can." The old woman nodded. The Doberman whined and followed her down the street, his tail between his legs.

Elizabeth's knees were shaking so hard she could barely stand. Tears poured down her cheeks. Ian took Spike from her arms.

"You're a nervous wreck," he declared in a tone almost as stern as the one he had used on the other woman. "Did you take any of the pills Sue gave you?" When she mutely shook her head, he took her arm and marched her back to the apartment. He'd take Spike out later.

He force-fed her two of the pills, ordered her to strip and go to bed. Meekly, she obeyed, and by the time he returned from an uneventful, successful walk, she was sleeping peacefully.

Ian looked down at her for a long time. Then he took off his clothes and climbed into bed with her, drawing her against him. They couldn't make love while she was unconscious, he reasoned. And he couldn't stand another night alone.

Spike settled happily on the pile of clothing at the foot of the bed, and soon Ian was the only one in the dark bedroom who wasn't asleep. He thought briefly of the alpha-wolf strategy he had used on the Doberman, cursed the crowded city where he couldn't even walk his dog in peace, and ached for the day when their problems were over, when he held this woman in his arms as his wife. Sleep came only in the early morning hours.

CHAPTER THIRTEEN

"REALLY, I AM JUST FINE," Elizabeth insisted the next morning. "Those pills and sleeping close to you gave me the kind of rest I needed. I feel like a new woman. Honestly."

"I can stay home with you if you want." Ian repeated his offer. "I'm two days ahead of my work schedule, and Crown thinks I'm the greatest thing since sliced bread. It wouldn't affect my job, love."

"Are you sure you're not also offering because you aren't crazy about going in?" she countered.

Ian looked away. She was right. This morning, she looked terrific. Her old, energetic, optimistic self. He ought to leave her alone to work on her phobia. But today it was the panther, a breed he respected deeply. A cat that should never be confined to a limited area. He'd give it a tree, but that was about all he could do. He could already see the anger and contempt in the creature's eyes.

"At least I'm giving it something better than what it had before," he muttered. "I guess that counts for something."

Elizabeth touched his hand, the first contact she had dared since waking and finding Ian asleep beside her. She had showered, dressed and made breakfast before he stumbled out of the bedroom, looking as if he hadn't slept a wink. "It counts for a lot, darling. There are people in this city who probably think concrete and steel are a natural part of a captive animal's life. You're showing them otherwise."

"City people." The contempt in his voice was obvious. "Present company excepted, of course," he added hastily, seeing a flash of pain in her eyes. "I'm still mad at that woman and her dog." he lied.

"Tell me how you did that?" she asked, eyes alight with curiosity. "I've never witnessed such a scene. I thought you'd be torn to shreds. Bitten at least."

Ian grinned. "You have to understand dogs," he said. "Even old Spike here is descended from wolf-like creatures. They ran in packs, just as wild dogs today will, and one is the leader. The one with the most strength, intelligence and just plain chutzpah. He's called the alpha-wolf. When one of the lesser ones gets out of line, the alpha attacks him, gets direct eye contact and cusses the very devil out of him. Unless the alpha's term of power is weakening, it usually doesn't take the other animal a moment to realize that he has made a *big* mistake. Fortunately, Dobie last night was smart enough to give in immediately. You watch. If we run across him again, he'll even kowtow to Spike because he's under my protection."

"Fascinating." She brushed a stray lock back from her face. "I could listen to you talk about these things for hours."

Ian glanced at his watch. "I could talk for hours, but if you're sure you're all right, I'd better get a move on. Not coming in is one thing, being late is another. And I want to do the panther in one day. I hate the idea of leaving him in the holding pen overnight.''

"I understand." She rose and kissed him goodbye.

After he and Spike had left, she went to the phone directory and looked up Jane Duggin's number. She called the psychologist and declared her desire to start the flying lessons as soon as possible. Jane protested, but finally agreed to find a reliable school that Elizabeth could visit before she committed herself. Elizabeth also asked that it be located a good distance from the city—she didn't want anyone she was close to to know what she was doing. Ian would have a fit, as would Sue.

The next call she made was to Sue. They argued for several minutes about Elizabeth resuming a sex life with Ian, then the doctor gave in. "But no going to work yet," she declared.

"I promise," Elizabeth lied.

After hanging up the phone, she took a taxi to her office, greeting a surprised Nancy.

"I thought you were on leave," her secretary said.

"Not anymore. I'm undertaking some outside projects and need to cut back on my work here. Hold any calls until noon, please."

In her office, she started working on a few clients' cases that simply couldn't be left any longer. The last one was Ian's. She bought him a few solid stocks and some government bills, a modest investment certificate and put the rest in his checking account. Then she began to plan.

If she could learn to fly, they could stay based in the city, live in her apartment, and he could travel with her anywhere he wanted, take any job offered. He could get away from his hated zoo and be free. They could have a wonderful relationship. She could adjust her client load to enable her to be just as free as he was. Elation filled her.

Until she thought of his marriage proposal and her idiotic mistake of telling Robert about it. Now the entire family expected a wedding. She could hold off until after the baby came in July. But after that . . . ?

Shelve it, she told herself. *You've got enough right now to worry about. Leave that one for later.*

She left at midafternoon and did some grocery shopping. Tonight Ian was going to be fed a decent meal. And something more. She stopped at a nearby boutique and bought the sexiest gown she could find.

Ian arrived home in a reasonably pleasant mood, one Elizabeth knew would improve shortly. He explained that the panther had seemed pleased with his new environment. The sleek animal had immediately climbed the tree and laid down on a branch to nap. "He'd probably worn himself out, pacing in the holding cage," he added grimly.

"You look a bit worn yourself," she said, giving him a light kiss. "Go shower and get comfortable. Dinner will be ready in a few minutes."

"Dinner? Didn't you rest today?" He frowned.

"Just go." She gave him a gentle shove. "I'm fine." He looked at her skeptically, but went, Spike at his heels.

By the time he returned, the roast was on the table, the salad was to the side of their plates, the dishes of baked potatoes and peas were in the middle of the table and she was pouring the wine. "Would you please carve?" she asked with a smile.

All through the delicious and satisfying dinner, Ian studied Elizabeth. She seemed like her old self. Gone was the weary, tormented woman of yesterday. Had one night's sleep in his arms accomplished all this? And could he stand sleeping with her again platonically?

After they had washed the dishes, she suggested sweetly that he walk Spike alone tonight, she had to do some things around the apartment. Ian wondered what possibly needed doing, since the place was immaculate, but he didn't question her. He was too tired from lack of sleep and working at a demon's pace to ready the panther's cage.

The walk was peaceful—the lady with the Doberman apparently having decided to take a different route. But what he found when he returned to the apartment snapped him out of his serenity.

Soft music played. Sweet perfume filled the air. The lights were low. And Elizabeth . . .

She greeted him dressed in the clingingest, sexiest, most revealing nightgown he had ever seen. It was a light aqua color, and its silkiness followed every soft curve of her body. Ian swallowed hard.

"This isn't fair," he said in a strangled tone.

"I have permission," she replied archly. He put Spike down and reached for her.

He made good his promise to love her cross-eyed. At least that was what it felt like. Elizabeth heard herself sighing and sobbing and moaning as he took her from one peak of pleasure to the next. His loving seemed to have no limits, even after he had spent himself several times. Recovery took minutes and a touch. Finally they fell asleep in each other's arms, twisted sheets and lights ignored, and slept the peaceful sleep of reunited lovers.

During the next couple of days, Elizabeth found that she could handle the literature on planes with less and less emotional discomfort, sometimes even reading at night after Ian had loved himself into an exhausted sleep. Her work was not physical, so she understood why she wasn't as tired as he was each night, but his almost brutal pushing of himself on the job worried her. When he'd describe his day's accomplishments, she'd shudder inwardly, wondering if even a man as hardy as Ian could keep up the pace he was setting. His boss certainly liked it, though. He gave Ian a generous raise, which Ian absolutely insisted on using for his share of the rent. He had been so adamant that she had finally taken it, but the next day had used it to buy him some more stock for his portfolio.

They spent a pleasant weekend at the estate, agreeing regretfully that good taste dictated they should sleep apart Saturday night. However, Friday they dropped Spike off with Jennifer and drove farther up the island to spend the night in a charming inn, decorated completely in Early American.

On Saturday Elizabeth was relieved to find Robert at least civil to Ian. Adelaide wouldn't leave her alone about the wedding, but she hedged around her questions without being rude to her beloved grandmother. Jennifer was wrapped in a cloud of happiness, and even Michael seemed in better spirits. Ian told her that Michael had confided that his attitude toward fatherhood was mellowing as the days passed. Elizabeth was delighted, but the lack of any practical joke bothered her. She wouldn't believe he had fully accepted his status until she saw at least a hint of the old Michael.

On Monday she received a call from Jane, asking her to come in to her office. When she arrived, Jane told her that she had located a flying teacher who came highly recommended and who ran a small school on the outskirts of New Jersey. Would Elizabeth like to take a day to visit the place and meet the woman? Eagerly, Elizabeth agreed. They talked for a while longer, and then she left, confidence filling her.

The next day, she and the psychologist drove in Elizabeth's Mercedes to the flight school. "This really is in the backwoods," Elizabeth commented as they passed fields and forests that contrasted with the factories and cities closer to the coast.

"You said you wanted anonymity," Jane replied. "Well, you've got it here." She gestured at the small airstrip that came into view.

Elizabeth gulped. This was it. In a few minutes she would know if she could go through with it. At least the sight of the several small planes near the small corrugated metal building didn't make her nauseated or sweaty.

And after meeting the woman in charge of the operation, she felt even better. Bette Marsh was a wiry, tanned woman of indeterminate age. Her face was weathered, but her figure was trim and tight. After introductions, they accepted her offer of coffee and went into the building.

"I don't run much of an operation, Elizabeth," Bette explained as they sat around her cluttered office. "I take on a student now and then, care for some weekend pilots' machines, run someone up for a joyride once in a while. But your case sounds interesting. If you think you can handle it, I'll do my darnedest to get you aloft." They shook hands on it, and Bette gave her a set of instruction books, telling her that there were lessons inside she should study, complete and get back to her as soon as possible. "After Thanksgiving, we can start with a ground model." Elizabeth drew a deep breath and thanked her.

"I was afraid I'd have to start in the air," she confessed.

"No, ma'am," Bette declared firmly. "You'll get to know the cockpit better than your own face in the mirror. *Then* we talk flying."

Since it was nearly dark by the time they left, Elizabeth suggested they eat dinner at one of the country inns they had passed on the way down. Jane agreed. At the restaurant, she tried calling Ian several times, but didn't get an answer. He was probably working late, she decided, fixing a home for one of his beloved animals. Over dinner, she told Jane about Ian's obsessions and caring spirit. Jane declared that she was lucky to have such a man, and that since he was the catalyst in starting her on the road to wholeness, she was very optimistic about Elizabeth's success.

It was after ten when Elizabeth finally shoved the key in her door. The flying instruction material was safely hidden in the trunk of her car, and she planned to secrete it in her office the next day. There she could work on the lessons without Ian getting suspicious. She closed the door and turned to face a tornado.

"Where in hell have you been?" he yelled, grabbing her shoulders. "I've been combing the streets between your office and the apartment, looking up alleys, in back doorways, even...trash containers." His expression was a mixture of dread, anger and relief, and he embraced her tightly. "Lizzie, I was scared sick. Your secretary said you never made it in to your office, and I assumed something terrible had happened to you."

Elizabeth didn't know whether to laugh, cry or be mad. They might be lovers, but she didn't *belong* to him. On the other hand, his concern touched her deeply. "Ian, I went out to Kennedy to watch planes with Jane," she lied. "I tried calling you, but when I couldn't get you, I assumed you were working late. Jane and I had dinner together."

He held her at arm's length, studying her face as if he was trying to read the truth. "All day at Kennedy? Wasn't that a little much?"

"I...I had a little trouble in the beginning. We talked for a while. Time got away from me." More lies. How in the world was she going to cover her actual lessons...providing she made it that far.

"Okay." He dropped his hands. "I'm sorry I overreacted. It's just that New York City makes me nervous. I never really feel you're safe alone."

She stood on her tiptoes and gave him a kiss. "Don't start your own personal 'I hate New York' campaign, Ian. You yourself have lived in much more dangerous places."

He looked at her, a thoughtful expression on his face. "Would you ever consider leaving here after we're married? Not going any place weird, but settling near another city."

"New York's my home! My job is here, my family. How could I leave?" And how was she going to break it to him that she wasn't marrying him? Each day that she put it off, the subject would be harder to face. "Ian, I ... I'm happy with the arrangement we have now. I really am not sure about the marriage route in spite of what I said to Robert. I was upset then, and it just slipped out." She began to explain, telling him of her concerns: they simply hadn't known each other long enough; she was afraid she wasn't cut out for motherhood; all the differences between them, particularly the kind of place they liked to live. Ian listened, but his expression darkened with each excuse, and he was silent when she finished.

For the first time since they had begun to sleep together again, they didn't make love that night.

The rift lasted several days, and Elizabeth felt her heart would break at his coldness. He was pleasant and polite, but distant. She had too much pride to back down, and threw herself into her studies, staying later and later at the office to complete the lessons. Then one night she returned to find the apartment empty. Some of Ian's belongings were missing, and there was a note from him that told her that he still loved her dearly, but he had to get away from her to think. He poured out his feelings about his job and city living, making her realize just how much of a daily sacrifice he was making to be with her. Crumpling the note, Elizabeth sat down in a chair and cried her heart out. Then she called Jennifer.

"I know it's late," she apologized when Jennifer answered sleepily. "But I need your help." Jennifer listened as she explained the situation. "Tell me, do you think it's hopeless?" Elizabeth asked when she had finished.

"Only if you're unwilling to compromise," Jennifer answered, now sounding fully alert. "You'll have to meet each other halfway, just as Michael and I are learning to do over the baby. Elizabeth, for the most part, you're a levelheaded person. Sit down and make lists of where you and Ian agree and disagree. Apply some of that cold financial wizardry, view the situation as distantly as you're able, and see if you can't come up with a solution."

"I can't live without him, Jennifer."

"Then solve your differences. Bend, give, compromise." Jennifer sounded stern and very mature. She would, Elizabeth thought, make a good parent. They talked for a while longer, then she hung up and went to bed, resolving to work on her problems in the morning. She slept fitfully.

The next day when she arrived at her office, she gave Nancy strict orders that she was to be disturbed by absolutely no one.

Not pausing for lunch, she pondered her relationship with Ian. The problem about flying was low on the list now. Marriage was number one. Why was she so determined not to commit to him legally? Maybe a session with Jane could give her an answer to that one. She called the office and made another appointment.

Then she addressed the problem of Ian's hating New York though she loved it. City life suited her and suited her business. She could not live off in some wild empty place, doing nothing. Not even with him as companion. She would go as crazy as he seemed to be going here. But what was it that Ian had said. Settle *near* some other city? She had been so caught up in telling him she didn't want matrimony that his words had somehow slipped by. She made a note on paper. That was definitely a compromise possibility.

Her stomach grumbled, and she glanced at her watch, surprised to see that it was after five. She had quite literally puzzled the day away. Suddenly, the sound of sirens, honking horns and shrieks drifted up to her window from the street. She hurried over to look out.

A dozen police cars were complicating a terrible rush-hour traffic jam. And the reason for their presence was halfway up the side of the brick wall, clearly heading for her window.

The monster appeared to be a huge gorilla, but Elizabeth knew better. Her office was in one of the older buildings with windows that still opened, and she was quick to throw hers wide. The cops were beginning to aim weapons.

She screamed for them not to shoot, waving her arms and praying they understood her over the horrendous racket of the traffic. To her relief, they slowly lowered their guns.

The gorilla finished his climb, jumped agilely into her office and removed his furry mask to reveal a grinning Ian.

"You wouldn't take my calls," he said. "So I decided to get your attention by a more direct approach."

"You could have waited until I came out!" she shouted. "You nearly got yourself killed, you idiot!"

His eyes were slaty. "Would it really have mattered to you?"

"Of course!" she yelled, completely furious now. "I love you!"

Furry arms pulled her close for a passionate kiss, and she forgot her anger and fright in the magic of his embrace. Ian was back. *Loving* Ian was back, and she knew now that she would do anything not to lose him again.

She heard the sound of her office door being opened, and a dozen policemen swarmed in. But Ian didn't release her until they were pried apart.

"Just what the hell is going on here?" the officer who seemed to be in charge asked angrily. "Lady, do you know this maniac?"

"He's my lover," Elizabeth said defiantly.

"Soon to be husband," Ian growled. "I climbed up here to make one point, Lizzie Marlowe. If you don't agree to marry me—and I know you love me, so it's ridiculous not to be my wife—I'm going to keep on pulling crazy, embarrassing stunts until I finally—"

"Mister, if you don't shut up, I'm going to run you directly to Bellevue!" the burly officer in charge shouted. Ian ignored him.

"Well, Elizabeth, what'll it be? Marriage, or visiting me in the booby hatch?" Ian gazed down at her.

"Lady," the officer said, "are you in on this? Did you know he was gonna pull this stunt? Because if you did, you're an accessory. You already admitted you was sleeping with him."

Ian turned on the man like a wolf protecting its mate. "She knew nothing about it," he declared. "You've no business casting aspersions on her good name."

"Look, gentlemen," she said in her most dignified, upper-class tones. "I think if we all just sit down and talk for a few moments, we can have this straightened out in no time, and you officers can go back to fighting serious crime instead of innocent tomfoolery." With her last words, she turned and glared warningly at Ian.

"He caused a public disturbance," the commander claimed. "Traffic's backed up for blocks."

"Were there any accidents, damages?" she asked smoothly.

"Well..." He shrugged. "None that I heard of yet, but..."

Elizabeth strolled over to her desk, giving Ian a none-too-gentle shove to move him behind her chair. She sat and folded her hands together. "Then, since there seems to be no reason for you to swear out a complaint, I see no reason for wasting your time any longer."

The policemen looked baffled. The commander took off his hat and scratched his head. "I guess you're right lady."

"*Ms* Marlowe." She corrected. "And this is *Dr.* Bradshaw." She pointed at Ian. "He may act like an idiot at times, but he's a world-renowned ethologist." She paused, enjoying the further confusion the strange word brought.

The commander looked around the office, clearly impressed by the trappings of wealth he saw there. "Ms Marlowe, you any relation to Marlowe Industries?"

"Yes. My uncle and adopted father is Mr. Robert Marlowe." For once she didn't regret the use of the family name and the power that went with it. She'd do anything to keep Ian out of jail.

"Uh..." The commander looked down at his shoes and then up at Ian. "You ever been in trouble in this city before, Dr. Bradshaw?"

"Yes," Ian replied, knowing that he'd be checked out, anyway. "Call Sergeant Wilson down at the Central Park Station. He'll fill you in on the details." The commander asked Elizabeth if he could use her phone. She turned the instrument in his direction.

The commander got Wilson and listened. When he hung up, he looked at Ian oddly. "He wanted to know how the little dog was."

Ian grinned. "Fat and sassy. Smart as a whip."

"He recommended I let you off as long as you promise not to pull this kind of stunt again."

"I swear." Ian's eyes twinkled mischievously and Elizabeth knew he was cooking up another scheme.

Just before the police left, an awful thought struck her. ''Is this going to be in the papers?'' she asked. Robert would have a fit.

The commander nodded. ''Ma'am, there are hoards of news people out there behind the police line. Once we take it down, I can't guarantee they won't try for an interview. They sure shot enough footage of the doc here doing his wall bit. And I bet they got you when you stopped us from plugging him with tranquilizers.''

''Oh, Lord,'' she moaned, slumping in her chair. ''Ian Bradshaw, you've done it now!''

CHAPTER FOURTEEN

IAN FOLLOWED the police to the outer office and bolted the doors behind them. Then he returned to face Elizabeth.

She was sitting with her head in her arms, face-down on the desk. He had no idea what she was feeling or thinking.

"Being, as you know," he said, "a man of little honor, I have to confess that while you were snowing the cop, I peeked at the stuff on your desk. Elizabeth, do you know we've been doing exactly the same thing?"

She looked up, a mixture of love and anger on her face. "What are you talking about?" she whispered.

"Your notes." He pointed to the list she had been making all day. "When I ran, I ran with a purpose, love. I went to John Adam's place—he's a prof friend—and asked if I could use his computer expertise to run off a data sheet on our likes and dislikes. I brought the results over to the apartment to show you, then remembered you'd be here. I tried everything with Nancy save giving her my body as a sacrificial offering, but the little gal is loyal to you, Lizzie. I couldn't even get her to tell you I was calling." He gestured at his fur-clad body. "Hence the dramatic entrance."

Elizabeth felt a bit dizzy. "You mean you've been trying to find a compromise, a solution, too? Ian, that's almost uncanny."

He bent down and kissed her throat. "'Tis fate, my love," he murmured. "We were destined to be together from the very beginning. You can't escape me clutches, darlin'."

She shivered in sensual response and smiled at his teasing. "I missed you so," she confessed. "Even before you actually left physically. You were so cold and distant."

Straightening, he gazed down at her. "You nearly broke my heart when you said you still had reservations about marriage. I've never felt such rejection or pain. But I didn't love you any the less."

"I'm so sorry." Her eyes filled with tears. "But I made an appointment with Jane to see if she can help me find which loose screw in my head is making me marriage-shy."

"I can tell you that," Ian began. But a pounding on the door and the ringing of the phone in the front office interrupted him.

"It's the reporters," Elizabeth said, groaning. "We're going to have to face them eventually. I guess we might as well get it over with." She looked up at him. "You don't by any chance have anything on under that costume, do you?"

Ian smiled wryly. "Just my skivvies, I'm afraid. You know, the little bitty ones that barely cover—"

"I get the picture." She rose, gathering her notes. "Put your head on and don't you dare say a word.

Just get us through the mob and into a taxi with as little commotion as possible. *Please.*"

Ian had just picked up the headpiece when something else on her desk caught his eye. Her back was to him, so he took the opportunity to sneak a peek. The envelope was large, big enough to hold several pieces of paper, and the return address read, Bette Marsh, Marsh School of Aviation, Springton, NJ. What was going on?

"Hurry up, Ian." Elizabeth's voice interrupted his scrutiny. "Not only do I want to get this over with, but I haven't had a thing to eat since breakfast. I'm famished!"

"Me too." He slipped the mask over his head. "But for more than just food." He put his arm around her shoulders protectively and led her toward the door.

It was far worse than Elizabeth had dreaded. The reporters were so thickly packed in the hallway that there was no way for them to get by. Questions were shouted at her with such rapidity and in such volume that she instinctively moved closer to Ian, seeking comfort from him.

Ian lost his temper completely. Jerking his mask off, he told the mob exactly what would happen to them if they didn't get lost immediately. He left no expletive in the English language out of his warning. Reporters scattered like leaves in a strong wind.

Elizabeth sighed with relief as she watched the last of them disappear around the corner. "That wasn't exactly commotionless, but I'll have to grant you that it *was* effective."

Ian lowered his head and gave her a long kiss. She returned it, thinking at one point that she heard a soft click, but dismissing it as passion rose to cloud her mind to everything but her spectacular lover.

They made it back to the apartment without further trouble. The cab driver was startled by Ian's appearance, but he said nothing. Elizabeth tipped him generously for his silence.

Once inside the apartment, Elizabeth headed for the fridge, asking Ian what he'd like for dinner. In answer, Ian stripped off his costume, leaving his powerful body naked except for brief briefs. "I think," he said in a seductive tone, "that at the moment it's more important to feed our love than our stomachs." He reached for her, and she was unable to resist the tantalizing kisses and caresses he lavished on her. One hunger replaced the other, and she made no protest as he lifted her in his arms and carried her to the bedroom.

"I've been *starving* for you," he said, stripping her with maddening slowness. "And I'm going to relish every moment of this to the fullest."

"Could you relish a little faster," she pleaded, her body already on fire for his. "I'm not made of ice, you know."

"Melting fast, are you?" His lips touched her breast. She tangled her fingers in his hair and writhed against him, desire making her wild.

Ian didn't relent. He moved over her half-clothed body with his hands and lips, driving her insane with passion. She cried out for release with a fervor he hadn't heard from her before. She was his forever, he was certain now.

Hours later, Elizabeth staggered into the kitchen for a sandwich and a glass of milk. She knew she didn't have the strength for anything more complicated. When she returned through the living room, she noticed that Spike had settled for the night on the discarded costume. She ought to buy the thing for Ian, she decided. It would make a grand Christmas gift.

Ian was deep in sleep, his strong features relaxed and a small, satisfied smile on his sensual lips. She wanted to ask him so many questions. What had the computer given him? What had he meant when he had said that he knew why she was reluctant to marry? A thousand things. But she got into bed and snuggled next to him, knowing they would all wait until morning.

Morning came far too soon and far too abruptly. The telephone rang relentlessly, and she finally reached to answer it, even though Ian muttered for her to pull out the plug. Her number was unlisted, so she knew it would be a personal call and possibly important.

It was personal. "Have you seen the front page of the *Times*, young lady?" Robert roared. "This time the two of you have gone too far!"

Elizabeth sat up, brushing hair out of her eyes. "What are you talking about, Robert? I don't—"

"You and that...that ape man kissing. And a splendid shot of that idiot climbing the side of your office building. Do you have any idea how embarrassing all this is to your family?"

"What about me?" she retorted. "How do you think I feel, having my private life splashed all over the place for anyone to see? Robert, you have to understand that Ian and I aren't following the normal rules of society in our courtship. This...incident arose out of a misunderstanding between us. I can promise you—"

"Give me the phone," Ian commanded, taking the receiver from her hand. He put it to his ear and lay back down. "All right, Robert," he said firmly, "I apologize again for upsetting the rules. She was hedging on the marriage, and I wanted her to know for certain that I meant business. I admit it was crazy, but it got the job done. We're back at the negotiating level again."

A lengthy silence followed. Then, "I just don't see the world the way you do, Bradshaw. You seem to view it as a playground where you can get away with anything. Frankly, I'm surprised you aren't behind bars for causing a public disturbance."

"It almost happened. Elizabeth talked them out of it."

Robert sighed, sounding defeated. "I suppose the two of you are still planning to come out for Thanksgiving dinner?" he asked.

"Wild horses couldn't keep us from it." He took Elizabeth's hand and squeezed it. Robert sighed again and asked to speak to her.

"I'm sorry to have yelled at you," he told her. "I had no right to be angry with you, since it was hardly your fault. I only wish you hadn't let that photographer catch that kiss."

She suddenly remembered the soft click. "Honestly, we thought we were alone. Ian told them all to—"

"I know what he told them. A censored version is part of the article."

Elizabeth stifled a giggle. "It was spectacularly effective. You should have seen them scurry. He was so big and intimidating in that costume and he really looked like he meant every word he said."

"I did," Ian commented, his hand lazily stroking her bare back.

"I'll try to calm down before Thursday," Robert said. "I am looking forward to seeing you, at least."

"Thursday?" she asked, then remembered the holiday. A little frisson of anxiety claimed her. After Thanksgiving, she was to start working with Bette in the flight simulator. Her long-distance teacher had declared her lessons perfect, but the problem between Ian and herself had washed the flying thing completely out of her mind. "Oh, yes," she amended quickly. "We'll see you then."

After she hung up, Ian started to initiate another bout of lovemaking, but Spike appeared in the doorway, an attitude of desperation about him. "Walk time," Ian muttered, getting out of bed. "Some things just won't wait."

"I'll still be here when you get back," she said, a saucy expression on her face. Spike received the fastest walk of his life.

Later, they breakfasted and called in to both their places of work to say that unexpected family matters would keep them away for the day. Then they sat down with her list and his computer printout.

"It seems that if I don't stick you out in the middle of nowhere, you are willing to change urban sites," Ian observed.

"That's true," she conceded. "I don't like the idea but I love you enough to make the change. I just need access to a healthy business community with investors who can use my expertise."

Ian thought for a moment. "Let me do some checking around. I've really been giving some serious thought to starting a fauna park on my own. If I could find a place that would be interested in such a project and could come up with the grant money to build it, I know I'd be doing something extremely satisfying for myself. And it would have to be near a city, because I'd need access to an international airport for delivery of the animals."

"And it would have to be someplace warm."

"And you would have to be the business manager." He grinned. "You know me and money."

They discussed possibilities awhile longer, then Elizabeth asked him what he had meant yesterday about understanding her reluctance to marry.

"I'm probably not entirely correct about all the reasons," he said. "And I'm an observer, not an analyst, but I think it has more to do with your past than your present desire to be independent and free."

"My past?" Another ghost, she thought.

"You lost your parents. Robert lost his wife, Michael his mother. Your family is littered with broken romances and loss. You see Michael reluctant about parenthood, and you yourself have expressed fears that having children would be terminal to your career, which just isn't so, Elizabeth. Look around you, and you'll find plenty of women able to combine family and career. Your sex is tough and adaptable. Maybe more so than mine."

His words brought a lump to her throat. He could be right.

"There's one more thing," he said quietly.

"What?" She blinked back tears.

"I'm hardly a rich man, as you well know. Your fortune is almost beyond my comprehension. Sub-consciously, you could be wondering if that's part of your appeal to me." He stood and started to pace the room. "I can't change our pasts, Elizabeth. I come from the kind of stock I do, you come from yours. But if our positions were reversed, I swear I'd love you just as much. I'm no fortune hunter!"

"I *never* thought you were!"

He stopped and looked at her. "Others will. I think Robert suspects it, and that's one reason he resents me. Before we go any further I want to make it clear that I won't use one dime of your money on my project."

"But, Ian..."

He held up his hands. "No argument. You can help pay for a house, groceries, things like that. But your money goes into your business and mine into mine. Period. Agreed?"

She smiled through tears. "I don't suppose I'm going to be given a choice, am I?"

"No." His look was stern.

"I admire your pride. I agree on the condition that you feel free to borrow from me if you get in a bind. You'll pay me back, of course."

Ian shook his head. "That won't work, Elizabeth. It would be the same as taking handouts from you. If I need money, I'll do what everyone else does and go to a standard lending institution. You've done me a great service by building a credit rating for me with that portfolio and checking account. Shortly, I'm going to take out a loan and pay it back in monthly installments to prove I'm a reliable financial risk. No, your money and mine must be separate except in domestic matters. Then we're equals."

Finally, she agreed, knowing his pride would have it no other way. Then he urged her to think about marriage again.

"I'm not asking for a final answer today," he said gently. "But, darling, I don't want any other woman. I want the specialness of family life. For all your tragedies, you've known it. So have I. My parents are nothing like your people, but their love is still strong after almost four decades of hard work and living together. I stopped off to see them about six months ago, and you know, they take walks every evening, holding hands. Lizzie, I want that for us." The fervor in his voice stirred her deeply, and she almost impulsively plunged into a promise. But something made her hesitate.

"Please give me a little more time, Ian," she asked. "I need to think about what you said. To be fair to you, I need to be so sure that I have no doubts." He nodded understanding, but she could read disappointment in his gray eyes.

They spent the rest of the day talking and loving, then went out to an exotic Indian restaurant on the West Side where Elizabeth stuffed herself with strange and spicy dishes, which Ian explained as they arrived. His knowledge of the world and its people was almost as extensive as his knowledge of the animal kingdom. Not to marry this remarkable man would be stupid, given her feelings for him. But her heart had to decide, not her head.

At the office the next day she was teased unmercifully by her friends and clients about the picture and article in the paper, but she took it good-naturedly. That evening, Ian confessed that he had taken the same ribbing, but that his co-workers had been impressed with his lady friend. It was almost, he told her, as if he had suddenly acquired some kind of royal status because of her. He had been viewed as a skilled worker and knowledgeable scientist, but now he feared he would be kept at some distance because of the upgrading of his social position.

"That's tough," she said sharply, not wanting him to start wallowing in their differences again. "If you can't stand the heat, don't cook!"

"Hell, woman," he said, gathering her into his arms. "I'd love you if you made me a complete outcast. Forgive my mood. I won't be there forever, anyway." He proved the change in his attitude in his usual loving fashion.

Thursday arrived, and they drove out to the estate. Their greeting from Robert was warmer than Elizabeth expected, and she attributed it to the fact that Michael seemed more of his old self. He had even agreed to attend childbirth classes with Jennifer. Ian went out of his way to spend time with Robert, and Elizabeth guessed that they were discussing the plans she and Ian had wrestled with earlier that week.

Cook outdid herself, presenting a Thanksgiving feast so delicious and elegant that everyone, including the indomitable Charters, who never admitted to physical weariness from overeating, took to their beds after the meal for a recovery nap. Cook had even prepared a tiny turkey shaped out of dog food for Spike, and the dog seemed as weary as his master when Ian kissed Elizabeth and started toward the guest room.

"Wait a minute." Robert, who had been lingering, summoned them back. "I'm old-fashioned, and it does go against my grain, but since the two of you are living together, anyway, it seems a foolish pretense for you to sleep apart here. Go on to the guest room with him, Elizabeth. Just don't flaunt this in front of your grandmother."

Amazed, Elizabeth threw her arms around her uncle. "I never thought you'd bend this far, dear, dear, Robert. Thank you for being so understanding."

Robert gave Ian a strange look. "Ian and I have spent some time discussing the nature of human love," he admitted. "He reminded me of how dearly I loved my wife. So much that no other woman has ever interested me." Moisture appeared in his eyes. "Have a good nap, you two," he said, turning abruptly and heading up the stairs to his own solitary bedroom.

Elizabeth let Ian take her by the hand and lead her down the hall to the guest room. Tears threatened in her own eyes. Love made one so damn *vulnerable*, she thought. Even after all the years, Robert still grieved. Was she afraid of having to live like that someday? With Ian's penchant for reckless action and wild places, his life was and would be frequently in danger, more than the average man's. But then Ian was hardly average, and that was one reason she loved him so.

"Miracles do happen," Ian said softly as he closed and locked the door. "Maybe someday Robert and I will actually become friends." Spike scampered over to the little dog bed Jennifer had bought for him and immediately flopped down for a snooze.

Elizabeth started to pour out her troubled feelings to Ian when she caught sight of a new picture over the bed. It was a large blowup of the newspaper photograph of Ian and herself, locked in an embrace. Laughter replaced the sadness in her heart.

"Miracles *do* happen," she declared. "That has to be Michael's handiwork. What do you think? Has he finally come to his senses about the baby?"

Ian put his arm around her. "Looks a lot better, love. I'll try to get a few minutes alone with him later this afternoon. But right now, I insist on taking advantage of Robert's thoughtfulness." His lips covered hers, drawing her into a dream of passion that left no room for fears or doubts.

They awoke about four and joined Jennifer and Michael for a stroll in the garden. The day was sunny and unusually warm for the time of year, so only light jackets were necessary.

"So when are the two of you going to make honest individuals of each other and officially tie the knot?" Michael asked.

"In due time," Ian answered. "Certainly not until after Jennifer pops. Elizabeth says, and I agree, that it would be too much of a strain on the family to have two exciting events too close together."

"Manure!" Michael declared. "Listen, I set up you two. I knew Elizabeth would fall for you and vice versa. She needed a rogue male to interest her. Everyone around here is too... normal."

"Michael!" Jennifer chided. "That's no way to talk to your friend."

Elizabeth watched a wicked gleam grow in Ian's eyes. "No, Jennifer," he said. "Mike's right. But he's wrong in claiming credit. Elizabeth and I are soul mates, destined for each other. We'd have found each other somehow without his help."

Laughing, Michael taunted him, saying that he was wrong. Ian made a grab for his friend, intending to punish him with a mild roughing-up, but Michael took off into the woods at a dead run. Ian followed, realizing that this was a perfect opportunity to have time alone with his friend... as well as teach him a lesson.

Elizabeth turned to Jennifer. "Do men ever grow up?" she asked. "Honestly, the way Ian has carried on lately, I wonder if women have to raise their husbands as well as their children."

Jennifer sat down on one of the stone benches. "It is hard to tell at times. But I can assure you that Michael has changed for the better. You know about the classes, and as you can see, he's also returning to his old mischievous ways. And I can take that to be a good sign." She smiled sweetly.

"I do, too," Elizabeth agreed. "Did you see the new work of art in the guest bedroom?"

"I took it in to be framed," Jennifer confessed. "But what were you doing in there?" Elizabeth explained about the arrangements Robert had permitted. After Jennifer had finished expressing her amazement and pleasure at his unbending, Elizabeth told her of her misgivings about marriage.

IAN CAUGHT UP with Michael after a few minutes. He had given his friend enough time to get them both out of earshot of the women, and then had easily caught him and thrown him playfully to the ground. Michael was laughing too hard to put up much of a struggle, and Ian pinned him quickly, straddling his chest and locking his wrists to the ground.

"Thanks for the new decoration in the guest room," he said. "Can I ask a favor and take it home? I'd like to put it in Lizzie's living room." Michael burst into fresh chuckles and agreed. Ian released him and sat beside him.

"How's the fatherhood thing really going, Mike?" He watched the other man's face for signs of his feelings. Elizabeth and her cousin were alike in many ways, since they had grown up together. If he could understand Michael better, then maybe he'd have more keys to Elizabeth.

Michael sat up and shrugged. "I feel better," he said. "I still feel queasy when I think about being in the delivery room, but I'm slowly getting used to the idea. My only worry is Jennifer. Ian, if something should happen and I should lose her..."

Ian put his hand on his friend's shoulder. "A century ago, you'd have been right to worry. But today, maternal death in childbirth in this country is extremely rare. And Jen's in fantastic shape. She'll do fine and give you a bunch more as the years go by. Then you can get gray while they all go through puberty and adolescence. I bet every one of your boys will be a devil just like you." Michael groaned and looked heavenward.

"I understand why you and Elizabeth are obsessed with the concept of losing your loves," Ian went on. "This family has suffered terrible losses. And I think it's one reason why she's holding out on marriage. An affair is one thing, but in her mind, I think, marriage would immediately put me on some hit list."

Michael nodded slowly. "You may be right. I guess I need to deal with that, too. My mom—" He broke off.

"Let's talk about something else, buddy," Ian said understandingly. "I need a little help from you...some detective work. I saw an envelope in Elizabeth's office. The return address was an aviation school. You've got a hell of a lot more contacts than I do. Could you get the place checked out? I want to know what she's doing corresponding with it."

"Ask her."

"I don't want to rock the boat. She's been following her doctor's orders and reading about flying, but I want to know what else is going on without her knowing I know. I doubt the psychologist will tell me, so I need to sneak. Are you willing to help me?"

"Sure." Michael winked conspiratorially. "Where Elizabeth's welfare is concerned, I'm your man." Grinning, they shook hands firmly.

CHAPTER FIFTEEN

"ALL RIGHT, LIZ. You're doin' great," Bette congratulated her as they began the completion of her first flight in the simulator: the landing.

"That's because I know I'm really on terra firma," Elizabeth replied, licking her lips and keeping a close watch on the altimeter and airspeed indicator. "If this thing was one inch off the floor, I'd be a basket case, I swear."

"You keep up that negative yappin', and I'm gonna put you over my knee and spank your britches, woman," Bette threatened. "Judging from your lessons and from the work you've done today, I'd say you're the best dern student I've ever had. You'll be just fine. Now bring her in."

Elizabeth did, the simulator indicating that even if the landing was a bit bumpy, it was within acceptable parameters. As the "plane" slowed and halted, she felt a rush of elation.

"I did it!" she exclaimed. "We didn't crash!"

"Course not." Bette unhooked her safety strap. "I told you that you were good, and I meant it. Don't give out compliments I don't mean."

Elizabeth believed that. Bette Marsh was the most open, uninhibited woman she had ever met. Not a dishonest or deceitful bone in her body.

They went into the office to arrange for Elizabeth's next session, and Bette offered her coffee. "No, thanks," she said. "I'll have a glass of water instead. My nerves are jangled enough without adding caffeine."

"I know you're doing this for therapy, Liz," Bette said, "but would you mind a nosy busybody asking why? I mean, a gal could live in New York all her life and never need to go noplace in a plane. Your job at stake? I've had a few students with that problem. Would be fired if they couldn't travel."

Elizabeth suddenly felt like opening up. "Believe me, if it was just my job, I'd quit and find another. No, Bette, this is for a man. A very special man." Ian's image rose in her mind. She had lied to him this morning, knowing she was going to be late getting home. She hoped that her excuse—having to visit an elderly client in a hospital in Connecticut—had rung true. He had raised his eyebrows skeptically, but had wished her a safe drive.

Bette made a derisive sound. "Man, huh. Listen to the voice of experience, honey. There ain't one of them out there worth the trouble and expense you're putting yourself to."

"This one is." Elizabeth took a sip of water.

"He know you're doing this for him?"

"No. I don't want any of my family to know until I've flown solo." The thought made her sweat. "I've got a lot of pride, Bette. Too much, really. But if I fail—"

Bette slapped her hand down on the cluttered desk. "None of that! Remember?"

Meekly, Elizabeth apologized. Then she went on to tell Bette about Ian's qualities, explaining his love for animals and his crusade for fauna parks. As she spoke, Bette started to nod.

"He don't sound so bad," she conceded. "He treat you as good as that pup of his?"

Elizabeth just smiled. Bette laughed.

IAN FILLED OUT THE PAPERS for the loan he needed to buy a ring. On Christmas Eve he intended to ask for her final answer. That would give them a full seven months to prepare for a new life, if they planned a late July wedding. Jen's baby would have hatched by then, so it should work out well with the family. And it would give his own parents plenty of time to plan to come for the ceremony. Briefly, he wondered how Sam Bradshaw and Robert Marlowe would get along. And he would have to warn Michael to keep pranks to a minimum. His parents' senses of humor were the earthy ones of people who had spent their lives close to the soil, but Mike might prove a bit much for them if he got carried away.

The loan approved and the money transferred to his checking account, he went shopping. The stone he chose was a small one, tiny compared to what a woman of Elizabeth's social standing would normally wear, but it was perfect, without flaw, and he could afford it. Returning home, he hid it carefully in his backpack in the depths of the closet. Then he prepared a solitary meal.

Elizabeth had looked funny when she'd told him of the trip to Connecticut that morning. She had acted cheerful and affectionate, but there had been a strained set to her eyes, and she kept dropping things. He wondered what was going on.

The phone rang, and he went to pick it up. Michael's voice greeted him. "She's taking flying lessons, old buddy," he said conspiratorially. "She enrolled weeks ago at this Marsh woman's flight school. I checked it out, and it's got a fine reputation."

Ian was silent, absorbing the information. She was actually learning to fly. How far would she go to fit in with his way of life? This was a major sacrifice; he had seen firsthand how terrified she was of being in the air.

"Ian, are you all right?" Michael's voice called him back to reality.

"Yes. Yes, I'm okay, Mike," he replied. "I just . . . just am having a little trouble absorbing the news."

"You aren't the only one. Ever since her folks were killed, Elizabeth has been freaked out by heights and planes. That was one area I stayed completely clear of when I was pulling pranks. Nothing that would even hint slightly of falling. I've known her all her life, and I can't believe she's doing this. You might as well set a date. If she's learning to fly, she's going to marry you."

"When's Jennifer due?"

"Around the first week of July." Michael's voice was firm and sounded self-assured. A good sign, Ian told himself. Both Marlowes, it seemed, were healing.

He got the location of the school from Michael and cautioned his friend to speak of the matter to no one, not even Jennifer. "If she's gone to this much trouble to keep it a secret, we may foul things up if we let her know we're on to her," he said. "And that's the last thing I want to do."

"Me too," Michael agreed. "I know what it's like to deal with deep-seated fears. Good luck, old buddy."

After he had rung off, Ian sat back and thought for a long while. Then Spike interrupted him by standing by the door and whining. "Okay, fella," he said. "I understand all about calls of nature. Let's go out." While he strolled with his pet, he decided that the next chance he had, he was going to visit Marsh's place personally. Michael's information was all hearsay, and even though it might be reliable, Ian wanted to make sure his love was in good hands.

ELIZABETH RETURNED to find the apartment empty, but the dishes in the sink indicated that Ian was probably just out with Spike for his after-dinner walk. She quickly took off her clothes and showered. The scent of perspiration clung to her, and he was sure to question why she had worn jeans and a sweater to visit a client. Thank God for good timing, she thought. When he returned, she was clad in a housecoat and negligee and was fixing a light supper for herself.

"How'd the business go?" he asked, giving her a kiss.

"Fine. She bought several more blue-chip shares. When the dear soul passes on, her heirs are going to be quite wealthy."

Ian kissed her again. *You sweet liar,* he thought.

The days passed rapidly, and the city was transformed into the annual pre-Christmas frenzy. The
usually crowded sidewalks were even more packed as
shoppers struggled to find the right gift for friends
and loved ones. At times, Ian thought he'd lose his
mind as bodies pressed against him in subways and
on the streets. His only solace was his time with
Elizabeth.

He had begun to send out query letters to potential urban areas in the south, detailing his proposal
for a park and making it clear that no state or mu-
nicipal monies would be needed. Once he had a positive response, he would start grant-hunting.

The week before Christmas, he told Elizabeth that
he had to run an errand upstate for the zoo, rented a
car at a place just outside New York City proper and
drove down to check out the Jersey flight school. The
moment his vehicle left the main highways and entered the peaceful rural area and woodlands, he felt
his spirit soar.

He was, he realized, like those animals at the zoo.
A wild creature who had been trapped. Here in the
countryside, he felt free at last. When he and Elizabeth settled, he decided, it would have to be *near* a
city. Not in one.

The modest airfield surprised him. Just a small
runway and a few single-engine planes. There wasn't
a soul in sight. He got out of the rental and signaled
Spike to heel.

"Anyone here?" he called. No answer. He strolled
over to the metal building that he assumed served as
a hangar and office. The hangar door was shut, but
the office was unlocked. Quite a change from the

city, he mused wryly, where everything was bolted up and chained down. No one was inside, and respecting the owner's trust in others, he returned to the car to wait. Spike roamed outside within view.

Soon the sound of an engine filled the frosty air. Ian got out and looked up into the sky. A small plane approached from the southwest.

It landed and taxied to a stop. A wiry figure wearing an aviator's jacket similar to his own got out and strode toward him, removing a flight cap at the same time. Brown, graying hair, hard-featured, but a handsome female face. Undoubtedly Bette Marsh.

"Hello," she said, giving him a nonsexual appraisal. "What can I do for you, mister?"

"Tell me about Elizabeth Marlowe," he said. Her brown eyes widened.

It took some doing, but he finally gained her trust. All he wanted, he explained, was to be notified of the date of his love's first solo flight. He wouldn't let her know he knew, but he told Bette that she would probably need extra solace the days and nights prior to the daring experience, and that he also wanted to be waiting when she returned to congratulate her immediately.

"You believe in her more than she believes in herself," Bette said. "I guess that speaks pretty well for you. She's a whiz—just too jumpy."

"I believe Lizzie Marlowe can accomplish anything she sets her mind to," Ian declared. "I love her, and I want to give her all the support in this I can." Bette agreed to notify him, but she added a warning.

"You two might be in love, Bradshaw, but you keep too many secrets from each other. Take my advice—you'd better start being more open with each other, or you're gonna run into trouble down the line."

Ian pondered her words on the drive home, and thought about their future together. It was a week yet before he intended to pop the question. Maybe he'd better start paving the way so she'd have time to prepare her answer.

She greeted him warmly, not giving him a chance to bring the subject up, but dragging him into the bedroom. First she showed off her purchases for her family, hinting that she had something very special for him. But before he could reply in the same terms, he found himself pulled down on the bed and kissed into a state of wild passion during which he could barely reason, much less talk coherently.

Much, much later Elizabeth sensed that Ian wanted to talk. She turned on the light, then slipped on a filmy negligee and sat next to him, stroking his thick black hair lovingly. "Something on your mind?" she asked softly.

Ian grinned weakly up at her. "I only wish that what I had on my mind was physically possible at the moment. You look outstandingly delectable in that excuse of a nightgown."

She ruffled his hair. "No, now, come on. I know you better than that. You came in the door with a determined look on your face. I didn't give you a chance because I was so excited about my shopping spree, and then..."

"Then my future bride was overcome with desire for my form and ravaged me on the spot."

She slapped him gently on his head. "I noticed no unwillingness on your part. In fact, once I initiated, you took the lead, so I don't want to hear any complaining."

"Who's complaining?" Ian rolled over and laid his head in her lap. The silk of the gown and the warmth of her body began to renew his vigor. He smiled to himself. She hadn't protested his calling her his future bride. *Pave the way one step at a time,* he told himself. Then he launched into a discussion of the cities from which he'd received the most positive replies to his letter, telling her that Atlanta seemed to be the best prospect.

She listened, her feelings mixed. The idea of moving, even to as cosmopolitan a place as Atlanta, still bothered her. The shopping trip that afternoon had reminded her how dearly she loved New York. But then, she thought, she loved the man whose head rested on her lap far more. Atlanta would be a good place to live, and she would get used to it.

Ian began to intersperse his words with kisses on her bare ankles and silk-veiled calves and thighs. She had a feeling that he was still keeping something to himself, but his caresses were, as usual, irresistible. She let the unfinished business pass and gave herself over to his seductive touch, reveling in their love until they both fell into exhausted sleep.

The next morning she could feel Ian watching her with an unwavering gaze as she moved around the kitchen, preparing the large breakfast his body required. Finally, unable to take the suspense any longer, she turned to him.

"Ian, what is it?" she asked. "I've been...sensing that you have something special on your mind ever since you walked in the door last night. Can't you tell me what's bothering you?"

Ian studied her. Dressed for the office in a tweed suit made utterly feminine by a lavender froth of a blouse, she looked beautiful. His love. His woman, who was willing to do the one thing in the world she was most frightened of to ensure she could stay at his side. For a brief moment, he toyed with the notion of telling her that he knew of her sacrifice, but then dismissed it. Her triumph would be even greater if she wasn't aware he knew until she had made that first solo.

But the lady was no dummy, and he realized he had to tell at least part of the truth. "Elizabeth, I got an engagement ring for you for Christmas. I want to know if you'll accept it," he declared, keeping his eyes fixed on hers.

"A ring. As in marriage band to follow?"

Ian nodded, his heart pounding in his chest. Elizabeth frowned, then smiled, then frowned again. Clearly, she was thinking furiously. He waited.

"You know how much I love you," she said quickly, turning back to tend the sausages. "And if we're moving south, where I understand social standards are a bit more conservative, it would only make sense to marry. It would save some occasional embarrassment."

Ian's heart sank. *Embarrassment.* What a cold excuse for joining for life. Why couldn't she see that they were mates and should make a permanent commitment to each other? He was so angry that he almost shouted that he knew about her secret flying lessons, but good sense kept him in check. He had developed a lot of patience over the years, working with and observing animals. He could give his love the same gift.

She finished cooking in silence and served the meal, her portion a fraction of his. He could tell that she was mulling over his repeated proposal, so he let her eat in peace.

But when she was at the front door, ready to leave for her office, she regarded him with a frank expression. "I'll marry you, Ian. After Jennifer delivers, and because I love you. I can't imagine life with anyone else or life alone again." The moisture in her eyes belied the coolness of her voice. Ian whooped and grabbed her, mussing her makeup thoroughly.

Elizabeth spent most of the morning unable to work. Why the idea of matrimony bothered her, she couldn't figure out. Even a discussion with Jane about it hadn't helped. Maybe it was connected to the rebellion she had inwardly declared against the socially correct way of life her relatives had been ramming down her throat since she had made her debut. *Oh, damn,* she thought, pacing her office. *Why do I have to be such a mess of emotions? Why can't I see things simply? Just make decisions for my life the way I do for my finances?* She worried and paced until she was thoroughly grumpy, and it took an effort not to snap at Nancy when she ushered in her first client of the afternoon.

However, once settled down to business, she found she functioned efficiently. The client departed, pleased and thanking her effusively. She picked up her flight-training manual and spent a while studying before the next person arrived. She hadn't been able to give much time to Bette since the first simulator run, but promised herself that after the madness of the holidays was over, she'd buckle down again, literally. A quiver started in her stomach, but it wasn't wholly due to anxiety. She was actually a little excited.

Ian spent the day in a state of euphoria. He knew Elizabeth had a long way to go to change her prejudices, but she was a woman of her word. If she said it, Elizabeth Marlowe meant it. They would be man and wife in a little more than six months!

On the way home, not even the bustling crowds jamming the subways and sidewalks bothered him. He just cheerfully made his way through the mass of humanity like a tank, carrying Spike and making the crowd part for him without effort. He even stopped in a shop and picked up another gift for her—a gown even sexier than the one she had worn the night before. He could barely afford it, but now that she knew about the ring, he wanted to have at least one surprise for her on Christmas Eve.

That night, they made love with a tenderness and passion that surpassed anything they had shared before.

ELIZABETH TOOK the day before the holiday off and went grocery shopping, planning a private feast for them. She also bought and decorated a small Norfolk Island pine. Ian was delighted and regaled her with tales of the day-long journey he and his father would take from the Nebraska grasslands to a place where evergreens grew in abundance. They cut their own tree and brought it back for his mother to decorate. Elizabeth found herself deeply moved by the picture he drew of a close, simple family life. Although the Marlowes were as close, their lives were hardly as simple. She knew the tree that graced the living room in the mansion would be artificial, and that Charters would have done most of the decorating.

Christmas Eve arrived, and Ian hovered at the kitchen door, savoring the sight of his love and the mouth-watering aromas of the dishes she was preparing. Elizabeth was no wizard in the kitchen, but she was good, and he knew the meal would be scrumptious. Just like his Lizzie.

It was. Ian stuffed himself on turkey and the trims, knowing from what she had told him that they would be having a meal more gourmet and less traditional at the Marlowes' the next day. He had spent so many Christmases sweating in a jungle dining on tinned ham and a beer that this was a very special meal, made more so by anticipation of what was to follow.

Elizabeth felt a sudden nervousness as they cleaned up together. Exchange of gifts would be coming soon, she knew, and in a short while, her free, bare left-hand ring finger would proclaim to the world that Elizabeth Marlowe was committed to marrying the man she loved. As much as she chided herself for her ambivalent feelings, she could no more help them than sprout wings and fly.

Ian sensed she was deliberately dragging out the clean-up process, and when they had almost finished, he took Spike out for his walk, then settled the dog on his jacket for the night. Elizabeth was still puttering in the kitchen.

He ambled in and put his arms around her waist. Her apron was damp, and he could feel the warmth of her through it and her soft blue challis dress. "Let's go into the living room," he murmured, nuzzling her earlobe. "I can't wait any longer to see what you got for me."

In spite of her nervousness, Elizabeth giggled. He was going to be so shocked when he opened his gift! She turned in his arms and let him kiss her, feeling all the love she had for him warm her heart.

"I guess this is the first of many Christmas Eves together," she said, emotion making her voice husky. "Will we be able to have a real tree in Georgia, if that's the place that works out?"

"Love, if I have to go clear up to Minnesota to cut you one, I promise you'll have the real thing for the rest of your Christmases." He kissed the top of her head, imagining future holidays with a growing family.

But he said nothing of his dream to her. She was skittish enough about legalizing their relationship. Time to face the issue of children would come later. *Patience, Bradshaw,* he cautioned.

Elizabeth pressed herself against him, and she suddenly and unexpectedly pictured children—small Ians and miniatures of herself. The emotions that gripped her became so strong that tears filled her eyes. For as long as she could remember, she had never wanted children, never wanted to bring an innocent child into a world that could hurt him as she had been. But now...

Ian sensed that something was going on. He held her tightly and whispered words of love and comfort. He wanted to take every burden she bore and put it on his own shoulders, but he respected her too much to ask her to unload. She was a woman of great strength and determination, and she would find her own way out of whatever was troubling her. If she asked for his help, he would do anything for her. But he would not fight her personal battles.

Elizabeth clung to him for a while longer, until the tempest of emotions subsided. Her eyes still teared, but she wasn't really crying. "I guess I'm getting sentimental in my dotage," she said with a lightness she hardly felt. "Opening presents was one of the things I remember best about—" She broke off and sniffed.

Ian reached for the box of tissues on the counter. "I love you, Elizabeth," he said softly. "I think I know what you're feeling. Sentiment isn't a weakness. It's a sign of a sensitive spirit. Don't you think there were times when I was out in the boonies, thousands of miles from my own parents, that I didn't shed a tear for the warmth of a crackling fire in the stone fireplace my dad built with his own hands? For the sight of my mom stringing cranberries and popcorn? For the midnight service in the little country church we attended? We'd all be given small candles, and the pastor would turn off the lights as we lit them. Then everyone would sing 'Silent Night.' Lizzie, it was so holy and beautiful.''

His words released the tears. "Oh, Ian," she mumbled against his chest. "How could you bring yourself to leave such a warm, wonderful life?"

"I had my own destiny," he said, stroking her back. "It led me away, but it never hurts to look back. I think it only makes one stronger. My family's love and the way I grew up are part of the reason I can love you the way I do, with *all* my heart."

She felt emotional control returning. "Well, Dr. Bradshaw, I may be a bit messed up inside, but I return your love. Let's open the presents!"

They went rummaging for their gifts and piled the boxes on the coffee table. Elizabeth put some Christmas music on and went over to sit beside Ian on the couch. "You first," she declared, handing him the huge box containing the costume.

Ian took it, a puzzled frown on his face. He had expected a unique gift, knowing his love, but for the life of him he couldn't imagine what was inside the brightly colored box. It was enormous and made no rattling sound when he shook it. "Let me guess," he hazarded. "A year's supply of toilet paper?"

"No, you nut." Elizabeth laughed. "Open it and see for yourself. Unless you want to try another guess."

"Year's supply of underwear?"

"Ian, open the box. You have a very *earthy* mind."

"'Deed I do." He leered at her. "Know what we're going to do after this is over?"

"The box." She pointed at the present.

He stopped teasing and removed the wrappings. When he saw the gorilla suit, he started to laugh. "I'll be damned," he said, holding the garment up. "Think of all the money I'll save when I have to climb walls now. No rental fee." He kissed her noisily. "My very own ticket to public mayhem."

"Don't you dare, Ian Bradshaw! Once was quite enough." She gestured at the framed photograph of the two of them that hung over the bookcase.

Ian held up his hands. "I promise, never again. We'll save this baby for Halloween parties and the like. I've had my day in the sun." He reached for the small box containing the ring. "Now, love," he said. "Please accept this." He handed her the box.

Elizabeth held the future in her hand for a moment and then unwrapped it. The ring was gold, the stone small but perfect. "Put it on," she whispered.

His large hand took her small one, and he carefully removed the ring from its box. He looked at her with love and reverence for a moment, then Elizabeth felt a totally new warmth and love fill her as he slowly slid the jewel down her finger. He drew her to him and kissed her with a tenderness that melted her completely. All doubts and fears for the moment were gone from her mind, heart and soul.

The sexy negligee provided a convenient excuse for the passionate night that followed.

CHAPTER SIXTEEN

THE RING ON HER FINGER caused a flurry of excitement when they arrived at the Marlowe home. Adelaide hugged her, saying that she never thought she would see the day her granddaughter would come to her senses and commit herself to a man. Then she hugged Ian, welcoming him to the family.

"That's a bit premature, Mother, don't you think?" Robert broke in. Elizabeth thought her uncle seemed rattled by her engagement. Michael and Jennifer, of course, were delighted and enthusiastic.

"Oh, Robert," Adelaide said in a scolding tone. "If she's gone this far, you know she'll go through with it. When shall we set the date, dears?" she asked, turning back to Elizabeth and Ian.

They were all seated in the grand main living room, the large artificial tree skillfully decorated, gracing one corner. Charters was serving eggnog prior to dinner.

Her grandmother's question made Elizabeth uneasy. It had been one thing to talk about it with Ian. Now, with her family included, cold, hard reality set in. She looked over at Jennifer, who was wearing a loose dress, though she still didn't look pregnant, only exceedingly happy. Could she herself, Elizabeth wondered, be happy like that someday?

"We thought it would be best to wait until after Jennifer's baby came," Ian declared, taking Elizabeth's hand. He knew this would be hard for her. Facing a group of people she loved, but whose way of life she had rejected. And now it looked as if she had finally succumbed to their plans for her. Of course, they didn't know the entire story...yet. He took a deep breath. "By then we'll also know where we'll be moving and—"

"Moving?" Robert's voice was full of alarm. "Why can't you just settle here? Or in the city, if you must."

"Because of Ian's plans," Elizabeth said firmly. "When we know for certain, we'll let you know. But he can't build the kind of park he wants to in this region. The climate's too severe."

The conversation lagged after that declaration.

Dinner was a bit more cheerful. Cook had prepared a feast of pheasants and wild rice, and Charters made sure that no wineglass remained empty for more than a few moments. While Robert and Adelaide were subdued, Michael, Ian and Jennifer grew steadily merrier. Elizabeth felt detached, as if she were watching a movie.

After dinner, callers started to arrive, and the main topic of conversation the rest of the afternoon was Elizabeth and Ian's engagement. Her old friends, most of whom were already married and raising children, seemed delighted that she would be joining their ranks soon. Nothing was said about their moving away.

Callers of Robert and Adelaide's age group were politely congratulatory, but Elizabeth could tell that

Ian was not entirely approved of by the local gentry. She suspected that most of them remembered the splashy picture and article about his outrageous climb to her office. No proper young man would behave in such a way.

And he was an outsider. As she endured the afternoon, she mused that most of her married friends had joined to men they had known as boys. Men from the same social rank, the same society. With Ian, she was going rogue.

Gradually the visitors departed, and the family was left alone again. They exchanged presents—Jennifer laughing with pleasure at the teddy bear Ian had bought for her, and Robert deeply touched at the prize etching of nineteenth-century Crystal Cove that Elizabeth had discovered in an antique store. Harmony was restored. Then Robert asked Ian if he would mind speaking with him for a few moments in his study. Ian agreed cheerfully, and Elizabeth watched them leave with a feeling of apprehension growing in her.

In the study, Robert made certain the door was closed behind them. Ian declined an offer of a brandy, saying that he'd already had too much to drink. The older man poured himself one, however, and Ian saw that his hands were shaking slightly.

"I'll come right to the point," Robert said. "You and I have had our differences, but if you truly believe you can make Elizabeth happy, I'll not stand in the way of your marriage."

"I appreciate that." Ian took a seat in one of the leather wing chairs. Robert remained standing.

"But as you must know," Robert continued after taking a sip of his drink, "social matters aren't as simple here as I imagine they are where you grew up."

Ian was annoyed. "I'm not sure I see what you're getting at," he said.

Robert took another sip and faced the window, his profile to Ian. "This afternoon, when some of my friends learned of the engagement, they hinted—hinted, mind you—that you might not be after Elizabeth at all . . . merely her money."

Ian rose out of the chair and instinctively assumed a fight/flight stance. "That's a *lie*!" he exclaimed. "I may be living in her place, but I kick in my share for the groceries and rent as best I can. I don't give a damn about money, Marlowe! Hell, Lizzie keeps my financial records. I don't even know how much I have. Dammit, I'm on an *allowance*. She gives me money at the beginning of the week, and I hand over my paycheck at the end."

Robert turned and looked at the man in front of him. Anger and honesty were written all over him, but Robert still had doubts. Elizabeth's fortune was considerable, and with her keen sense of management, it probably grew daily. Could she secretly be keeping Ian on a dole? The situation was very awkward. He didn't want to get her in trouble with her future husband over the issue, but he wondered if his unpredictable niece was really using her best judgment. "I believe you, Ian," he said. "But what of the future? Can you offer her any kind of security, a solid home? Can you get a job that will keep the two of you and any children you may have together?"

Ian's shoulders sagged. "I don't know the answer to that yet." He sat back down and outlined his plans, emphasizing that none of Elizabeth's money would be touched for his fauna park. "And as for a family, that's the one thing in the world I crave more than the park. I love her, and I want for us to share the same kind of life my parents have had. Loving, living, working together." He paused, remembering Robert's loss. "Growing old together and watching our children make their own way through life."

Robert sat in the chair opposite him. "I think I'd like to meet your parents," he said. "Different as they must be from the people I generally associate with, I believe I'd like them." He bowed his head for a moment. "They're fortunate to still have each other."

"Yes, they are," Ian said quietly.

When the two men finally emerged from the study, Elizabeth was relieved to sense peace between them. A tenuous peace, perhaps, but better than bitterness and open warfare.

Adelaide and Jennifer had been planning her nuptials, a task she was content to leave with them. She knew that she and Ian would be busy enough trying to get their future together without having the extra bother of wedding plans.

They returned to the city that evening, and the next few days flew by, their love growing stronger daily.

New Year's Eve, they returned to the estate for the annual formal ball at the club. Ian had a problem finding a tuxedo large enough to fit him, and Elizabeth decided that next Christmas, wherever they were, she would buy him one custom-made for his unique physique. They settled discreetly into the guest bedroom, and she spent an enjoyable time helping him into the unfamiliar outfit. He complained from start to finish, but when Elizabeth stood back and observed him, she was astounded.

"You look like royalty," she told him. "A count at least, or maybe a duke. Even a prince. All you need is one of those sashes they wear. Ian, you're simply stunning."

He grinned sheepishly. "Sorry I was such a pain while you were helping me. And thanks for the compliment. I'll shoo out of here now so that you can get gorgeous." He kissed her warmly. "More gorgeous, I mean."

The evening was a success beyond Elizabeth's wildest expectations. Ian might be unfamiliar with a tux, she discovered, but he was no stranger to dancing. He led her through the most complicated of steps with a grace and ease that was surprising for his size. She could tell that she was the envy of every woman there. And once, to her amazement, she heard Robert telling some of his friends about Ian's work. It actually sounded as if he was bragging about his future son-in-law.

The only embarrassing moment came at the stroke of midnight when she and Ian remained kissing long after everyone else had finished singing "Auld Lang Syne." It took a number of discreet coughs from people around them to make her realize how lengthy their embrace had been. When they parted, Michael solemnly led the crowd in a round of applause.

New Year's Day was frigid, so everyone stayed indoors. For the first time Elizabeth felt that Ian really belonged, that he was truly welcomed at the estate. She suspected that everyone with the possible exception of Adelaide knew where she was now sleeping, but it didn't seem to bother anybody. Ian was as good as a clan member now that he had claimed her for his future bride. When they returned to the city, she felt a new inner peace.

During the next weeks, Elizabeth was increasingly busy with clients who had put off investment decisions until after the holiday season. Ian was as loving as ever, and they did manage to squeeze in some leisure time together. But he was busy, as well, planning and corresponding, trying to fit the pieces of his dream together. They shared their love at night, if no other time.

Elizabeth did manage to sneak off to the New Jersey airfield once in a while, in spite of her work load. Late in January, on one fine clear day, Bette took her up for her first flight. Elizabeth sweated, but otherwise was able to control her anxieties. It was her complete trust in the wiry woman at the controls, she told herself, not believing that she could have improved her own attitude so quickly.

Valentine's Day evening, Ian took her to a small, romantic French restaurant where they shared a cosy, quiet corner and a fabulous meal. After dessert, he ordered brandies and then took her hand.

"I have two gifts for you tonight," he said, love glowing in his eyes. "One verbal and one concrete."

"You're giving me a sidewalk?" she teased.

"I'm giving you a new home. Atlanta has agreed to host the park. The city and county were reluctant until they understood that no local monies would be needed. Now they're welcoming me with open arms."

Elizabeth frowned. The reality of having to move struck her hard, as did Ian's lack of foresight about funding. "How do you intend to finance this venture?" she asked.

"Grants. I've applied to every place I could think of. I don't have much promised yet, but I have faith. Something'll turn up."

His easygoing optimism bothered her. "You could borrow from—"

"Hush, love." He touched his fingers to her lips. "I don't intend to go into debt one dime on this project. I know it's meant to be. The money will be there when I need it. Now, on to the other present."

He reached into his inner coat pocket and took out a small paper bag. "I wish it could be diamonds and emeralds," he said, handing it to her, "but this is from my heart to you."

She opened the bag. Inside was an object wrapped in tissue paper. She took it out and unveiled it. Then she gasped.

A necklace lay in her hand. The chain seemed to be a copperlike metal, and dangling from it was a pendant, a circle about two inches in diameter. Painted on it was a woman's face, her face, but not as she saw herself. This woman was wild and free and passionate. Every line was true to her actual likeness, but the spirit... "How?" she whispered. "Who?"

"Me and a guy I work with. I found out he does miniatures for a hobby, and I commissioned this piece from him. He took a few hours of ethology lessons in return.''

"But how did he ... I mean ... That's not *me*."

His gray eyes held hers, and she felt as though he could see all the way to her soul. "That's the woman I see you as, Elizabeth. That's you, my love. Your hair blowing free, your heart beating in time to mine, your true inner nature finally released in my arms.''

She looked at the pendant. How could she ever return a love that saw her this way? How could she measure up? Ian's expectations were far too great. Dismal doubts started to plague her for the first time in weeks, but she managed to put on a grateful expression and thank him with words and a kiss.

But that night, not even their shared passion could remove her fears. Ian clearly thought she was the woman in the painting, a creature as unfettered as he. *I'm not,* she mourned, unable to find sleep. She was city born and bred. Long-term happiness for them was impossible. She would have to find a way to break the engagement.

But her love for him was too great. Torn emotionally, Elizabeth spent the following weeks in inner turmoil. She doubted she could live with him forever, but she knew she would wither and die without him. Her family went gleefully ahead with the wedding preparations, and Ian continued seeking grants while he drew up plans for his park. No one seemed to notice her problem, and the only sympathetic ear she found was Bette's. The flight instructor wouldn't let her talk about anything but flying while they were in the air, but once the lesson was over, if Bette had time, she always invited Elizabeth into her office for a cup and a chat.

"I'm literally on the horns of that old dilemma," Elizabeth confessed one March afternoon. "I don't know if I can live with him, and I *know* I can't live without him. I tell you, Bette, now the future scares me more than the damn planes do."

Bette tapped a chipped nail against her coffee cup. "I haven't known you all that long, Liz, and I've no idea what your man is like," she lied. "But I do know that I see more of you in that pendant than you seem to."

Elizabeth fingered the necklace. Since he had given it to her, she had worn it as faithfully as her ring, even if at times her outfit deemed it necessary for her to wear it underneath her clothing. Perhaps she was hoping some of the character she saw in the portrait would rub off on her, she mused.

"I'm no mouse," she agreed. "But *this* is an Amazon! I definitely don't qualify for that rating."

"Selling yourself short again," Bette warned.

As March became April, they traded places in the Cessna, and Elizabeth began to fly on her own, secure in the knowledge that Bette was right beside her, ready to take over in case of an emergency. She had a bad night after the first time and sought the comfort of Ian's arms for many wakeful hours, even though her lover slept on, unaware of her condition. She had exerted iron control over her jitters, determined that she would give him no reason to question her nervousness. A single slip and she knew he would figure out what she had been up to on all the fake trips to the "client" in Connecticut. He would learn the truth soon enough. Bette was preparing her for her first solo. After that, providing she survived physically and emotionally, she would announce her triumph to everyone!

But the very idea kept her awake at night, sweating.

Ian watched strain eat away at her and prayed for ways to help her cope. He wasn't even sure that it was the flying lessons that were causing her anxiety. A part of him wondered if she was having second thoughts about their relationship. She had been acting strangely ever since he had given her the pendant, but he restrained himself from questioning her, since she was going docilely along with her family's plans for a late July wedding. Whatever was bothering her, he believed that his love would eventually heal it.

Then one day when she had taken off for "Connecticut," he got a call just before he left for the zoo. "Bradshaw?" It was Bette Marsh. "Your lady's going up by herself today. You wanna see her, you'd best get your hind end down here."

"I'm on my way to steal a car right now!" He slammed the receiver down, scooped up Spike and headed out.

ELIZABETH SCANNED the cloudless spring sky. Something deep inside told her that today was likely to be the day. As she drove, she occasionally fingered the pendant. Superstition, she told herself harshly. But Ian's gift brought her some comfort, anyhow.

The countryside was beautiful, the pale spring leaves filling out the winter skeletons of the trees, the grass turning from brown to green, and new life sprouting everywhere. She'd seen it so many times from the air while Bette had piloted. What would her reaction be when she was alone? Would she have the courage to look down? Hell, would she have the courage to even get off the ground? She ground her teeth, determination forcing the fear from her mind.

Bette was waiting in her office, a half-smoked cigarette fuming in the ashtray. She greeted Elizabeth casually, almost indifferently, and for a few minutes Elizabeth thought she had gained a reprieve.

But instead of relief, she experienced a wash of disappointment. She was ready! She knew all she needed to know. Bette had been a fantastic, patient teacher. It wasn't fair!

"Bette," she began, knowing it was against the rules for the student to ask for her first solo, but feeling too strongly about it to be able to contain herself. "Bette, I'd really like to—"

Bette looked up, a slightly bored expression on her tanned face. "Yeah, Liz? What is it?"

"Iwanttosolotoday!"

Bette's brown eyes lighted, and she grinned broadly. "You got it, kid. Sit down and let's run through the whole thing again."

"But I know procedure like the back of my hand."

"No exceptions, Ms Genius. Plant it."

For the next half hour, Bette had her run verbally through each and every step she would take on her solo, twice. It almost seemed to Elizabeth that her instructor was stalling.

Finally, Bette stood and walked over to the dusty window. She squinted and looked up at the sky, then seemed to study the heavily wooded area to the right of the runway. Nodding, she turned back to Elizabeth. "Let's go," she said.

Elizabeth's mouth was dry and her heart was hammering, but she made herself move coolly through all the preflight procedures, first checking the exterior of the Cessna, then mounting the small metal step and entering the cabin. She strapped herself in and began the long, well-memorized cabin check. Then it was time for action.

Since Bette had placed the plane in takeoff position, and since the day was windless, all Elizabeth had to do was go. She took a deep breath, sent up a prayer, smiled at Bette, gave her instructor a thumbs-up signal and let the throttle out.

Ian hid behind the trees, watching with his heart crawling up his throat. He had left Spike in the car, knowing that his own nervousness would be conveyed to the animal, and that in spite of his orders, Spike might bark, giving them away. Elizabeth musn't know...yet. When the Cessna began to move, he had to grab hold of a tree trunk. Elizabeth had more guts than any man he had ever met, including himself. To have gone in a few short months from getting the heebies-jeebies just from watching him climb to her bedroom window, to this!

At exactly fifty-five knots, Elizabeth lifted the nose and felt ground contact disappear. She was airborne, if only by inches! She could feel panic trying to grip her, but she forced herself to remain cool, following every step for lift-off and initial climb precisely. Out of the corner of her eye she could see the earth receding below her... and the empty seat beside her. She was on her own!

Climbing to six hundred feet, she began the traditional first flight rectangular pattern, using the airstrip as home base and taking the Cessna along the lines she and Bette had drawn earlier on the map.

She could never exactly say at what point in the maneuver she began to enjoy it, but as she smoothly completed the third side of the rectangle, exhilaration replaced fear. She, Elizabeth Marlowe, was actually piloting, flying, an airplane!

Ian stepped out of the woods and walked over to Bette. The instructor was shading her eyes with one hand, the other cocked on her lean hip. A small smile of triumph was on her face.

"Glad you made it, Bradshaw," she greeted him, not taking her eyes off of the plane. "She's doing perfectly, just as I expected."

"That's pretty much the way she does everything," he replied proudly. "She's a special woman."

"If she wants, she could go on with this," Bette commented. "She's good enough and smart enough to get a private pilot certificate, maybe even go for a cross-country license."

Ian's interest perked. "What would that mean?"

Bette shrugged, her eyes still on the plane as it began to turn into the descent pattern. "Just that she'd be able to fly anywhere."

"Anywhere?" Fresh excitement filled him. "You mean like in the world?"

"There're different regulations and systems in other places, but there's no reason why she couldn't eventually take a larger private plane to Timbuktu, if she wanted.''

Plans for the future filled Ian's thoughts, but he warned himself to let Elizabeth make the decisions. He would keep his mouth shut and wait to see what happened. But he couldn't help thinking it was possible that in the years to come he'd be regally chauffeured around the world by his beautiful wife.

Elizabeth bit her lip in concentration as she neared the runway. She was perfectly lined up, but she had to be alert in case an expected breeze threw her a bit off course. Next time, she would choose a slightly windy day to test her skills and mettle.

Next time! That she was even planning more of this was astonishing. She slowed to just above stall speed and sent up a silent prayer of thanks for Jane Duggin and her persistence. Without the Elf pushing her gently, she would never have made it this far. The little woman had known what she was doing. The wheels touched down with only a minor jolt. Elizabeth applied full back pressure to the yoke when she was certain that all three wheels were solidly on the ground, then she relaxed it as she rolled down the runway. She felt she was still traveling a bit too fast, but she didn't panic. Using the flaps, she slowed gradually and came to a complete stop just a few yards farther than she should have. Still maintaining control over her emotions, she went through the procedure of deactivating the machine.

She was almost finished when a banging noise startled her out of her methodical mental checklist. Looking out the side window, she was astonished to see Ian, a broad smile on his face and pride clearly gleaming in his eyes. She unlocked the door.

"You did it!" he yelled, reaching for her and dragging her from the seat. He lifted her in his arms and swung her around in a circle, laughing and whooping with joy. Then she was given a sound and thorough kiss. Letting all questions go for the moment, she gave herself over to the embrace. She had flown successfully, and she was in his arms. Nothing else mattered.

Bette's dry voice interrupted the kiss. "Good thing your seat belt was already unfastened," she said, moving past them and getting into the plane. "He'd 'bout torn you in half otherwise."

Ian put her down and still holding him tightly, Elizabeth looked anxiously at her instructor. "How did I do?" she asked.

Bette studied the instrument panel, then turned and cocked an eyebrow at her. "I'll give you a B-plus, maybe an A-minus, Liz. Your landing speed was just a hair over the line. Next time take it a little closer to stall."

"Yes, ma'am!" Elizabeth threw Bette a mock salute. Then she looked up at Ian. "What in the world are you doing here?" she asked.

"You can't keep any secrets from me, love," he replied, grinning shamelessly. "I spotted Bette's name and address on your desk by accident the day I gorillaed you. Suspicion grew, and I finally discovered that your little old lady client was really healthy as a horse, tough enough to chew nails and teaching you to fly. Imagine my surprise."

"You're a snooping rat, you know," she said, giving him a hug. But she was so very glad that he was here to share this special triumph with her.

"Sad, but true," he agreed. "But, Elizabeth, once I knew, I *had* to be here. Do you understand?" She nodded.

Ian turned to Bette. "Is there anyplace nearby where we could celebrate in a suitably romantic way, Ms Marsh? Where not too many eyebrows would be raised by a couple with no luggage and a small dog in tow."

Bette's face broke into a rare smile. "Liz, you really got yourself one here." She told them of an inn run by a friend of hers. "I'll call ahead and warn them you're coming."

As they drove away from the airfield in Ian's rented car, Elizabeth let all her excitement out. Raising her arms above her head, she shrieked, "I *did* it!" Spike jumped onto Ian's lap and eyed her warily. Ian just joined her shouts of triumph, thinking how deliciously he was going to reward her for her struggle and victory.

CHAPTER SEVENTEEN

THE INN WAS SECLUDED, the hosts welcoming, and they ended up spending the entire night there. In the morning, Ian drove her back to the airfield and her car, and they went home separately.

Saturday, they drove out to the estate to visit and to share the news of her triumph. She wore her pendant proudly, feeling that maybe she could measure up...someday.

After amazement and pleasure had been expressed all around about Elizabeth's successful solo, Jennifer quietly announced that Sue had told her that her delivery date might be sooner than they had originally thought. "You may want to move your wedding date up, Elizabeth," she said. "It seems as if the first Marlowe grandchild will be a June baby."

An alarm bell went off in Elizabeth's head. "Aren't the ceremony dates set in stone?" she asked Adelaide.

Her grandmother's eyes twinkled. "You don't think I could get them changed if I wanted to?" Knowing her influence in the community, Elizabeth realized that Adelaide could probably change anything she wanted.

"Then by all means, move it up," Ian said. He took Elizabeth's hand, noting that it was cold. "I'm willing to run down to the church right now, my-self.'' Elizabeth gave him a weak smile.

It was decided to leave the rearranging to Ade-laide, who fairly reveled in another challenge. Eliz-abeth was a little dizzied by the turn of events and began to resent being swept along at too fast a pace. With his usual perception, Ian noticed her mood, but didn't query her about it. He assumed she was just having trouble facing the fact that her life was going to change drastically sooner than she had expected.

Besides, he had his own problems. Grant money seemed to have disappeared into a great black hole. In spite of enthusiasm about his project, he could only get vague promises of funds and none of them sufficient to seed the park. Somewhere, somehow, he had to come up with a big donation before others would follow. For the next several weeks, he applied himself with diligence, but was unable to find any-one to back him.

Toward the middle of June, he received another bonus from his boss at the zoo and decided to use the money to fly down to Atlanta to meet with the city council and explain his problem in person. Maybe face-to-face he could get them to suggest a source he hadn't thought of. He didn't ask Elizabeth to join him because she was clearly too busy getting her of-fice affairs in order for the move and heeding her grandmother's requests for help with wedding de-tails, like dress fittings, which seemed to annoy her immensely.

In fact, he mused as he packed a few clothes for the two-day trip, Elizabeth had seemed uncom-monly snappish lately. Several times he'd had to hold his temper in tight rein to keep from letting one of her remarks degenerate into a full-blown argument. And then there were those lengthy sessions in the bathroom every morning from which she emerged pale and declaring she must be suffering from pre-marriage nerves. On a couple of occasions she had even seemed ready to spurn his amorous advances. But once he had her in his arms, her passion matched his. He knew she loved him, and when all the hoop-la surrounding the wedding was over, she'd settle back to normal, he was sure.

But Elizabeth knew differently. Their lovemaking at the New Jersey inn had brought her more than pleasure. In her nervousness the day before the solo, she had forgotten her pill. Then in her elation after-ward and the wonder of Ian's romancing at the inn, she had forgotten again. And that forgetfulness combined with their lovemaking had created a new being. A minute life that was part her and part Ian. She was pregnant!

When Sue had confirmed her suspicion, Eliza-beth had been aghast. How, she had asked, could it happen when she had only missed a pill or two? Sue shrugged and smiled consolingly, telling her that the human body is no machine. She was going to have a baby, and since she was getting married shortly, was that so bad? Elizabeth wasn't sure.

The first night Ian was gone, she sat home and brooded. Just when she got one aspect of her life and their relationship in order, another problem reared its head. She hadn't told him about the pregnancy, not certain how he'd take the news that he was not only getting a bride, but a baby within the year. Spike sat on her lap, and she stroked his silky fur. The dog seemed contented enough with her company, but she could tell that he missed Ian.

Well, darn it, so did she. His problems with funding were getting to her. If he would only dump his damn pride and let her lend him the money—*give* it to him—he wouldn't have a problem. Resentment simmered in her. Then the phone rang.

She almost didn't answer it, figuring it was Ian checking on her. She didn't want to be shrewish long-distance the way she had been at home. Her temper seemed to have a will of its own these days. And the morning sickness was a *real* treat. Hiding that from him had taken some skill.

The ringing continued, and she sighed, putting Spike down on the floor. She might as well answer it now. Knowing Ian, he'd just keep at it until he got her. As he always did, she thought, smiling. In spite of everything, she did love the man.

But the call wasn't from Ian. It was Robert. Jennifer had gone into labor, and he and Michael were bringing her in. Could Elizabeth join them at the hospital? She heard the plea in his voice and understood at once that he was asking for her presence as a stabilizing force. She agreed.

She settled Spike on one of Ian's old sweaters and told the little animal that she would be back as soon as possible. Then she left a message on her answering machine, telling Ian what was happening.

She took a taxi to the hospital, fully expecting to find both Robert and Michael half out of their minds. To her surprise, however, her cousin was very much in control of himself. He disappeared into the labor room, declaring that he was ready to help Jennifer through the experience. Elizabeth joined Robert in the waiting room.

"I can't believe this is the Michael I know," she told her uncle. "He seems so much more..."

"Mature?" Robert smiled at her. "It's taken a while, but I think my son is finally ready for fatherhood." Elizabeth shifted nervously, wondering if she was ready for motherhood.

They didn't have to wait long. A new male Marlowe arrived in the world after what Jennifer later described as the most fantastic experience of her life. During the wait, however, Robert wormed out of Elizabeth the problems Ian was having with funding. Her uncle had remarked that she didn't look well, and she had quickly thrown Ian's troubles out as the excuse. Tonight was not the night to let Robert know he'd soon be twice blessed with heirs. After her confession, he grew thoughtful.

But all other matters left both their minds when a nurse led them to a viewing room. Behind a glass wall was Jennifer, Michael and the baby. Michael, dressed like a doctor in surgical greens and a mask, could only show his delight by the expression in his eyes. Clearly, he was ecstatic. He unveiled his son for them, a small, fighting bundle of boy with reddish skin and curly blond hair. Jennifer looked tired, but she was smiling and waving at them.

"He looks like Michael did," Robert whispered, his voice thick with emotion. "Elizabeth, will you go call my mother and tell her all's well?" Pleading extreme weariness, Elizabeth said she'd make the call from her apartment. She was no longer needed here, she told him, and with one last look at the happy couple and child, she left.

Adelaide was so happy that she was almost speechless, a rare condition for her. But she soon recovered sufficiently to tell Elizabeth that her wedding date had been moved to the first Saturday in July, and that she had better tell Ian right away so he could readjust their honeymoon plans. Elizabeth said she would, though she knew that he had already planned on taking her to a cabin up in Maine owned by a friend of his, who had said the place would be free all summer if they wanted it. No problem there.

After she hung up, she turned on the answering machine. Ian's voice filled the room, and Spike jumped up and began to search for his master. Elizabeth laughed, stopped the machine and picked up the dog, telling him that it wasn't really Ian, just his voice.

"Here," she said, holding him near the recorder, "I'll show you." She let the tape run without really listening to the words. Spike sniffed at the plastic suspiciously, then lost interest and returned to his place on Ian's sweater. She rewound the tape.

"Darling," Ian said, "I'm so happy for Mike and Jen and can't wait to see the baby. I almost feel like hopping on a plane tonight, but I have meetings tomorrow. I'll try to catch you at a decent hour tomorrow night. I love you, Elizabeth, and I miss you like mad! Give Spike a pat for me, but hold me in your arms in your imagination tonight, love. I know I'll feel better for it."

When his message ended, Elizabeth sank into depression. She should be happy, she knew. Part of her was. Michael and Jennifer's son was healthy. Ian loved her and declared that he missed her. They would be married in a couple of weeks.

And would be a family in a few months.

She brought Spike into the bedroom to sleep on the floor by her side, feeling his company was no substitute for Ian, but better than nothing. She readied herself for bed, then cried herself to sleep.

The next day, she paid a quick visit to Jennifer, but hearing the details of birthing did nothing for her spirits. Unable to share her problem with the deliriously happy other woman, she left and spent a grumpy day at her office.

When she returned home, Spike indicated his displeasure at being left alone all day by standing by the door and barking. Rather than risk a mess on the carpet, she took the leash and started out. Just as she was locking the door, the phone started to ring, but she ignored it. In her present mood, she would probably snap the head off the person calling, and it could well be Ian.

Spike seemed mollified by the outing, and they shared the evening together in a relatively peaceful atmosphere. Ian didn't call, and she assumed that some of his meetings included dinner and politicking. Loneliness consumed her, but she consoled herself with the knowledge that he would be back the next afternoon. He had told her he would take the bus from the airport, but she decided to shuffle her schedule around and meet him herself. She ached for him and his loving arms.

WHEN HE GOT OFF THE PLANE and saw her waiting for him, Ian's heavy heart soared. His visit had essentially been a waste of time—he was loaded with promises, but no cold hard cash. Many of the businessmen and philanthropists he had talked to had expressed an interest, once he had the program seeded. But not one of them was willing to risk the initial investment. Ian had alternately seethed and moped on the flight back to New York.

But the sight of his love restored his spirits. Without a word, he wrapped his arms around her, feeling renewed strength from her return embrace.

"I love you," she murmured against his chest. "Oh, Ian, I missed you so!"

He put his hand under her chin to lift her face for a kiss and was framing a teasing comment when he saw the tears brimming and the dark circles beneath her eyes, not quite concealed by makeup. He limited his kiss to a tender one, embraced her again and asked what was wrong.

"I just missed you," she whispered, and Ian knew she was lying, covering a deeper problem. Cold feet, he worried. Was she questioning her commitment to the marriage again?

But when she informed him on the way home that the date had been moved almost a month closer and showed no signs of being unhappy with that, he decided he was off base.

"Could we stop by the hospital and see the new addition to the great Marlowe clan?" he asked. "You know, since I missed talking to you yesterday, I don't even know if it's a boy or a girl."

"Boy," she said curtly. Ian recognized a touched nerve. Was she jealous? That was insane.

"He is a little doll," she said in a softer tone. Wrong again, Ian thought. "Robert says he looks just like Michael did. We'll go over this evening when the proud father will be there. Sue has gotten us all special dispensation, and if you're willing to get into sterile coveralls, we can actually go in the room and visit."

"That'll be great." Ian looked out the window, watching with distaste as the city passed. Atlanta was an urban place, too, but within minutes of the city's outskirts he'd found wilderness that made him feel right at home. The area the county had designated for the park was perfect. If only he had the money...

"Since you haven't said anything, I assume you didn't have any luck," Elizabeth commented, interrupting his thoughts. He grunted an affirmative. Neither of them, he reflected, were in top form moodwise today.

Greeting Spike cheered him, and even made Elizabeth laugh. The little dog was one enthusiastic wagging tail and licking tongue. Ian tussled gently with him and patted the dog until he settled down. Then Ian stood and looked at Elizabeth.

"You know all about my problem, love," he said. "I haven't kept a thing from you. But you haven't told me what's really bothering you." He held up his hand when she started to retort. "Only when you're ready, Elizabeth. When you feel you can come to me and honestly reveal what's in your heart, I'll listen. Until then, no more half-truths, please. They hurt more than not knowing at all."

"I...all right," she whispered, tears forming again. "But I will say this here and now. It's not my love for you that's the problem." She held out her arms, and he felt all his worries disappear in a flash flood of love and desire. With this kind of bond between them, he believed no obstacle was impossible to surmount.

But when they were at the hospital visiting the proud parents and the baby, her moodiness returned. In a way she reminded him of the way Michael had been when Jen first discovered she was pregnant. He couldn't put his finger on it, but he suspected it had something to do with babies. Perhaps she was wrestling with the fact that she might not want them.

He sincerely hoped that wasn't the case. Clad in an outlandish suit of baggy sterile clothing, he was allowed to pick the tiny human up and enjoy the feel of an infant in his arms. Michael and Jennifer looked as if they were sure they had produced the finest baby in the world, and Ian reassured them that their offspring was strong and responsive.

Elizabeth watched him with the baby and felt a turmoil of emotion. Clearly, he took as easily to children as he did to his animals. Ian was natural father material. She sighed, hoping that he could make up for what she was sure she lacked. She declined to hold the baby, claiming that she thought she was coming down with a cold. If she held the tiny thing, she was afraid her emotions would run wild and betray her. And she wasn't ready for that by a far sight.

When they made love again that night, she did it with a fierceness designed to drive all other thoughts

from her troubled mind. Ian seemed startled at her
fire at first, but it took him only moments to understand her need and contribute to a vigorous bout of
lovemaking that put them both to sleep almost immediately afterward. Elizabeth spent a peaceful night
nestled in his arms.

The next morning she felt almost as good as new.
No nausea, and she caught herself humming a lilting tune as she prepared breakfast. Her appetite had
increased, and when she served the meal, her helping was almost as large as Ian's.

Ian sensed the change in her mood at once, putting it down to memories of the night before. When
he started to make some discouraging remark about
his fauna park, she surprised him by firmly and
cheerfully insisting that the resources would come
from somewhere. "You have too much stake in this
dream to give up," she scolded him lovingly. "If I
could learn to fly, you can have your park. I honestly believe anything is possible if you want it badly
enough."

Ian stared at her. At that moment she looked exactly like the beautiful maenad on the pendant
around her neck. A passionate, fighting woman! He
began to smile. "Together, we *can* do it, love," he
declared, reaching across the table and taking her
hand.

That afternoon, he gave an unhappy George
Crown two weeks' notice.

Elizabeth had her monthly appointment with Sue
that same afternoon, and she asked about her mood
swings. Sue reassured her that it was perfectly normal, especially considering the other pressures she

was under. "Just ask your man to be understanding," she advised. "He's your best medicine for getting through this sane." Elizabeth didn't reveal that she hadn't had the courage to tell Ian of her condition yet. They made arrangements for her records to be transferred to a colleague of Sue's in Atlanta when the move finally came.

Earlier, Elizabeth had done the same thing with Bette, explaining that in her condition, she didn't feel she should continue the lessons, but that after the baby came and they were settled in the south, she wanted to resume training. Bette recommended a teacher and told Elizabeth that she would forward her records to the man whenever she got the go-ahead. The two women exchanged farewells regretfully. Although Elizabeth had included her on the wedding guest list, she wasn't sure the instructor would show up at the affair, since it was extremely formal—not Bette's cup of tea.

Elizabeth had also arranged for Nancy to work with a young rising star in the financial world—a man Michael had known in school. Nancy wouldn't have the prestige of being his personal secretary, but she seemed pleased with the new position. Especially since the man was handsome and unattached.

Her clients were all dismayed that she was leaving, some even insisting on keeping their portfolios with her long distance. But for the interim, which she figured would be lengthy considering everything going on in her life, she turned them over to a trusted friend in the same line of work. With mixed emotions, Elizabeth closed down her office. The act put a stamp of finality on her life choice, and she felt both elated and anxious. Not even leaving home had been so emotionally wrenching, and when she returned to the apartment that evening, she sought the solace of Ian's embrace wordlessly. He seemed to understand.

Before the wedding, they moved out to the estate. Elizabeth sublet her apartment to a young couple who were ecstatic to find a place at all, much less such a nice one.

In spite of Robert's broad-mindedness in the matter, they decided to sleep apart at the mansion, since Ian's parents were arriving a few days before the ceremony, and also to heighten the meaningfulness of the ritual, a point they both felt important.

After dinner their first evening there, Robert asked them both if they would mind stepping into his study with him. "I want to announce to the two of you my choice of a wedding gift," he said. Curious, they followed him.

Robert shut the door, then drew Elizabeth close for a fatherly embrace. "I've always sensed this time would come," he said, his voice slightly husky. "You became my daughter through tragedy, and I never really thought I could hold on to you as I have my own son. But it doesn't mean I love you the less, Elizabeth."

"I understand," she replied, tears in her eyes.

Robert turned to Ian. "We've had our differences," he said. "I suppose we'll always have our differences, Ian, but I want you to know that in spite of them, I trust her to you." Ian nodded somewhat stiffly, wondering what was coming next.

Robert clasped his hands together and stood between the two of them. "I've given this a great deal of thought, and I've come to the only logical conclusion. Ian, Marlowe Industries will fund your park, provided it is named after my late wife, Irene. I've searched for years for a suitable memorial for that wonderful woman, and I believe her spirit will be pleased to be associated with giving God's creatures a home."

Ian was speechless. This was the last thing in the world he expected. He recovered his composure slowly, trying to find the words to express his feelings.

Elizabeth, on the other hand, had no trouble. She flung her arms around her uncle and thanked him over and over. Ian looked as if he had been hit with a crowbar, but she wasn't going to let Robert's generosity go unrewarded.

"I...I *really* don't know what to say, Robert," Ian confessed finally. "I can't tell you what this means to me." He felt a flood of overwhelming emotion and turned away for a moment, jamming his hands into his trouser pockets.

Robert looked at the broad back of the man who had so annoyed, embarrassed and at times even frightened him. A spark of affection surfaced, and he knew that eventually they would be friends. "You don't have to say anything right now, Ian, only that you'll accept my gift in Irene's memory."

Ian lifted his head, his back still to them. "Of course I will, Robert. And knowing that you felt about your wife the way I feel about Elizabeth, I'm only too honored to name the park after her. I'll make it a place she'd be proud of,'' he added, determination in his voice. Then he turned to face them. Elizabeth thought she caught a glimmer of moisture in his eyes.

Ian tried to smile and held out his hand to Robert. When the older man shook it, their eyes met, and Ian saw a new warmth in Robert's expression. Impulsively, he pulled the man in for a quick bear hug, then released him quickly.

Robert grinned. ''Let's go tell the others,'' he suggested.

TINY ROBERT FARRINGTON MARLOWE II was a constant reminder to Elizabeth that she would be a mother soon, too. The baby had grown considerably since his birth and was now cooing and occasionally smiling, an event that brought pleased sounds from all the adults present. Gradually, Elizabeth let herself be drawn into the little charmer's spell, and the first time she held him, she felt that old, familiar mixture of emotions—pleasure and anxiety. She knew she would have to tell Ian soon, before the wedding. He had a right to know.

His parents arrived the Wednesday before the wedding. Elizabeth and Ian drove down to Kennedy to pick them up, and Elizabeth took an instant liking to the couple. Sam Bradshaw was a tall man—nearly as tall as his son—but without the musculature that made Ian's body unique. He had a full head of gray hair and brown eyes that snapped with pleasure and approval when he met Elizabeth. Nora, Ian's mother, was a large-boned, tall woman, with a serene manner that gave her a special dignity. Her face was lined and tanned, as was her husband's, but the smile and hug she gave Elizabeth were as sunny as the Nebraska skies.

"I never could figure my boy out," Sam told her on the drive back to the estate. "But seeing the wife he chose, I guess he ain't too far off the real world, after all."

"Dad," Ian commented good-naturedly, "there are real worlds of all descriptions. You have yours, I have mine."

"Don't you two get into it, for goodness' sake," Nora scolded gently. She patted Elizabeth's hand. "Elizabeth here'll think all you do is argue. She's never seen you working together at haying or bringing a new calf into this world." Her words made Elizabeth's heart jump. These warm, down-to-earth people were going to be grandparents. The grandparents of the baby she and Ian had made during a night of abandoned passion. Speaking of real worlds...!

The Marlowe estate and family didn't faze the Bradshaws in the least. They settled into one of the upper floor guest suites with no more fuss than if they were visiting neighbors down the road. Part of Ian's adaptability, Elizabeth concluded, came from his heritage.

The next two days were hectic. There were last-minute plans, visits, a bridal shower, and on Friday evening the rehearsal at the church. That experience nearly unnerved her, but she kept her dignity and let no one, not even Ian, know of her inner tempest.

But Ian knew. When he took her hands, they trembled and were icy in spite of the warm July air.

Her smile looked genuine enough to fool the others, but he could see tremors at the edges. Was it just prewedding nerves, he wondered. Or something more serious?

Earlier in the week, he had asked Michael to join him on a walk with Spike and had used the opportunity to convince his friend to lay off the practical jokes. Michael had agreed, saying that fatherhood had brought a certain seriousness to his life. Although he thought he saw a gleam in his friend's eyes, Ian reflected that recently Michael had seemed to have settled down. Maybe once Elizabeth came to terms with having children, the same thing would happen to her.

After the rehearsal dinner, which was held at a restaurant of Ian and Elizabeth's choice, everyone went to bed, since the next day would be so filled with festivities. But Elizabeth lay sleepless.

Finally, about two, she could stand it no longer. Putting on a robe, she made her way barefoot down the stairs and hall to Ian's room, letting herself in as silently as possible. Both Ian and Spike awoke the moment she closed the door.

"Elizabeth, what—"

"Darling, I have something to confess." She hugged the robe tightly around herself. "I'm two months pregnant!"

CHAPTER EIGHTEEN

IT WAS TOO DARK to see Ian's expression, but when he immediately leaped from the bed and embraced her tenderly, then covered her face and throat with kisses, she had no doubt about his feelings.

"Elizabeth," he murmured, "why didn't you tell me before? I thought I was the happiest man in the world. Now I *know* I am. Oh, love, a child! A baby of our own! How...?

Laughter and tears bubbled in her voice. "Remember the night at the inn? I'd skipped a pill that night and the day before, as well. Nervousness tends to make me forgetful, and I knew that solo was coming up."

Ian touched her cheek gently. "Maybe deep inside you really wanted to get pregnant, but that logical mind of yours was telling you to decide yea or nay, or wait for the 'perfect' time."

"Ian, I'm not so sure I'll be any good as a mother," she confessed, feeling the hot tears spilling down her cheeks. "I'm just glad that you seem to have a strong parenting instinct."

"Listen, Elizabeth," he said, lifting her chin with his finger. "You will be just fine. I've seen the flightiest of creatures settle down and become incredibly nurturing after they've given birth. And one thing you are not is flighty. You almost take life too seriously and your duties too grimly. I'm no fortune-teller, but I predict you're going to find family life the most rewarding thing you've ever experienced."

"Oh, I hope so," she whispered. "Hold me, Ian. I just can't go up there to that lonely room." He gathered her into his arms and carried her to his bed. They didn't make love, but just fell asleep in each other's arms.

Ian woke with a start to a sharp rap on his door and the sound of it banging open. Michael, son held securely in his arms, strode in.

"Okay, groom," he said, jerking the curtains open to let in the morning sunshine, "time to hit the deck. Gonna get the old ball and..." His words trailed off as Elizabeth sat up, rubbing her eyes.

"Morning, Mike," Ian said dryly, giving his friend a miffed look. "Care to step outside while Lizzie comes to?"

"Whoops." Michael grinned broadly. "Couldn't wait, huh? Don't worry. Your tryst is safe with me. Won't say a word."

"Out," Ian ordered. "I'd hate to give my best man a black eye." Michael gave them one more amused look and scooted.

"He's certainly back to normal," Elizabeth commented, swinging her legs over the side of the bed. "The perfect joker."

"And the perfect father." Ian put his arm around her shoulders and kissed her. "Just as you'll be the perfect mama. How are you feeling? I could kick myself for not figuring this out before, but I just assumed you were popping those pills with your usual efficiency."

"I'm only human, darling." She laid her head on his shoulder, a sense of peace coming over her. Peace and a bubble of joy at the thought that in a few hours she would be joined to this strong, loving, kind man for life. "I'll continue to need your love and support as long as I live."

Ian's heart dropped every concern and worry it had borne when he heard her words. "And I'll always need you, Elizabeth. We were meant to be husband and wife." He gazed at her tousled beauty. "And are our kids going to be something else!" Their laughter made music in the sunlit room.

Elizabeth managed to sneak back to her room without being seen. Shortly after she showered, a tray arrived from Cook with a note saying that she knew the nervous bride would eat better in solitude. Gratefully, Elizabeth took the tray from the maid and lit into the delicious breakfast. She was famished!

Just as she finished, Jennifer came in. "I thought you could probably use a little help getting ready. I know my hands were shaking so hard the day Michael and I were married that I could barely get my dress buttoned."

Elizabeth rolled her eyes. "Wait until you see the thing I have to wear. Adelaide chose the design, and it must have ten thousand itty-bitty pearl closures . . . up the back!"

"You need me," Jennifer said firmly, but with a wide smile.

Elizabeth did her own makeup while Jennifer took the gown from the protective bag and laid it on the bed. "Oh!" she exclaimed. "It's just beautiful! And that off-white color will look so much better on you than a pure white."

"I'm hardly a virgin bride," Elizabeth commented wryly, combing her hair out. She knew Ian would prefer it down, and the veil would look better with it long, too. She put on underclothes and then let Jennifer help her into the gown.

"My goodness, this is tight," Jennifer complained after struggling for a while with the buttons. "Have you gained weight or something since it was..." Elizabeth gave her a look over her shoulder.

Jennifer burst into delighted laughter and whirled Elizabeth around for a hug. "I understand why you didn't tell us," she said. "And I'm so happy for you! You won't know how much you can love your husband until the two of you share the birth of your baby. Ian knows, of course?"

"Not until about two this morning," Elizabeth said. Then, as Jennifer finished closing the gown, Elizabeth confessed her fears and feelings. "But that's all behind me," she concluded. "Now the only thing that worries me is what kind of goofy trick Michael has planned for us. To have escaped his pranks so far makes me highly nervous. It's like waiting for something to pounce on you."

"He'll behave." Jennifer didn't meet her eyes. "Ian warned him a while ago to behave." There was an odd note in her voice, but Elizabeth put it down to her delight in finding out that another baby would be joining the family.

She drove to the church with Robert, everyone else going in other cars. Clearly, he wanted her to himself one last time before giving her over to Ian.

"You are a beautiful bride, Elizabeth," he said. "Even though you're moving away, I can't begin to tell you how proud and happy I am today."

"You've been my father for so many years," she replied. "I'll miss you all, but probably you the most . . . Oh, darn, I don't want to cry."

"It's a day for laughter *and* tears," Robert said. "I'm about the happiest man I know. Both my children are joined to people I love and . . . admire. And I have a healthy grandson."

Elizabeth debated for a moment. "What would you think if I let you in on a little secret?" Robert slowed and looked at her, a smile slowly forming on his face.

"When?" he asked, no censure in his voice at all, only joy.

"Late December. Long enough away to keep gossip at a minimum."

Robert chuckled. "Damn good thing we moved this ceremony up on the calendar. This is absolutely wonderful!"

The wedding went without a hitch. Ian looked magnificent in a formal cutaway morning coat and gray trousers. Both he and Robert fairly glowed with joy. When the minister finished the ritual and Ian and Elizabeth each wore a gold band, Ian slowly raised her veil, his gray eyes filled with a love deeper than anything she could have imagined. His kiss demonstrated that love—tender, sweet and passionate. Then the organ began the stately music for their walk up the aisle. Head held high, Elizabeth moved proudly, arm in arm with her husband, to the arched doors of the church. They rode in the back of the family limousine, driven by Charters, who insisted on the honor, to the party at the club.

Later, all Elizabeth could remember of the party was being whirled in dance by one partner after another, but always ending up in Ian's arms. She heard wishes for all the best until the words rang in her ears, and she was certain that if even a tenth of those blessings came true, she and Ian would live a life of happiness together.

During one break, she noticed a guest who hadn't come through the receiving line. Hurrying over to her, she gave Bette Marsh a hug. "I'm so glad you came," she said, taking in the woman's lovely long silk dress. "I was afraid this kind of thing wasn't your style."

"Isn't." Bette lit a cigarette. "But I wouldn't have missed it for anything. You're a special gal, Liz, and I wanted to see you sent off proper." She nodded in Ian's direction. "I don't have much use for romance myself, but I'm willing to bet both my Cessnas that you're gonna have one hell of a great life together."

That blessing meant more to Elizabeth than all the others put together.

About five, Ian slipped her away, getting Charters to take them back to the house to change. He wanted to make it to the cabin before too late in the evening, he explained. His friends had told him that it was ready for the honeymoon couple, fully equipped with food and drink and clean sheets. And he was starved for Elizabeth.

He helped her out of the dress, laughing when she told him that Jennifer had discovered her condition because the gown fitted so snugly. "Robert knows, too," she said.

"His reaction?" He kissed her shoulder.

"Total happiness. He's mellowed considerably, Ian."

"I know. He even insisted that my folks stay over a week or so in order that the two families get to know one another better. Wonder what'll happen when Mom issues him an invitation to come to Nebraska."

"I bet he'll go."

They dressed hurriedly, smoky tendrils of passion weaving between them, but both wanting to hold off until they were alone in Maine. Ian hefted the suitcases and led her downstairs.

A crowd, consisting of both families and the Marlowe staff, awaited them in the vestibule. Elizabeth found herself weeping and hugging them all. So much love radiated in the room that she was dizzied by it.

"Well, cousin," Michael said, taking both her hands. "I hate like the very devil to see you go, but if it had to be, I couldn't have chosen a better guy. Ian's the tops."

"I couldn't agree more," she replied. "And thank you so much for holding off on the jokes. I know it must have nearly killed you."

Michael shrugged. "It was easy. Ian threatened to pound me into the pavement if I messed around, so I didn't."

Ian heard the words and gave Michael a searching look. His old friend was lying through his teeth. Something was afoot!

The final moment of farewell came. Charters announced that Elizabeth's Mercedes had been brought to the front of the mansion. He handed Ian the keys. Michael scurried to pick up their luggage. Elizabeth sensed a current of expectation join the love in the room. What was going on?

When Charters opened the mansion door with a grand gesture, she let out a scream of combined outrage and surprise.

Her beautiful, dignified silver-gray car was covered in gaudy orange and black tiger stripes. The grill had been painted black and white to resemble sharp teeth. Green tiger eyes gleamed on the front fenders. Across the driver's door was scrawled, "Just Married, After a Primitive Affair." Spike bounced around happily on the back seat.

"Michael!" she yelled, whirling on her helplessly laughing cousin. "How *could* you? You can't expect us to drive to Maine in that! We'll be stopped by every highway patrolman who sees us."

"It's removable, Mrs. Bradshaw," Charters interjected in a calm tone. "And please don't blame Mr. Michael entirely. I must confess to being a co-conspirator." A tiny smile twitched at his lips.

"Take it to the car wash down on Channel Street," Robert advised, merriment in his eyes.

"Wait a minute," Sam Bradshaw said. "I gotta get a picture of this. Beats any wedding prank I ever saw." He hurried away for his camera.

Finally, showered by rice, Ian and Elizabeth drove off in the outlandish vehicle. They made it to the car wash with a minimum of embarrassing honks from passing motorists. Ian tipped the operator twenty dollars to ensure that all the paint would be removed.

"And while you're working," he said, "I'm going to get back inside and kiss my wife."

"Ian, I swear, you're shameless," Elizabeth declared as he pulled her to him while the Mercedes moved into the huge rolling brushes. "You'd make out anywhere, wouldn't you?" she added, laughing as he started to nibble her earlobe.

"With you, love, anywhere at all." And then Ian Bradshaw proceeded to make good his promise.

HARLEQUIN HISTORICAL

Explore love with Harlequin in the Middle
Ages, the Renaissance, in the Regency, the
Victorian and other eras.

Relive within these books the endless ages of
romance, set against authentic historical
backgrounds. Two new historical love stories
published each month.

HIST-A-1

ATTRACTIVE, SPACE SAVING BOOK RACK

Display your most prized novels on this handsome and sturdy book rack. The hand-rubbed walnut finish will blend into your library decor with quiet elegance, providing a practical organizer for your favorite hard-or soft-covered books.

Only $9.95

Approximately 16″ x 8″ when assembled

Assembles in seconds!

To order, rush your name, address and zip code, along with a check or money order for $10.70 ($9.95 plus 75¢ postage and handling) (New York residents add appropriate sales tax), payable to *Harlequin Reader Service* to:

In the U.S.

Harlequin Reader Service
Book Rack Offer
901 Fuhrmann Blvd.
P.O. Box 1325
Buffalo, NY 14269-1325

Offer not available in Canada.

BKR-

Take 4 best-selling love stories FREE
Plus get a FREE surprise gift!

Janet Dailey

Americana

A romantic tour of America with Janet Dailey!

Enjoy the first two releases of this collection of your favorite previously published Janet Dailey titles, presented alphabetically state by state.

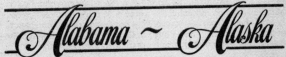

Available in June wherever paperback books are sold or reserve your copy for May shipping by sending your name, address and zip or postal code, along with a check or money order for $2.75 per book (plus 75¢ for postage and handling) payable to Harlequin Reader Service to:

Harlequin Reader Service
In the U.S.
901 Fuhrmann Blvd.
P.O. Box 1397
Buffalo, NY 14240

In Canada
P.O. Box 2800
Postal Station A
5170 Yonge Street
Willowdale, Ont. M2N 6J3

JDA-A-IRRR